The Girl Beyond the Gate

The Girl Beyond the Gate

Becca Day

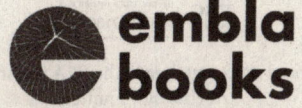

First published in Great Britain in 2022 by

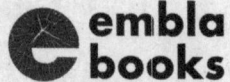

An imprint of Bonnier Books UK
5th Floor, HYLO, 105 Bunhill Row,
London, EC1Y 8LZ

Copyright © Becca Day, 2022

All rights reserved.
No part of this publication may be reproduced, stored or transmitted in any form or by any means, electronic, mechanical, photocopying or otherwise, without the prior written permission of the publisher.

The right of Becca Day to be identified as Author of this work has been asserted by them in accordance with the Copyright, Designs and Patents Act 1988

This is a work of fiction. Names, places, events and incidents are either the products of the author's imagination or used fictitiously. Any resemblance to actual persons, living or dead, is purely coincidental.

A CIP catalogue record for this book is available from the British Library.

ISBN: 9781471415449

Also available as an ebook and an audiobook

This book is typeset using Atomik ePublisher
Printed and bound by CPI (UK) LTD, Croydon CR0 4YY

The authorised representative in the EEA is Bonnier Books
UK (Ireland) Limited.
Registered office address: Block B, The Crescent Building,
Northwood, Santry, Dublin 9, D09 C6X8 Ireland
compliance@bonnierbooks.ie
www.bonnierbooks.co.uk

For Nan, who always believed in me.

Prologue

Unlike my neighbours, I'm not interested in catching a glimpse of the dead body in the community centre. My stomach is twisting itself into knots, and the last thing I want to see right now is a black sheet-covered gurney being wheeled out. Part of me doesn't even want to look out of my bedroom window, I just want to hide away and pretend none of this is happening, but I need to get an idea of what's going on – and just how much I ought to worry.

From my view, I can just about see the residents crowding behind the yellow tape while the flashing lights of the police cars and ambulances illuminate their faces. Marisa Diaz's arms gesticulate wildly above her head. I can just imagine what she's saying. Marisa tends to drift into her native Spanish when she becomes passionate about something, and if anything is going to bring out the passion in the women of Kensington Grove, it's a murder. For a community that never experiences any excitement beyond the annual duck race, two unexpected deaths in less than a month is to the local gossip machine like mother's milk to a baby. First the suicide, or at least what they said was a suicide, and now this. The residents are, of course, expressing the appropriate amount of concern. Some are even wiping tragic tears from their cheeks, but everyone knows the main reason they're standing out in their slippers and dressing gowns on this frosty November morning is to find out all the juicy details. Perhaps even sneak a peek.

I wonder if any of them are talking about Lacey. The longing to check on her, to make sure she's okay, tugs at my heart.

Blinking away a few stray tears, I pull my attention away from the residents and instead train my eyes on the grim-faced police officers, attempting in vain to read their lips as they mutter to one another. I recognise a couple of them; that's how complicated my life has become. One of the officers glances this way and for a fleeting second, I'm sure he's looking straight at me. I'm imagining it, of course, but panic roils in my stomach all the same. No doubt the police will want to speak to every resident of Kensington Grove, and, with everything that's happened over the past few months, I know I'm going to be the prime suspect.

It's true, the list of potential suspects is pretty much confined to the residents. That's the whole point of a gated community. No one can get in unless they have a key card, and that fact means crime levels tend to be low to non-existent. The worst crime previous to this, as far as the other residents are concerned at least, was when Sally's son Markus set fire to the old shed out on the allotment. She'd been the talk of the community for days, and almost seemed pleased when the suicide became the hot gossip as it took the heat off her and her son. The low crime rate is one of the things hiking up the house prices so much – the promise that it's one of the safest places you can live.

And then, no, I'm not imagining it. Now some of the women are turning to look at me too. Heidi, Sally, Marisa. I flinch away from the window, concealing myself behind my curtain, and take three slow measured breaths. I need to go down there. It looks odd me not joining the residents, especially given everything that's happened this year. Like I've got something to hide. Of course, I do, but they don't need to know that. My plan is already in motion. Everything is resting on what happens over the next twenty-four hours. I can't afford to make a single mistake.

Chapter One

108 Days Before the Murder

Jodie

'Jodie Madison?' A stylish guy, in his late thirties at a guess, dark hair flecked with grey, smiles through the arched gates as I sit in my car waiting to be admitted. Kensington Grove sits at the top of a fairly steep hill, and my poor Mini has struggled. The engine is whirring furiously from the strain. On top of that, my air conditioning is broken so I'm having to make do with the windows rolled down, but it's not making a difference. There's not a hint of wind; the stifling air around me is stagnant. England is in the grip of a heatwave; it's just gone midday and it's thirty-two degrees outside. Just gross.

I'm not entirely sure what to expect in moving to Kensington Grove. When I came to look around a few weeks ago, I wasn't in quite the right headspace to ask all the sensible questions or properly explore. I just felt this instant pull, like it was the ideal place for my new start. The house itself was far less important than the gates, and the privacy that comes with them. So, I signed the rental agreement and paid the deposit there and then.

I've heard of gated communities before, though I don't think they're that common in the UK. The estate in Hull just a few streets down from where I grew up was a gated community, though the gates were often left open and the supposed security was a simple code that really didn't mean much once it had been handed out to the pizza delivery boy. Kensington Grove, on the other hand, is prized for its safety and security.

The man flashes his card at the reader and the electric motor kicks into gear, the gates sliding open before me as I drive up to him.

'Paul Downhurst. I'm the development manager for Kensington Grove. Here's your issued key card.'

He hands me the piece of plastic which I slide into my purse, and my immediate thought is that I will most definitely lose it at some point. I'm sure I must hold a world record for the amount of times my bank has had to issue me a new debit card. As if Paul can read my thoughts he says, 'David Timson over there is our head concierge. He and his team operate this main gate between the hours of 7 a.m. and 7 p.m., but if you come home outside of those hours without your key you'll need to phone someone to let you in. If you need to admit anyone – visitors, service people and the likes – just phone the concierge desk and he'll add them to the list.'

I nod, trying to process the flood of information as Paul plonks a set of keys and a spiral-bound, laminated manual into my hands. 'Here are your house keys and your handbook. Have a read of it at your earliest opportunity. It takes you through the various regulations of the estate; noise levels, cleanliness and hygiene, external decorations, what have you. There's 24-hour CCTV on the gates. The community centre is just down there which holds daily activities, and of course there's plenty to do outside the gates as well. Some beautiful footpaths and cycleways in the woodland over there. Do you cycle?'

'Um, no. Not really.' I'm listening to him but my mind is focused on the handbook and trying to ascertain how many pages it is. I start flicking through, and my eye is particularly drawn to the big red letters at the footer of each page, detailing the potential fines that could be handed out should 'the rules' not be adhered to. For a brief moment, the desire to hand the keys back to Paul leaps through my thoughts, willing me to run, sprint, out the gates and never look back, just like I did before. Kensington Grove isn't me. I'm not this person. I've changed my mind.

I swallow down the thought, allowing it to sit in the pit of my stomach as I remind myself why I chose a gated community in the first place. No unannounced visitors. That in itself is enough to put up with the ridiculousness in my hands. It's not quite on the scale of A-list celebrities with gym perks included, but it's not far off. If only I had someone to show it off to.

I wonder what you'd think about it all. I imagine you'd like the kooky, eccentric vibes.

Paul is still rambling on about all the estate has to offer, as if I haven't already sold my soul to the place. I force a smile. 'Thank you, I'll be sure to give this a thorough read.'

I feel like that's a good signal for him to let me go, but instead he just smiles back at me. I'm desperate to get out of this oven of a car and splay myself half-naked on the sofa with an ice-cold drink. This weather calls for a beer, but I told myself before I set off this morning that I was going to knock lunchtime drinking on the head when I moved.

'Well then,' Paul says eventually, 'I suppose all that's left to say is welcome to the Grove. My office is the first building, just over there. Feel free to pop in if you have any questions or concerns, and the office phone number is on the front of your handbook as well.'

I offer him a nod of appreciation and roll my car forward, past the threshold of the Grove. As the gates slide closed behind me and Paul retreats to his office, a weird feeling falls over me, a strange unease in the air. I start moving through the estate at a crawl, taking in my surroundings. There are very few people out on the pathways considering what a nice day it is, certainly no one to make me feel on edge.

It's the buildings. That's where the tension is coming from. It's seeping through the old bricks, flowing around the gothic structures.

Along with the glossy brochure that I'd flicked through at the estate agent's, I had googled as much information as I could on Kensington Grove before coming to view it. Apparently, it's one of the UK's most successful urban renewal projects. On one site I found photos of the original Victorian buildings; red brick serving as a stark contrast to the surrounding greenery; all high ceilings and spires pointing skywards. In its previous life it was an asylum. Of course, they didn't use that word in the estate agent's brochure. They simply referred to it as a hospital, as if knowing the estate's true heritage might contaminate the living experience. Now, the main building has been converted into flats and the surrounding buildings into seventy-five slightly odd houses.

Along the edge of the main road runs a stream leading to the huge pond which takes pride of place in the centre of the estate. The stream is the only natural thing in the entire community. It runs out, under the gate on the east side, into the surrounding meadows. The rest of Kensington Grove has been designed, supposedly, to counteract the old hospital atmosphere. The rowan trees are planted at measured intervals, the grass is systematically checked to ensure it never grows too long, the immaculate driveways are all perfect copies of each other. Everything is required to be neat and orderly, a complete rejection of anything wild.

I pull up to my new home and shake off the tingles mounting in my limbs. Mine is one of the smaller, rented houses on the far end of the estate. It's still a decent size, and fits in with the aesthetic perfectly, but the distance from the main entrance and the fact that the view out of the kitchen window is hindered by the gate means it's less desirable and, luckily for me, more affordable. Once inside, I lean against the closed front door and take in the sight before me. My larger furniture has already been moved into the house, and the rest of my boxes are piled up neatly beside the bay window in the main living area. Something I hadn't noticed when I came to view this place is that I can see straight into next door's house through the living room bay window. The layout of these houses is weird. Apparently, the architects thought having windows on every single wall would be good for the patients, a way to encourage healing.

I try to silence the panic that is bubbling away in my stomach. There had been decorators in when I came to have a look around, large painter's dust sheets and ladders obstructing my view, otherwise that's definitely something I'd have noticed. So much for my private sanctuary. I make a mental note to get a floor-length curtain to block the view. Maybe I won't be lying on the sofa in my underwear today as I had hoped.

I glance wearily at the boxes, trying to decide whether to tackle them now or after lunch, and decide on the latter. There's little use trying to do anything productive on an empty stomach anyway, and it's too hot to exert that amount of energy. Instead, I sink down onto my red sofa and lift my legs to rest my heels on the coffee table. I trace the stitching on the cushions, circling the worn areas that I've vowed for at least two years I'd get patched up. Sweat clings to the back of my neck; my top is unflatteringly skin-tight around my stomach rolls. My head falls back, allowing my hair to fall over my eyes, dull blonde and, I notice, a few grey streaks have appeared. Barely visible, but I wonder if it's time to start dyeing it.

I close my eyes and listen to the chirping of the birds, allowing myself to feel the first twinge of excitement. Day one of my new life. I feel like a child, playing with a doll's house, creating a backstory from scratch for each of the little dolls. Perhaps I should have gone further; got a different job, gone on a diet, pretended I was twenty-five instead of thirty. It isn't every day you get to start again – I could have made myself some reclusive ex-celeb if I'd been creative enough. Instead, I'm still the same old Jodie – doesn't like small talk, would order in food every night if I could, thinks I'm funnier than I am – but with fewer pitying stares to confront on a daily basis, and fewer reminders to have to avoid. That's good enough.

Despite myself, I reach over to the handbook and flick through it. The photo on the front is of the community centre, previously the hospital's chapel, sitting self-importantly in the middle of the estate. The original preserved steeple takes pride of place in the centre of the roof, but the front has been updated with modern expanses of glass glinting in the sunlight and reflecting the pond. The juxtaposition of the two building styles is quite striking. It looks as if someone has gone in and hiked up the exposure and saturation; it's almost cartoon-like. The first page of the handbook lists the regular gatherings that are held at the centre:

    Mondays – Kids' Club
    Tuesdays – Over 50s' Night
    Wednesdays – Rehearsals for Kensington Grove Am-Dram
    Thursdays – Coffee Morning
    Fridays – Quiz Night
    Saturdays – Residents' Association Meeting
    Sundays – After Church Tea & Biscuits

Also on this page is a sticky note, but not the fluorescent type you would buy in your average stationery shop. This sticky note has a silver embossed design around the edges and an almost pearlescent finish to it. In swirly handwriting, is the message:

> *Dear Jodie, we are so looking forward to meeting you. We'll see you at the community centre at 2 p.m. today. It's the last residents' meeting of July. Heidi Downhurst.*

My eyes flick to my phone. It's already past one, and the note isn't so much an invitation as an instruction. My foot taps on the floor as I dither about whether to attend or not. It's probably not a wise idea; being the new resident means I'm bound to be the subject of the town gossip, and attending this meeting sounds like it's just inviting unwanted questions. But then, if I don't go, will I come across as strange? Rude? Perhaps if I go, and they realise there is very little to know about me, they'll move on quicker than if I act like some mysterious recluse.

Taking it as an opportunity at the very least to put off unpacking, I haul myself up from my spot on the sofa, which is far too difficult and makes me realise how desperately I need to start working out again. I'm about to head through the front door when a movement in the corner of my eye makes me glance out of the window. A silver van has pulled up on the driveway next door, and behind the steering wheel is a woman maybe a few years older than me, sporting a sleek ponytail that's pulled so tight it makes my head hurt. The woman hops out and moves round to the back of the van, flinging the doors open with a flourish.

I watch with interest as she pulls a ramp from the back of the van and starts lowering a wheelchair down it. The breath catches in my throat.

The estate agent didn't mention any kids living next door.

Unable to tear my eyes away from the frail girl sitting in the wheelchair, I exhale slowly through pursed lips. It's fine. It doesn't matter. I just won't interact with them. I tend to keep myself to myself anyway, this will be no different. Steeling myself, I make my way back onto the street, ensuring to lock the front door behind me. Not that it's strictly necessary in Kensington Grove. It's the safest place I could be after all.

For some reason I'd expected the community centre to be modern inside to match the exterior doors, but as I enter I see they've kept all the original design elements of the old chapel. The domed ceiling is supported by dark wooden ribs, while thick stone pillars and crested stained-glass windows adorn the walls. Everyone seems to be standing in their own little group; the elderly residents are sitting on the plastic chairs which have been laid out in rows where the pews should be, the men are standing in shirts and ties over by the cork noticeboard, and a handful of women wearing stilettos are lingering by the tea table. I wonder what the former congregation would think of their church being used in this way. Perhaps their ghosts are glowering invisibly by the tea table, dripping ectoplasm over the scones.

Before I can take even a few steps into the hall, a brunette woman, whose burgundy suit jacket contrasts beautifully with the string of white pearls around her neck, totters over to me.

'Jodie!' she cries in a sing-song voice, her arms spread wide as if we're long-lost friends. I can't help but take a step back, my defences flying up at the prospect of an uninvited hug, but I'm little match for the determined woman careering towards me. She wraps one arm around my shoulder and squeezes, turning back to the other residents and beaming. She smells of hairspray and tangerines. 'Everyone, this is our newest addition to the Grove. Jodie Madison.'

I half expect the others to come swarming at me in the same overly friendly way, but to my relief they don't. Instead, they all turn in sync to scrutinise me. Some, at least, make the effort to nod and smile, but others, particularly the group of women the hugger broke off from, are studying me like I'm a scientific specimen. I try to keep my body language as open and unreserved as possible. The pressure of 'fitting in' shouldn't really bother me at my age, but I'm overcome with the distinct sense of starting at a new school and trying to slot into one of the existing cliques.

'I'm Heidi Downhurst,' the hugger says, her plump, crimson-coated lips spreading into a smile which reveals a set of perfectly straight, perfectly white teeth. She looks like she's been put through an Instagram filter, from her bouncy curls which boast rich shades of chocolate and caramel to her almond French-tipped nails. I try not to think about my own nails, chewed up, right into the skin.

'I believe you met my husband, Paul, already,' Heidi continues. I nod and a smile creeps onto my lips. Of course. Paul is so the Ken to her Barbie. And even though he may be the development manager of the estate, I have a sneaky suspicion it's Heidi who is actually in charge of how things run around here.

'It's very nice to meet you.' I don't mean for the words to sound forced or strained, but the lump in my throat has returned. I don't do well in situations like this. Right from when I was a child at school, I always stood to the back of group photos, never put my hand up in class, always kept to the same small group of friends in the playground. One school report said I was 'quiet as a mouse', which was evidenced by the fact that my teachers often forgot I was even there. Heidi, on the other hand, evokes memories of the girl who always volunteered to read off the board, the one who was head of the school council and who only needed to flash a smile to get what she wanted.

Heidi leads me over to the group of women, who shuffle in their circle to make space for the new addition. 'This is Sally.' She gestures at the blonde wearing a turtleneck, who simply raises an eyebrow in my direction. 'She's the nosiest one, for sure.'

'Hey, cheeky cow!' The women all laugh, and I laugh along too, though in my mind I'm making a mental note to steer well clear of Sally. Marisa, I learn, is treasurer for the Residents' Association, and the only woman of the group who lives in one of the flats as opposed to the houses. She gives off much friendlier vibes than Sally, her dark, defined features always lighting up when anybody makes the smallest joke. Emma is the mum of the group, looking astonishingly composed despite the twin babies grumbling in their pushchair, the two other toddlers hanging off her sleeves and the disgruntled teenage boy sulking next to her with his hands in his pockets. Someone else I'll be steering clear of. I can only imagine the chaos in her house.

'You're going to love it here in the Grove,' Heidi says, not removing her arm from my shoulders. 'We're a sort of family here, aren't we, girls?' None of the other women respond, just smile whilst scanning me up and down.

Feeling suddenly very small under their scrutiny, I look past the women and my eyes land on a tall cabinet made entirely of glass near the old altar. At first glance I assume it houses decorations of some kind, but the longer I remain transfixed the more I realise that it isn't holding statues or trophies or any of the usual bits you'd expect to see in a display cabinet. I take a step closer and shiver. They're pieces of equipment they used in the asylum. An array of restraints, leather with chains dangling off them. Some kind of electrical probes. Metal collars. And then right in the centre, hanging at full height, a straitjacket.

'The Residents' Association thought it would be nice to give a nod to the Grove's history,' Heidi explains as if reading my mind. 'You'll see bits of memorabilia dotted around the estate. Quite artistic, I think, don't you?'

I nod and force my eyes away. I'm not the best judge of art. I don't tend to 'get' the message the artist is trying to convey and, no matter what Heidi says, she'll have a hard time convincing me that it isn't odd to have something like that in what's supposed to be a welcoming, communal space.

'It's going to be so lovely having someone living in that house again,' Heidi says. 'It's been empty for ages now. The lady who lived there before you passed away unfortunately. A tragic car accident.'

'Oh, I'm . . . I'm sorry.' I flush, not entirely sure of how to respond. I knew the owner before me had died. But I had assumed it was old age.

Sally cocks her head to the side. 'Tell us about yourself, Jodie.'

Straight away, my mouth fills with saliva. All thoughts of my new persona, my lies, vanish. I'm a blank slate. 'There's not much to know.'

This is clearly an unsatisfactory answer to the women, who begin bombarding me with questions; 'Are you married?', 'What's your job?', 'Do you have any kids?', to which I answer 'no', 'a journalist', and 'no' respectively. I'm sure they already know – I highly doubt Heidi didn't fill them in before I arrived – but I suppose they couldn't resist raising an eyebrow to the fact that I have neither a husband nor kids.

'So, you're a journalist? Which newspaper do you write for?'

I bite my lip, a bitter resentment settling into the pit of my stomach. I left my job at the *Guardian* along with my house, and it still stings. There hasn't been much else I've ever wanted to do. Other people's lives are fascinating. From my quiet little corner of the world I can sit and observe, I can figure out what makes people tick. A number of times my boss Dan suggested I take up a higher-paid position as managing editor, but each time I turned it down, preferring instead to stick to my human interest articles. Not only did it give me more time at home with you, but that's where the juicy stories come from. Governments arguing like schoolchildren and bombs going off on the other side of the world have nothing on the man who's been dating his girlfriend for five years but has never actually met her, or the couple who have been in a twelve-year *ménage à trois*. But it's no good dwelling on what I've turned my back on.

'I just started at the *Estate Reporter* a few weeks ago,' I explain. It's the small local paper, and once my rental agreement came through, I took up a position as health and fitness junior editor, more out of sheer need for a steady wage than of any particular interest in the field. The women all nod, undoubtedly a little underwhelmed, and move swiftly to the hot topic of the week.

'So, ladies,' says Heidi. 'We need to decide which kind of flower beds will be laid along the footpaths this autumn. I think chrysanthemums. Very versatile and they'd bring a lot of colour to the Grove.'

'Ooh, I'm not sure,' the blonde woman cuts in. 'The white pansies looked so beautiful last year. Really added a touch of class to the place.'

'Sally, white just doesn't scream "welcome". We want the place to look happy and full of life, not like something out of a funeral.'

As their conversation grows in passion, I take the opportunity to allow my mind to wander. I picture my old house which was tucked away right in the corner at the end of a cul-de-sac, and a tinge of sadness hits me. I loved that house. There was a huge leafy oak tree right outside that had completely covered the façade, so much so that if you stood at the entrance of the cul-de-sac, you wouldn't have even known there was a house there. This meant that visitors were rare; no trick-or-treaters came at Halloween, no canvassers knocked to make me feel crappy for not supporting a charity, and even the neighbours rarely uttered more than a brief 'good morning' in my direction. That had been exactly how I'd liked it. Selling it was a heartbreaking yet necessary step in affording to move to the Grove. That, and dipping into my mother's inheritance. As much as I'd have preferred staying put, at least here no one knows where I am. I'm a needle and I've created my own haystack to bury myself in. I get the feeling here, though, even with the lack of visitors coming through the gates, I'm going to have to deal with the residents of the Grove far more than I anticipated.

'Shall we begin?' Paul's voice pulls me out of my thoughts, and I glance over to see he has positioned himself at the front of the hall.

'We should wait for Norah,' Emma says.

'She texted me earlier.' Heidi waves her hand in a dismissive fashion. 'She's caught up at the hospital. She won't be joining us.'

Paul nods and gestures to the rows of chairs. 'Not to worry. Ladies and gentlemen, please take your seats and we'll begin.'

I try to focus on the meeting but my mind is elsewhere, focused on the chills slinking through my body. It's this place. This estate. My body is recoiling against something here, a breathing lifeforce woven into the DNA of the buildings. I can't help but think what it all once was, can't help picturing what the former residents went through. Victorian asylums certainly aren't a topic I've read widely about, but I know enough. Tormented patients and violent attendants. I wonder if any of the other residents stop to think about it, really think about it, beyond displaying the old equipment like some bizarre tribute. It wouldn't seem so, looking at them now as they passionately discuss whether the playground should have the addition of a rope swing or a fireman's pole, what the theme of the school dance should be and whether the Kensington Grove sign on the entrance needs a repaint. At one point, one of the residents receives a warning for leaving their bins out for a whole two days after they'd been emptied, but that's about the most exciting it gets.

'Perhaps Jodie could do it?'

Hearing my name makes my stomach flip. I look around the room and blink. All eyes are trained on me. Heidi, the one who said my name (whoever else?), offers me another of her wide, toothy smiles. 'What do you think? It would be a nice way to induct you into the community.'

I stare back at the sea of faces, probably only for a few seconds but it feels like an hour. My instinct is to just say 'yes, sure!' and work out what I've agreed to later, but I've been stung by that before. That's how I ended up organising Gabbie's leaving party back when I worked for the *Guardian*. It made sense that I'd be the one to do it. After all, she's the one who got me the job. But if they had known how clueless I am about music or party decorations or indeed any kind of social gathering, they probably wouldn't have asked me. Still, as I sit in the community centre and vow not to blindly accept whatever Heidi Downhurst is attempting to rope me into, the words 'Sorry, I wasn't listening' just won't come. So instead I continue to stare blankly.

Finally, Paul clears his throat. 'Jodie? Would you like to volunteer for the fundraiser for your new neighbour and her daughter Lacey? You can help run one of the stands or be on the decorating committee?'

My throat constricts. Lacey. That must be the girl I saw in

the wheelchair. The very thought of her makes me lightheaded. I want to get up and run out of the hall but the residents' glares are slicing into me, the expectation hanging in the air. I close my eyes and consider my situation. Asking the questions I really want to ask – like 'what exactly does volunteering entail?' – would make me appear cold and heartless, as if I don't want to help out with a poorly little girl's fundraiser. Even though that's true (I most certainly don't want to help out, but not for reasons that any of my neighbours would understand), the last thing I want is to make a terrible first impression. So, through gritted teeth and despite my better judgement, I smile and say, 'Yes, sure. I'll do whatever.'

Upon returning through the relative safety of my own front door, I'm already exhausted. Keeping up the appearance of someone who's not teetering on the edge of a breakdown is tiring. I briefly consider listening to my meditation app – it never works for me, I just enjoy the man's voice, it reminds me of Morgan Freeman – but then I remember that alcohol exists. Though I know it's probably a bad idea, I trudge over to one of the boxes in the kitchen and rifle through it until I find a bottle of rosé wine and a glass.

It's warm from its unrefrigerated journey, but I don't much care. Nor do I care that the sunlight is still streaming unfettered through the curtainless window, leaving boxy patterns on the laminate floor and serving as a reminder that now is not an appropriate time to be drinking. The slight fuzziness my second glass brings calms me and dulls my senses, which is exactly what I need, and before long I'm staring at the empty bottle, trying to convince myself that it wasn't full when I started. Now, without alcohol to indulge in, my fingers tap lightly on my knees as I contemplate what to do next.

I could watch television, but that involves sorting the wires and getting it all connected, and not only am I likely to blow the thing up if I attempt it myself (technology in general is not my strong suit), but I'd probably just spend an hour flicking aimlessly through the channels before switching it off again. That's what I usually end up doing. I could go to bed. After all, my eyelids are already drooping and I've moved into the realm of forcing myself to stay awake. But it's still only 4 p.m. Even if the comfort of my bed is inviting, I'm not about to turn in quite this early. That would officially mean I'm getting old. So, after dithering for ten minutes and telling myself that it's absolutely not an option to go to the corner shop for more wine, I resign myself to the one thing left for me to do. Unpack.

The box I pick is a random choice. The black ink scrawls on the exterior don't exactly give any clues as to what's inside. I simply wrote 'living room' or 'bedroom 1' on them when I was packing. I pull back the brown tape, the noise of it screeching through the silence of the house, and lift the cardboard flaps, expecting to start putting tins away in cupboards and socks in drawers, perhaps hang a couple of canvas paintings or scatter a few cushions on the sofa. But instead of doing any of that, as I open the box, I feel my old wounds that I've attempted to stitch up also reopening.

My fingers drift along the photo frames inside, as if they're greeting old friends with the caution that comes from time apart. Moments of perfection captured for eternity that cling to me like a coat fashioned from shattered glass. The tighter I pull it around myself the more it cuts into me. All it takes is seeing these pictures one more time, to see your face that I miss so much, to realise that I almost enjoy the sting of the glass shards. It reminds me how much I loved you. How much I still do.

Chapter Two

108 Days Before the Murder

Norah

It's very disconcerting having the unknown enter your life. Our routine is consistent, undeviating, as it is required to be. Medications, hospitals, assessments, forms, over and over again. I thrive off routine. I weigh myself each morning, ensuring my weight never fluctuates over a couple of pounds. Once a week on a Sunday, Laura from the beauty shop in town comes to my house and reapplies my gel polish, red, always red. And at precisely 2 p.m. every day I take a twenty-minute nap, the perfect amount of time to perk me up without causing me to feel more sluggish. But occasionally something crops up that is out of the ordinary.

I didn't even notice her car on the drive when we got home. There were many things distracting me. Firstly, we arrived home to find the builders waiting outside. Lacey had one of her tantrums on the way home from the hospital, causing me to completely forget we'd booked them for today. Not five minutes after letting them in and guiding them to the garden did Lacey start, wheeling herself after them, following them like a puppy within seconds, as she does when anyone visits the house. I could see their expressions from my view at the kitchen window; pity mixed with the uncertainty of having a child in a wheelchair outside with them. I should have known that no amount of coaxing would get her inside while they were there, and that any attempts to do so would inevitably end in a row, but the concern on their faces was growing. Perhaps they were thinking of the risk assessments involved in having a minor on a building site (even though the extent of potential injury at this point is slicing a finger on the tape measure), or perhaps they were pegging me as a bad mother for letting her stay outside with two strange men.

'Please, just do as I say,' I practically begged. This seems to be my most used saying at the moment, always with the pleading tone. She enjoys pushing me to my edge, like a child testing a loose tooth. Eye rolls and sour expressions. The insistence that she knows best. The over-dramatic slams of doors. I know I need to surrender to this part of pre-adulthood. Efforts to slow it will only push her further away. Many a child behaviour book has informed me of that much. But it's one thing to say you have accepted your child is growing up, it is quite another to do it in practice.

Now, the thumping of her music reverberates through the walls between the kitchen and Lacey's room. Some kind of metal nonsense. It sets my teeth on edge. As I drop the ingredients of tonight's dinner – mince and a tin of chopped tomatoes – into the slow cooker I glance out to the garden and try to picture how it will look once the builders are finished with it. The ramps they're installing for Lacey's chair are going to make our garden even smaller. In contrast to the likes of Heidi, whose garden could fit my entire house into it and still have lawn left over, these outskirt houses have such little open space. Still, I can't really complain. They were originally going to house us in one of the flats until I pointed out how impractical that would be with a wheelchair.

I wish we had the space for the swimming pool they're building for Lacey in our garden, as opposed to having to traipse over to the community centre. I've always wanted a pool. I think about it every time we go on holiday. Something about the way water glistens has always relaxed me, and having one in my own garden might have just been enough to make me feel as if I'm somewhere else. Again, I remind myself, mustn't complain. And anyway, it isn't about me. It's for Lacey. All this is for Lacey.

I grab her tube-feeding formula out of the fridge and pop it on the side ready, then pull out the sharpest knife from the drawer and start slicing mushrooms. The metal glints in the sun, and I find myself overcome with an immense desire to run it along my finger. Just to feel something. Shaking the thought, I place the knife back on the counter and trudge across to Lacey's room. When I open the door I'm greeted with the sight of her slumped back in her chair, head bobbing to the godawful noise coming from her stereo and her astronomy book propped open on her knees. If she spent as much time tidying her room as she does reading that damned book the place would be spotless.

'We'll do your tube in five minutes, okay?'

She doesn't acknowledge me.

'Can you turn that down a bit please?' My voice is calm, measured. I'm even impressing myself with my level of restraint. I've got good at hiding what's going on inside. I've had to.

The bolognese sauce is now bubbling nicely, and Lacey has yet to make a reappearance. I should really go and get her – if her feeding schedule varies too much it can mess with her digestion – but five minutes won't do any harm. I move out to the deck and settle myself on the daybed with my tablet.

My eyes drift to the time in the corner of the screen. The residents' meeting is in just over half an hour. I could really do without it today. The thought of getting Lacey to make herself look presentable, feeding her, getting her to the hall and then having to sit through Paul's weekly drivel is nothing short of torturous. Pursing my lips, I pull out my phone and type out a quick excuse to Heidi. Luckily, a mere mention of the hospital tends to make people uncomfortable enough not to press for details, and being at the far end of the estate should mean that hopefully no one will notice my car parked out front.

'We're all done here for today, Mrs Williams.' I look up from my phone to see one of the builders smiling down at me, the sun behind him plunging him into a dark, muscular silhouette.

'Miss,' I correct him with a quirk of the lips. 'Did you get everything you need?'

'Yep, it's not a complicated job. We'll start work on it Monday morning. Is there any particular time that suits you?'

'The earlier the better.' I like to get the important tasks of the day out of the way as early as possible, so that I can feel productive from the get-go.

I pull myself up from the daybed and make a start towards the house so that I can see them out, when something catches my eye across the fence through next door's window. There's someone in there. I squint and try to get a better view. It looks like a woman. I avert my gaze before she can catch me staring and go inside to see the builders out. Once I'm alone, I pick up the formula and roll it in my palms, darts of anxiety fluttering in my chest.

A new neighbour. Interesting. This brings a level of uncertainty to the coming weeks. My mind is instantly awash with questions, just as hers is likely awash with questions about us. I wonder if she expects me to do the neighbourly routine; knock at her door with a bottle of wine, invite her over for dinner, add her to the Kensington Grove women's WhatsApp group. Ten years ago, before everything happened with Alison, I might have done just that. But not now.

I think I'll do Lacey's feed in her room today.

Chapter Three

Heidi
Girls, I think next time I see Jodie I'll invite her to join this group. Is that okay with everyone?

Marisa
Sounds good. She seems nice.

Sally
I don't know about anyone else but I get a weird vibe off her. Just me?

Emma
You get a weird vibe off everyone who moves here.

Sally
What? I just like our group. I prefer not to mess with something that works.

Norah
You didn't like Alison when she first moved here.

Sally

Yeah and look how that turned out. Maybe it's just your neighbours, Norah. LOL! You're cursed.

Norah

I'm sure there won't be a repeat of what happened with Alison. Feel free to invite her Heidi.

Chapter Four

106 Days Before the Murder

Jodie

I wake up drenched in sweat, my heart thumping so fast it's threatening to burst through my ribcage. If only there was a pill I could take to stop me from dreaming about you. Alcohol used to do the trick, but it's becoming less effective now. Will it ever stop? It's been two years and still this is a regular occurrence. Jolting awake, screaming, sheets damp with perspiration.

After a few moments of just sitting and attempting to calm my breathing, I wriggle out of the bedsheets, which have managed to twist themselves spectacularly around my legs, and shuffle to the bathroom. My feet stick to the floor as I move. Without thinking, I flick the switch and light streams into my retinas. It makes me feel sick. Hand pressed to my now pounding head, I stumble to the sink and splash icy cold water in my face but it fails to wake me up properly. My mind is still asleep, still locked in that torturous scene. My hands stretching out, reaching for yours, but always being mere inches away. The space around me contracting, closing in. Then the water. So much water. Images on loop.

It takes another four splashes to the face to snap me properly out of my nighttime haze, and only then do I fumble about for my phone to check the time. 9.05. Well, shit.

When I eventually drag my heels over the threshold of the office at 9.37, my hair thrown up into a loose bun and my shirt hanging untucked at the back, the blast of air conditioning is a welcome reprieve from the stifling heat outside. At least the sheen of hangover-induced sweat lacing my forehead can be easily explained.

I can already sense the displeasure in the air mixing with the rich scent of coffee percolating. Luckily, I very rarely wear make-up, so getting dressed in the morning is a simple procedure, but when you're stumbling around with blurry eyes and the remnants of a hangover, even donning a suit skirt takes time. I can barely remember the car journey – the twenty-five minutes it takes has fallen into the auto-pilot fog with the rest of my morning – but I'm certain it wasn't safe. Still, I've arrived late but alive and I hurry to my desk. I even forgo the coffee machine, which I desperately want to stop at, in the hopes that I might be able to slip into my workstation without Andrew noticing.

Of course he does. He leaves me sweating for half an hour, just long enough for me to relax into the assumption that I've got away with it. Only then do his feet appear in my peripheral vision. His shoes always gleam under the fluorescent strip lights, as if they're made of oil instead of brogue leather, and on this particular day the gleam jiggles as his foot taps.

'Late, Jodie,' is all he says, prompting my ears to burn. I peek through my fringe. He's standing with his arms crossed, eyes scanning my desk, pausing at the untidy stack of papers before moving onto the empty Mars bar wrapper that's still sitting there from last Friday. The disapproval seeps off him. At the *Guardian* my boss was used to my 'haphazard nature' as he liked to call it, and he knew that a competent journalist such as me was well worth a messy desk, but here I have yet to prove my worth. All Andrew has to go on is a CV and a glowing reference, which is still to bear fruit.

'Sorry, I moved house on Saturday so things were a bit disorganised this morning.' That is technically the truth, but the rise of his eyebrows tells me he senses there's more to it than that. I wonder if he can smell the wine seeping through my pores.

'You need to be in the conference room in five minutes for the morning briefing. You can use that time to clean up your workspace.' He turns and kicks the nearby bin towards me so that it bumps against my ankle. I flip Andrew off in what I hope is a subtle fashion, but clearly not subtle enough because the intern at the desk next to me sniggers behind his hand.

I had every intention of cleaning up my desk, but the coffee machine is old and slow, and by the time it has sputtered out the last of the frothy milk for my cappuccino, it's already time to start heading to the conference room. The morning briefing starts as it always does, with Andrew tutting at figures and pacing back and forth in silence while us employees around the table sit and hope we won't be called on. The air in the room is as stale as my lukewarm coffee. As Andrew paces, I tap the edge of my cup with my pen, causing the thickening skin to break and reveal the cloudy liquid below. How sad that I could be so desperate for caffeine that I would force down this muck. Still, it suits the conference room. It matches the uninspiring beige walls and worn carpet.

I spend most of the meeting clock-watching, waiting for 11

a.m. to roll around so that I can take a quick swig from the bottle of flat Lucozade I keep in my top drawer. Just a touch of vodka. Not to get drunk; it helps take the edge off the hangover. An old trick I discovered after googling 'How not to feel like death after drinking' a few months back.

'The last thing on the agenda,' Andrew says after what feels like hours, 'is the leisure centre opening Saturday after next. The mayor will be in attendance. Jodie, I want you to cover it.'

Hearing my name snaps my eyes from the clock to the front. I nod with forced enthusiasm, then wince. 'Oh, I had sort of agreed to volunteer at this fundraiser for a sick young girl that weekend ...' I trail off as I realise what I'm saying. I could slap myself. This is the perfect excuse. No one can blame me for having to work.

I'm already rehearsing what I'll say to Heidi; how I'm gutted not to be able to attend but that I will make up for it by contributing a sizable donation, when Andrew stops pacing.

'Lacey Williams' fundraiser?' he says, and my eyes widen.

'You know Lacey Williams?'

'Everyone round here knows the Williams family. Mother's a bit weird, very intense, but they've kind of made a name for themselves. There were even television crews when they were gifted that house of theirs.'

I shake my head in disbelief. They've been given a house? Just how sick is this kid?

Andrew continues, his face lighting up the more he thinks about it. 'I'll tell you what, you go to the fundraiser and interview Lacey and her mother instead.'

'You want me to interview Lacey?' This has all gone very wrong. Somehow, not only have I got myself roped into helping out at the fundraiser, I've now volunteered to spend an hour or so talking to the very person I had hoped to avoid. 'I don't think it would be appropriate. I actually live next door to her. Surely that causes a conflict of interest, no?'

I think I've made a fairly good case for myself, but Andrew smacks his hands on the table, a grin stretching across his face.

'That's even better! Who better to get an inside scoop than her neighbour?'

I'm about to open my mouth to argue, but Andrew cuts in first.

'You said you wanted more human interest pieces, right?' he says, his lips quirking into a smile as if he knows I have no way to refuse. 'This is your chance.'

Chapter Five

94 Days Before the Murder

Norah

According to Heidi, my new neighbour has volunteered at the fundraiser. Since I wasn't at the residents' meeting I can assume one of two things happened. Either she was bullied into it by the lovely people of Kensington Grove, or she's noticed Lacey and we've piqued her interest. I'll have to keep an eye out for her today and see if I can decipher which it is.

I've been lying awake for the last hour, as I always do when approaching one of these events. Something about it makes me uneasy. I usually spend a few hours tossing and turning in bed the night before, opting to distract myself with a book, eventually falling asleep around two in the morning and then miraculously waking again at five. I'm bleary-eyed and achy, but I know there's no chance of getting any more sleep so I haul myself out of bed and creep out into the hallway.

Lacey's door is ajar as usual. It's been a rule in our house for years. I need to be able to see in to check on her. She's thrown the retorts of needing her own privacy at me more times than I can remember, but I won't budge and she knows it. I peek in and watch her for a few moments. When she sleeps she looks like my little girl again. Her cheeks puff up, giving her face the slight chubbiness of childhood, and her bottom lip sticks out, causing my heart to swell.

I ease away from the door and head to the kitchen where I pour myself a green tea. I've been trying to cut down on caffeine recently, and every morning I regret it. I'm so tired, not just physically from my lack of sleep, but mentally exhausted at the thought of the day that lies ahead. I need to remind myself why I'm doing all of this. The benefits greatly outweigh the effort.

As I sip my tea, a light flashes on next door. Another early riser. Perhaps she is anticipating today's events as much as me. My first impressions of the woman I share a fence with are thus: I'd say she's in her late twenties or early thirties at the latest; younger than me, but old enough that society would deem it appropriate for her to be in a committed relationship and thinking about children by now. There is evidence of hardship etched into the lines on her forehead. Her mousy hair is a touch unruly, and she doesn't care for make-up or ostentatious outfits. Still, despite her relaxed demeanour she is clearly business-minded, working long hours, though I have yet to discover what she does for a living. I'm not sure why I'm so intrigued by her. Initially I thought it was simply the fact that she is new, an unknown, but now I think there may be more to it.

Tea demolished, and my craving for a proper cup of coffee still not satisfied, I head back to the hallway and tap on Lacey's door. It's always a struggle to wake her, requiring at least two attempts. Steeling myself, I move closer and jiggle her shoulder, and before my eyes my pre-pubescent daughter adopts the mask of an angry teenager; sullen and scowling.

'Darling,' I say in as soothing a voice as I can muster. 'You need to get ready for the fundraiser.'

She lets out a groan and turns over, simultaneously rolling her eyes. I think she dislikes attending these events even more than I do. I jiggle her shoulder again – I've made the mistake of letting her drop back to sleep far too often to fall for it today – and unhook the dress that's hanging up on the back of the door.

'Come on, Lacey, put this on and we'll clear your airways before we leave.'

She opens one eye to scoff at the dress.

'I don't want to wear that.'

'What are you talking about?' I shake my head, unwilling to participate in yet another power struggle, especially not at this time of the morning. 'It's beautiful. You said you liked it when we were in Harrods.'

'I didn't. I said it was the best one of the outfits you showed me. But I still don't like it. It's childish.'

'You are a child!'

'Actually, I'm a teenager. You gave birth to me, remember?'

A flash of annoyance bubbles inside me at her ungrateful attitude, but I chew it down as best I can. I will not be sucked into an argument. I will not.

'Lacey, don't be ridiculous. Put it on. End of discussion.' I fling the dress at her and leave without another word, instantly feeling wretched. This seems to be increasingly the norm for us these days, and I'm not quite sure when it started. We weren't always at each other's throats like this. It's developed slowly, over time, like a sickness invading our home. I don't mean to snap. I hate that we seem to be drifting further and further apart, that what should be an easy conversation between mother and daughter so often ends in friction. But, try as I may, sometimes her attitude gets to me. I'm not yet used to having a child who is old enough to question me. I know what's best for her. I always have. Why won't she just surrender to me?

Chapter Six

94 Days Before the Murder

Jodie

The couple of weeks since I was assigned the interview have been a harrowing countdown. Each morning when I've headed into the office and checked my calendar, the bold red text highlighted on the Saturday slot has winked at me, taunting me. As it turns out, I barely see the Williams girl. It seems our schedules conflict somewhat, as every time I leave for work the curtains of their house are still drawn, and every time I get home their van is gone, not to be seen again until I'm safely out of conversation range. Had it not been for the fundraiser, I probably could have pretended there wasn't a child next door, as the other residents of the Grove have proven more than enough to distract me.

They fascinate me with their high aspirations and their effortless poise. Mornings, before the sun has even risen enough to switch off the streetlights, Heidi jogs past my house in skin-tight yoga pants, a bottle of Smart Water in hand and one of those fancy watches that track how many calories you've burned strapped to her wrist. She flashes her pearly whites at me watching through the living-room window, a knowing smirk on her face, as if she can tell that below the window all I have on my legs are my patched-up pyjama bottoms. She then continues down the road, bouncing up and down, probably to the rhythm of some poppy music blasting through her headphones, and disappears into the distance like an oasis blurring into a mirage.

I asked Sally Peters the other day what Heidi does for a living, to which she gave a snort of derision.

'Heidi? Work?' she said as if the very suggestion of it was laughable. At first, I couldn't figure out how they managed to afford their huge house if Heidi doesn't work. Surely Paul's job doesn't earn *that* much. But then I thought about how the Williams family had been gifted their house, and it all made sense. Paul manages the estate, and therefore it's reasonable to assume that they receive certain discounts. I wonder how many of the residents of Kensington Grove actually work hard for what they have. I've got to admit, it does irk me slightly when I think back to my days of drudgery; taking in ironing and cleaning houses just to make ends meet while I slogged away in the evenings at my journalism degree. It was one of the best days of my life when I first saw my name in the *Guardian*. Finally, I had tangible proof of my hard work sitting right before me in black and white.

But it isn't just the Downhursts that have that spark, that air of never-wavering confidence. When I go on a rare walk around the estate I notice even the children seem to have it. When leaving their homes they simply call out to their parents, 'I'm going to Laura's' or 'I'll be at the playground with Darren'. Statements of fact. No asking or searching for approval. A different world from the one I grew up in, where you couldn't even leave your bike outside without it getting nicked.

One thing I do notice is that none of the children ever call round to Lacey's. In fact, the Williams house never has any visitors, not that I see anyway, and it doesn't seem Lacey has many friends, which suits me down to the ground because I never have to worry about the other kids from the neighbourhood coming too close. As far as I can tell, Lacey doesn't even go to school.

Getting to Saturday both drags and comes about all too fast. Half of me wants to get it over with, while the other hopes that something might crop up that would excuse me with both my boss and my neighbours. Of course, luck has never been on my side, and it's not about to change any time soon. Throughout the morning, signs of the fundraiser going ahead are plentiful. For one thing, the gates are actually open, allowing visitors to enter without having to sign in, and the usually quiet streets are for once lined with parked cars and the occasional traffic jam. I also spot Norah and Lacey out the front window as they leave for the community centre. Norah glances up as she nears the end of the drive, and there's an awkward moment of eye contact where I know I should avert my gaze but can't help but stare. She smiles and nods by way of greeting, and I force myself to do the same. I imagine she's used to the stares when she pushes her daughter around in her wheelchair.

I've been putting off doing any prep for this interview in the hopes that I might not actually end up having to do it, but as the seconds tick by my desire to be the best journalist I can be starts to overtake my reluctance. I have just under half an hour before I need to leave; that gives me enough time to do some basic research.

Taking a deep breath, I sit down at my laptop and type 'Norah

Williams' into the search bar. The first few results are fruitless: a repair parts company, a few Facebook profiles, but then four down there is a news story. In fact, there are a few stories from different papers, some fairly reputable, and I begin to wonder how I haven't heard of them before moving to Kensington Grove.

MAKE-A-WISH HELPS LOCAL GIRL'S DREAM COME TRUE says one article, alongside a beaming photo of Norah and Lacey at Disneyland and even a clip from an interview that was aired on daytime TV about Lacey's brave battle with cystic fibrosis. MOTHER CAMPAIGNS FOR BRAVE YOUNGSTER TO BE HONOURED AT THE COURAGEOUS CHILDREN AWARDS says another. That one shows Lacey and seven other children grinning next to the prime minister. The parents are standing at the back in the photo, though the only one who catches my eye is Norah, whose hand is resting proudly on Lacey's shoulder. It's as if she's looking straight at me.

I head back to Google and type in a different search: 'cystic fibrosis life expectancy'. The result flashes up almost instantly, and my gut tightens.

> Currently, about half of people with cystic fibrosis will live past the age of forty.

Forty years old. That's no age at all. And only half will live past it? I shake my head and close the laptop. That'll do. As long as I know some basics about them I can at least wing the rest. Steeling myself, I jot down some questions in my notepad, sling the satchel I always take to interviews around my shoulder and leave the comfort of my house.

When I enter the community centre (for the first time since the residents' meeting the day I moved in, much, I sense, to Paul and Heidi's disapproval) I think I've stumbled upon a circus as opposed to a small-town fundraiser. It's a bewildering swirl of activity. Somehow the decorations have made the old chapel look about five times bigger, and have completely masked the eerie atmosphere from the last time I was here. Huge billowing curtains of sparkly fabric hang suspended from the ceiling beams, giving the impression of a big-top tent. At a buffet table, a burly man in an apron produces platters of burgers and hotdogs. At the omelette station, chefs whisk up eggs and pour them into a skillet, turning out fluffy omelettes stuffed with avocado, kale or pancetta. It's all very Gen Z. You'd have loved it.

The centre of the hall is taken up with fairground games like Whack-A-Mole and Hook-A-Duck. This is where I'm to be stationed according to the strict instructions written in Heidi's cursive that was stuffed through my letterbox this morning. They obviously didn't trust me with anything more complicated than dishing out prizes. The far-right wall plays host to the craftier residents of the Grove selling their homemade candles and beaded handbags. And on the stage platform at the back, a golden throne lined with red velvet stands in pride of place.

I've barely managed to nod a polite hello to the hot-dog vendor when a mass of glossy brown curls bounces into the corner of my eye. I don't need to turn around to know who it is. The perfume gave her away from the other side of the room.

'So glad you could make it,' Heidi beams, and I'm instantly glad I opted for the food first. At least if I'm eating I have a reason to not engage in conversation. I don't know what it is about Heidi. She's just not my kind of person.

'I wouldn't have missed it,' I say, then turn my attention back to the vendor. 'One large with extra onions, please. Ketchup and mustard.'

Heidi doesn't try to hide her grimace. 'Goodness, if I ate that you just know it would pass the lips and go straight to the hips.' She chuckles and her eyes drop pointedly to my hips before flashing back to my face. 'Doesn't the chapel look marvellous? We've been working on it for the past two days. Even had to cancel quiz night last night. Almost everyone turned up to help.'

I take a bite of my hot dog, purposefully not acknowledging the not-so-subtle dig about my lack of attendance over the past couple of days, and nod. A silence passes between us, and I'm almost impressed with myself. I doubt Heidi being lost for words is a regular occurrence.

Heidi gives an audible sigh of relief when Marisa Diaz makes her way over to us, a much daintier box of fries in her hand which she eats with a fork. 'We've already broken even,' Marisa says, biting the smallest end off one of the fries. 'The cost of the suppliers has been completely covered. This is going to be *muy bueno!*'

'Marisa's our treasurer,' Heidi explains, and I nod once more. 'Oh, it's so wonderful that people are being so generous with their spending. Jodie, your stall is the third one down. After you've finished your ... brunch, of course.'

I swallow my mouthful, scooping a stray onion off my lip and gratefully taking a napkin from the smirking vendor. 'I need to speak to Norah before I do anything else.' I reach into my bag and take out my camera; a Canon which I spent practically my entire savings on a couple of years back. 'I'm actually working today. My boss wants me to interview her and Lacey for the paper.'

'The *Estate Reporter* is covering this?' Heidi's eyes light up. Before I can say anything she flips her hair over her shoulder, plucks the fries from a bewildered Marisa's hands and places them on the table, and poses next to her with one knee bent. 'Be sure to mention I strung the fairy lights by hand.'

'Oh, it's actually more of a human interest piece about Lacey than about the fundraiser itself,' I begin.

Heidi's eyes narrow slightly. 'Human interest? Norah's pretty picky about which interviews she gives.'

I'm about to respond with some kind of sarcastic comment – am I not good enough for Norah? – but decide against it and offer up a smile instead. 'I'll definitely need a good photo of the fundraiser to include in the article. Do you want to stand there? You'll be framed by the lights that way.'

Having seemingly instantly forgotten her loyalty to Norah, Heidi resumes her pose in the suggested spot and I snap a few shots, marvelling at how her hair seems to glimmer even through the viewfinder.

Just as I take the third snap, two fingers forming bunny ears appear above Heidi's head. I lower the camera and frown, prompting Heidi to turn around.

'Dr Roth!' she simpers, oblivious, and I can't help a smirk.

'Nice to see you, ladies.' He flashes a smile at Heidi and Marisa in turn, nudging his glasses up his nose with his forefinger, then directs his attention to me. I don't recognise him. I'm sure I would remember him if I had met him before. He's attractive in a slightly unkempt way, though perhaps he looks better than he is simply for the fact that he isn't a carbon copy of all the other men in Kensington Grove. Where they all wear their hair slicked back as if they're in a retro edition of *Homes & Gardens* magazine, his is longer and shaggier, and he's allowed his stubble to grow to the point of it almost being considered a beard. He's like a cliché from a 1970s aftershave ad; there's even the tiniest hint of chest hair poking out where the top button of his shirt is undone. I am perversely turned on by it.

'I don't believe we've officially met.' He stretches out his hand and I fumble to put my camera away to shake it. 'Christian Roth. I'm the local GP.'

'Jodie,' I reply, deciding to keep my own introduction as detail-free as possible.

'I remember from the residents' meeting. You made quite the impression.' So he was there. I wonder how I could have missed him.

'I'm afraid I can't say the same for you.' The words come out before my brain can filter them and I wince. Not everyone appreciates my wry sense of humour, and I'm trying so hard not to make the wrong first impression here. To my relief, his face changes, amusement creeping onto his lips. I might be imagining things, but I'm sure his cheeks have reddened slightly.

'I was a little late, so I stood at the back. I'll have to try harder next time,' he says. He grins, but I'm not entirely sure if he's trying to be friendly or not. I wish I was a better judge of character.

Heidi, seemingly dismayed that her opportunity to feature in the local paper has been interrupted, steps between us and places a manicured hand on Dr Roth's shoulder. 'I meant to ask, how is little Daniel Baker after his fall? It looked ever so painful, poor little mite. Not that I'd let a child of mine climb on the picket fence, mind.'

At this point, I zone out of the conversation and instead turn my attention to movement on the stage platform. I swallow hard, attempting to keep my breath steady, and watch as Norah steps in front of the microphone and taps it to ensure it's working. And there, sitting in her wheelchair at the back and staring up at her mother with big brown eyes, is Lacey.

I can't quite pinpoint the source of my discomfort at seeing her again. Just being in the same room as her has caused the hair on my nape to stiffen, and the roiling in my stomach tells me the hot dog was probably not the best idea.

I suck in a breath and let it escape slowly through my teeth. Let's get this over with.

Norah takes to the microphone with the air of someone who is well-versed in public speaking. She stands tall in the centre of the stage, eyes shining as she stares out at the sheer volume of supporters who have turned up. Her voice, when she eventually speaks, is crisp and clear, enough to silence the chatter of the crowds and the whirring of the game stalls within seconds.

'May I have your attention, everyone,' she says, holding her hands up as if she's a preacher at the altar. 'I want to thank each and every one of you for attending today. The care and compassion this community has shown us since we arrived eight years ago has blown us away, and has restored my faith that true kindness really does exist.'

As she speaks, I find myself captivated, transfixed by her exaggerated arm movements, hanging on her every word, like I'm a schoolgirl awaiting instructions from my teacher. A quick glance around the hall suggests my fellow residents feel the same.

'As many of you are aware,' Norah continues, 'we have now reached the stage where Lacey is in her wheelchair full time, and the money you are so generously donating today will be used to not only renovate our home to make it disabled accessible, but also to build a specialist pool and wellness room here, in our much-loved community centre, which will allow her to train her muscles and build up her strength.'

At this, the entire room erupts into applause. Norah, now wiping a tear from her eye, nods to the side of the stage, and Paul steps over to help Lacey from her chair. When she places her frail, thin arm around his shoulders I fear it might snap in two. In fact, her whole attire – a glittery silver dress with ruffled skirt – looks as if it's about to drop straight off her tiny frame. She moves slowly and cautiously under Paul's support to the throne, and as she sits another round of applause rumbles through the hall.

'Thank you once again, from the bottom of our hearts, and enjoy your day.'

Ever the opportunist, I take the distraction of the speech as my chance to get away from Heidi and her overpowering scent. I shuffle through the crowds to the stage platform, where Norah stands watching over the residents.

'Norah,' I call, and the surprised look on Norah's face reminds me that we've never actually met. The extent of our relationship thus far has been the brief moment of eye contact this morning. Now that I'm closer to her, I can see the cracks in her put-together façade. She's naturally attractive, that's for sure, but there are bags under her eyes that she's tried a little too hard to cover with concealer.

'I'm Jodie, I've recently moved in next door to you.'

At this, she nods approvingly, though her eyes remain wary.

'Of course, I'm sorry I haven't been round to say hello properly. Things are so hectic.'

'Don't worry at all. I can imagine how busy you must be.' I don't say that I would prefer it if Norah would keep up the habit and never come and knock at my door. I've learned in my years of journalism that the key to getting a good story is building rapport, and even though I'm decidedly anti-social in my real life, I've learned to fake it when I need to.

A few pleasantries later and the three of us head to the smaller room just off the main hall in an attempt to find a quieter spot. Norah herself is yet another resident to fascinate me. Even now she's off the stage, her demeanour remains confident and self-assured. I take the liberty of setting up my camera to record the interview (I'm not one for taking notes, preferring instead to pore through the footage and pick out the gems later in the comfort of my own home), and the second I press 'record' Norah appears to sit a little straighter, to smile a little wider, to speak a little more clearly.

'Since she was a baby, really. She was premature and we've had issues ever since,' she says when I ask how long they've been dealing with Lacey's illness, and then to the rest of my reel of questions: 'Cystic fibrosis – it means her lungs are damaged, makes her muscles weak, it's also caused anaemia and diabetes.' 'No, no cure, just lots of support to make her life as comfortable as possible.' 'Yes, we couldn't have got through it if it hadn't been for this wonderful community.'

All the while, Lacey says nothing, instead keeping her eyes trained on her mother, a look of awe on her face as if she herself is surprised at how much the woman is willing to put up with. Norah's arm remains extended around Lacey's shoulders, hugging her close as if she's afraid if she lets go her daughter will crumble to dust. She holds onto her in the way only a mother can, clutching her entire world in her hands, a silent promise never to let go.

'Would it be okay if I asked Lacey a question?' I'm suddenly aware that Andrew specified I should interview both mother and daughter. Norah's lips tighten, and for a moment I expect her to say that the interview is over, but eventually the smile returns and she says, 'Of course.'

I lean forward, elbows resting on my knees. Lacey stares back at me, her wide dark eyes reminding me of a puppy waiting for its owner's instruction. From this distance I can see the constellation of freckles dusting her nose. She's very pretty, but she's thin, too thin, like she's been hollowed out, and her big brown eyes are disconcertingly similar to yours.

'Are you happy?' I ask.

There's a pause, long enough to bring to attention the ticking of the clock on the wall, before Lacey replies, 'Yes, I am happy.'

'How can you be?' This question is not on my list, but it escapes my lips nonetheless. Lacey smiles, as if she has finally been asked the question she knows everyone wants to ask but are always too polite or too nervous.

'Because everyone's so kind to me,' she says. 'My illness sucks, but it's made me realise how caring people are.'

I don't respond for a long time, just marvel at the girl in front of me, at how extraordinarily mature she is. Although, something tells me this isn't the first time she's said those words. Something about her inflection sounds robotic, as if it's been practised over the years.

I flip my notebook closed, stop the recording and clear my throat. 'Thank you for your time.'

'Not at all.' Norah stands up and positions herself once more behind Lacey's chair. 'I hope you enjoy the rest of the fundraiser.'

'Oh, I'm actually meant to be helping out.' I glance at the clock and try to figure out how long I need to stay in order to satisfy Heidi. 'I should probably go take my place at the Hook-A-Duck.'

'Ah, well, have fun anyway.' Norah gives me a firm handshake and starts moving toward the door. Just as they are about to turn the corner Lacey glances back at me and flashes me one last smile before disappearing with her mother back into the crowds.

Chapter Seven

93 Days Before the Murder

Norah

My eyes glaze over as I place the inhaler into Lacey's plastic mouthpiece. I go through these motions on auto-pilot now, barely even thinking about it as my arms move of their own accord. After a couple of puffs from her inhaler, we start with saline in her nebuliser and I brace myself with tissues. It doesn't matter how many times we do it Lacey always ends up coughing up chunks of mucus.

We've found ourselves in the exact situation I had hoped to avoid, and I'm struggling to shake the sense of unease that has been weighing on me since the fundraiser yesterday. It was what I expected; it had Heidi written all over it, not that I can complain. From what Marisa tells me the proceeds have been even more generous than usual, more than enough to cover all the renovations. I'm never sure how to react to news of how much these events raise. It's as if I've grown numb to it all.

Being interviewed by Miss Madison yesterday was a curveball to say the least. She stood out, not just because she was dressed in a casual get-up of jeans and a slouchy T-shirt instead of the semi-formal attire of her peers. There was a certain level of fragility about her. Though she was clearly adopting a professional stance, she shuffled from foot to foot and she intentionally avoided eye contact every time I looked at her. All classic signs of anxiety. She didn't want to be doing the interview any more than I did. What is it about us that makes her so uncomfortable, I wonder? Is it Lacey's illness, the fact she is in a chair?

Saline done, we start with Lacey's chest physiotherapy, which involves placing yet another plastic device in her mouth and having her breathe against hard resistance for a few seconds. I breathe in time with her, allowing the oxygen to flow through me and take with it my nagging anxieties. I check her blood-sugar levels, then pop the top off her insulin injection and press it against the skin of her abdomen. I used to hate needles, couldn't even watch them in movies without gagging, but like everything else, I'm now desensitised to it.

I thought I handled the interview rather well. I've become adept at answering questions in a satisfying yet vague way. Enough to allow the interviewer to form their story or their TV segment, but not so much as to allow excessive prying into our private lives. We've already had so much of us exposed, I need to be careful how things are worded. Miss Madison rattled through her questions, nothing we haven't been asked before. I could see her finger moving down her notepad as she ticked off each question, her speed serving as evidence that she wanted to get through it as swiftly as possible. Right at the end of the interview, something changed. A new question was asked, one that didn't seem to be pre-planned. And it wasn't for me, it was for Lacey.

Are you happy?

Those words jolted around me like an electric shock, sending tingles through my spine and fingertips. I knew the exact answer to every question prior to this one; the sentences have been rehearsed, reshaped, chiselled with care into an acceptable response. But I didn't know the answer to this question. Only Lacey knew the answer, and I wasn't sure I wanted to know what it was. Then, both during the questioning and again when we vacated the room, I saw it. Just like I've seen it time and time again. That look that Lacey gave her. The earliest signs of a fixation.

I pack up the nebuliser and place Lacey's food tray in front of her with a clatter. Breakfast consists of a bowl of porridge positioned next to a line of vitamins and antibiotics. She hunches over and begins to eat, while I move to the window and gaze out over our gate. When our neighbour moved in I had hoped to keep our lives as separate as possible, and was pleased to discover that she seemed to desire the same. She's never knocked to introduce herself. She's never attempted to engage in inane conversation over the garden fence. She has been going about her life and has allowed us to do the same, and I suppose it has resulted in me settling into a false sense of security. But if Lacey has decided she wants to befriend her, I'm afraid I'm going to have to put much stricter measures in place. I can't have a repeat of last time.

Chapter Eight

87 Days Before the Murder

Jodie

It's been just over a week since the fundraiser. The community centre is back to its regularly scheduled meetings. The streets are once again walked only by the residents who have paid steeply for the pleasure. But still, even though my involvement with the Williams girl is now complete, I can't help but be aware of her. A few days ago I spotted her out in the garden, watching with interest as Norah led her through what looked like some kind of chair-based yoga. Another day, I heard squealing outside the Williams house, and upon peeking out my window I realised Lacey was racing up and down her newly installed ramp, her mouth stretching into a grin as she allowed her wheels to free spin. Both times she noticed me watching her and waved, causing my heart to leap into my throat and the back of my neck to burn.

Ignore her, I tell myself every time. *Go back to pretending she doesn't exist.* But now that I've spoken to her I can't seem to switch it off. I think about her even when I can't see her; her upbeat personality, the sense that she's both just a kid yet mature for her age, the way her smile doesn't quite reach her eyes.

Tonight is a particularly hot evening. I'm trying to enjoy the warmth, but neither the thrown-open windows nor the fan I've set up in the corner of the room are helping to curb the sweat. I need a drink but it's not the right weather for wine. Pulling myself up, I rummage around in the fridge and thankfully find an ice-cold can of cider at the back, and settle down for an evening of staring vacantly at the TV.

I can just feel my eyelids getting heavy when a small voice calls to me. At first I think I'm imagining things. Eventually I realise the voice is coming from outside, and when I peer at the house next door my eyes land on Lacey, staring out at me through her own open window. I'm momentarily frozen, unsure of what to do.

'What are you doing?' I call back, shaking off the chills that are slinking through my body. Lacey lifts her finger and shushes me.

'Mum will wake up.'

I swallow. 'What are you doing?' I say again, this time at a lower volume.

'Can you angle your TV to the window?' she whispers, pointing eagerly at the set behind me. 'I'm never allowed to watch TV.'

I tilt my head, attempting to process what she's just said. Her mum doesn't let her watch TV? What on earth does the poor kid do all day? It's such a strange request that I can't begin to think of a sensible response. Instead, I glance back and forth a few times between the television and the girl hanging out of her window, silence the inner voice that's telling me not to get involved, and shuffle the set around.

I wake to the sound of resolute silence, the road outside my bedroom window devoid of any traffic. One of the benefits of being on the far end of the estate is no one has to pass to get to work. Living in the city, I'd been so conditioned to waking up to a cacophony of noise first thing – honking horns, stomping from the upstairs flats, the man from the fruit and veg stall yelling about his half-price bananas – that even after nearly a month of living here I'm still not used to this new, quieter pace of life.

I trudge into the kitchen, pour myself a cup of coffee, take a knife and start cutting up fruit, watching as the chopping board soaks up the juice of the strawberries. It looks like a splash of blood. I'm trying to eat healthier, and usually do a good job up until the evenings, when I get peckish and the day's efforts disappear down a crisp packet or biscuit tin. Still, I can but try.

It's my day off today, Sunday. I tend to not move much on Sundays. I never know what to do with my spare time. The most productive activity I have planned for my morning is to take a riveting Buzzfeed quiz on what kind of onion I am. I could use the distraction of work today too. I'm still not entirely sure if last night was real or not. Talking to Lacey through the window like that feels like a scene straight out of a dream, but when I glance at the spot where she'd been I know it did happen. My mind is whirring with questions. I can't quite figure out the set-up they've got going over there. Norah homeschools Lacey, which in itself isn't particularly odd, especially considering how ill the kid is, but there's something off. Some unease there, lurking behind closed doors. Perhaps it's just my journalistic side coming out, my desire to know each family's buried secrets, but something is telling me there's more to Norah and Lacey than meets the eye.

We watched a quiz show last night, nothing particularly special, but Lacey was all over it, transfixed by the set.

'Jupiter! That's the answer! Pick B!' she exclaimed as the player inevitably chose the wrong answer, and she had to remind herself to be quiet so as not to wake Norah. 'I love space. Do you like space? Did you know that space is completely silent? It's because there's no atmosphere so there's no way for sound to travel. Ooh, and did you know one day on Venus is longer than one year on Earth?' She talked so much and so fast, I got the feeling that kind of conversation is not generally encouraged by Norah.

Her overexcited chattering replays in my head as, fruit and a glass of orange juice in hand, I step out onto my decking. It's warm underfoot having soaked up the morning rays. We've not got long left of the summer, and we've been particularly blessed with good weather this year. According to Mr Weather Man, we should make the most of the remnants of our August heatwave because high winds and rain are expected later this week. I would expect nothing else from good old England.

Already I can feel the pull of my sun lounger. It's the only piece of furniture I've placed in my garden, and it's cheap plastic which means it's just as likely to burn you as it is to provide a relaxing place to stretch out, but I enjoy it nonetheless. I make the decision not to don my swimming costume and instead risk getting the glamorous socks effect from my jeans. I haven't shaved in a few weeks. I settle myself on the sun lounger and place my glass on the deck, a terrible idea considering how perpetually clumsy I am. The juice glows luminous in the sun. No sooner have I popped a slice of kiwi into my mouth when the silence of the morning is broken by a series of panicked voices. I squint against the bright daylight, trying to discern where the commotion is coming from but not caring enough to get up again now that I've sat down. That is, until I hear Lacey's name.

When I emerge at my front door, feet still bare and hair still in disarray, my gut lurches at the sight of Norah standing flapping her hands with a few of the other residents crowded around her. I immediately jump to the worst-case scenario. Lacey's lungs have given out, she's been given a terminal diagnosis, or maybe it's already too late and the ambulances are rushing towards us as we speak.

'What's going on?' I pad out to the group, which consists of Norah, Sally, Dr Roth, a couple of men whose names I can't remember and, of course, Heidi. The gravel from the pavement embeds itself into the soles of my feet with each step and I try not to wince. Norah doesn't respond, just shoots me a glance, one that I can't quite read. Instead, Sally turns to me and says, 'Lacey's gone missing.'

I don't know what to say. I stand there, dumb, and stare at Norah. She's welling up, tears threatening to burst from her eyes. I want to pull her into an embrace, tell her that I understand, give her a shoulder to cry on, but I can't bring myself to do it. Besides, Heidi's already got the comforting side of things covered, and I'm sure she's probably better at it than I am.

'Right, let's split into groups to search.' Dr Roth's calm voice booms over the confusion. 'She can't have gone far. Norah, you stay here in case she comes back. Call the police if you haven't already.' Everyone immediately scatters into pairs, and without thinking I run back to my front door to grab my shoes, hurry back to the group and latch onto Dr Roth. He seems to have it together. He's taking control. I'd rather stick with someone like that. Because if something bad has happened to Lacey, I might really lose it this time.

I try to silence the anxiety coursing through my veins, telling myself that Lacey's probably just gone off somewhere and will return shortly to a stern telling-off, but I can hear Norah weeping, saying that she hasn't got any of her medication with her. Surely she wouldn't have gone off without any of it? I attempt to shake the negative thoughts from my head as I run to catch up with Dr Roth, who is already charging ahead towards the main gate. I reach him, embarrassingly breathless after such a short distance, and start scanning our surroundings. I don't even know where to begin. Surely a child in a wheelchair can't be that hard to spot.

'When did Norah last see her?' I ask, my voice cracking a little.

'Last night. She went in to wake her up this morning and she was gone.'

I've reported on a few missing persons cases before. The first forty-eight hours are crucial where a missing child is concerned, and it's only been – I check my phone – ten hours since I chatted to Lacey through the window. I try to pull myself back to last night. Had she seemed different at all? Off in any way? Not that I'd be able to tell – I barely know the girl. I momentarily wonder if I should tell Norah, or at least Dr Roth, about last night. After all, there's a good chance I was the last person to see Lacey. But then I remember Lacey's insistence that we stay quiet so as not to wake her mother, and I decide against it. There's clearly some tension there. I don't want to be the cause of any issues between them.

My mind drifts back to our conversation. After the quiz show we watched an American college rom-com, I forget what it was called, and just after it ended and we were readying to say goodnight after quite possibly one of the strangest evenings of my life, Lacey went very quiet.

'Are you okay?' I asked, tilting my head to the side, a sudden worry settling in that I'd done something wrong, said something wrong.

'Can we do this again?' Her voice was tiny, barely even a whisper, and I had to ask her to repeat herself. When she did I spent a long time, probably too long, contemplating my answer. My immediate reaction was to try to come up with some kind of excuse, to put a stop to it right there and then. But then I looked at her face and her eyes and I couldn't say no.

'I don't see why not.'

My words brought an instant grin to Lacey's face, as if she had been expecting me to say 'no' just as much as I had expected it from myself.

'Thank you,' she said. 'I don't really have any friends. I never see anyone and when I do the others sometimes make fun of me.'

My heart ached for her in that moment, even more so than when I'd interviewed her. It's bad enough that a girl as young as her has to deal with her illness, but she's missed out on so much of her childhood.

'Why don't you tell me more about space? I never knew that about Venus.'

That was definitely the right thing to say. Her gloominess was replaced within seconds by pure joy as she reeled off more facts. I get it. If I was Lacey, I'd want to imagine jumping in a rocket and blasting off to the unknown too.

'God, if anything happens to that kid . . .' Dr Roth mumbles, his face wrinkling as he shields his eyes from the sun. Now that he's away from Norah his calm demeanour has shifted, and I feel like grabbing him and shaking him. He's supposed to be the expert. I came with him because I need someone strong. I can't be that person. I'm not strong, not where a child is concerned.

'You okay?' I venture, huffing and puffing a little to keep up with him.

'Sure, yeah, I'm fine,' he says. I raise my eyebrow, noting the definite 'not fine' tone to his voice. He glances at me and shakes his head. 'It's just . . . a worry, that's all.'

I nod, not sure of what else there is to say, but glad he seems to be relaxing a little. A man who cares. Makes a nice change.

'She can't have left the estate,' I reason, finding myself more grateful than ever that I now live in a small gated community. I dread to think what it must be like when a child goes missing in the city.

'Yeah. The concierge checked the CCTV, said no one unusual passed through the gates, so that's something at least.' He stops walking and rubs his face. Tiny beads of sweat are breaking out and glistening on his forehead, and I can't tell if it's because of tearing around in this heat or from panic. I need him to think rationally for the both of us.

'So, did you grow up around here?' I say, trying to break the tension. Christian regards me, his face creasing into an amused expression.

'Miss Madison, are you really trying to make small talk at a time like this?'

My cheeks heat up. Me and my dire social skills again. But Christian isn't judging me, I don't think so anyway. If anything, he looks amused. At least I've achieved my goal of calming him down, even if my pride had to take the fall in the process. I wonder how long he's known Lacey. Everyone here is so tight-knit. I'm probably the least qualified to look for her, but then again, how many of the residents here have chatted to her for hours while sharing their TV?

I stop dead in my tracks. Dr Roth almost doesn't notice, he's too busy marching along the street, yelling Lacey's name so loud the neighbours are all either peering through their blinds or flocking outside.

'Stop!' I call, and he swings round to face me.

'What's the matter?'

'I've got an idea of where she might be.'

Kensington Grove is littered with cut-throughs that weave around the houses like a rabbit warren. The parents of the estate are experts at navigating them to make the school run a little shorter. I learned that the hard way a few weeks back when I attempted to walk down one during school pick-up hour and nearly got trampled by a fleet of middle-aged women, schoolchildren and buggies. The cut-throughs twist and weave until they end up at the east gate, which coincidentally is the one point in the Grove where you can see right down to the foot of the hill where the local secondary school sits. I make my way, striding with purpose and with Christian trailing behind, to the east gate. Lo and behold, staring out through the bars, is Lacey.

I swallow down the emotions – relief and sadness – I feel at seeing her, and gesture to Christian to stay put as I approach her, cautiously. I don't want to startle her, and I'm acutely aware that she can wheel away from me much faster than I can run to keep up with her. I doubt I could even manage a light jog without my lungs imploding these days. The closer I move towards her, the more my heartbeat quickens. I don't want to be around her, I'd rather be doing anything other than walking towards her right now, but it's like there's something pulling me to her. I can't seem to stay away.

She spots me as I draw near to her left side but doesn't panic. She just offers me a half-smile, and then again at Dr Roth approaching behind me.

'Hey.' I move to stand next to her and follow her gaze. From this vantage point the holiday camp kids are actually visible in the grounds, albeit they're rather small and my refusal to wear glasses makes them look more like a collection of busy ants.

'Your mum's looking for you,' I say. 'She's worried sick.'

'No kidding, I could hear her from here.'

I give her a sideways glance. Her voice is laced with exasperation and it doesn't quite suit her.

'How did you know I was here?' she asks.

I purse my lips, not entirely sure of the answer. I'd just had a hunch, a random moment of clarity as I'd been charging around the estate with Dr Roth. But as I think about it, I realise what gave me the idea. I take a tentative step closer to her, then crouch by the side of her chair.

'The film we watched last night,' I say quietly, not wanting Christian to overhear. 'You kept talking about the school in it.' She nods but doesn't say anything. 'Don't you think you should have told your mum where you were going before taking off?'

She flinches, and I immediately regret my choice of words. It was accusatory, like I'm telling her off. I'm not used to dealing with a girl of Lacey's sort of age and it's so, so hard to know what to say, but I know my best bet is getting her to trust me. 'So . . . you just taking in the views or . . .'

'I just wanted to imagine what it would be like. I know it's stupid.'

'Not at all,' I say. 'Although, I've got to tell you, you're not missing out on much. My experience of school was a montage of dirty hallways, BO and not being cool enough to sit in the back row. Wasn't exactly the highlight of my life.'

Lacey lets out a small laugh, but there's no life behind it. It's hard to hear.

'I want to be an astronaut,' she says, her voice dreamy and far-off. 'I'd love to explore up in the stars, as far away from here as you can get. But I'll never be able to. I can't even go to school.'

'An astronaut would be pretty damn cool.' I follow her gaze down to the playground, at all the children who don't realise how privileged they are to have the opportunities they do. 'Is there anything else you fancy doing when you're older?'

Lacey considers my question for a moment, before looking up at me. 'I like writing.'

'Yeah? Well, that's a good way to escape, too, you know. If you write fiction you can make up your own worlds. And if you write about real stuff like me, well, you can lose yourself in other people's messes.'

Lacey laughs, properly this time, and I feel a burst of pride that I was able to cheer her up a little bit.

'Have you told your mum how you feel about school?' I say.

She shakes her head softly. 'I tried. She just says I'm too sick.'

I wince, searching for the right words. All that comes to me are cliché platitudes – *You'll get through this, I know how you must feel* – but I know I have no right to say any of them. Lacey's dealing with something that I can never understand.

'Come on, let's get you home,' I say, placing a hand on Lacey's shoulder. She jerks away.

'I don't want to go home. She doesn't want me there anyway.'

'Lacey, your mum is tearing her hair out.'

'I don't want to go back home! Please don't make me.' Her little voice is suddenly strong and unrelenting. A flutter of guilt, as if I'm meant to be doing something but I'm not quite sure what, settles into my stomach. I lower myself to her level.

'Listen to me. Your mum's doing her best. Even if she doesn't always show it she loves you. Believe me, my mum kicked me out on the streets. I know what it's like to not be wanted.'

Lacey absorbs this information but doesn't say anything. Tears start trickling down her cheeks and pooling in the corners of her mouth. I take another step towards her and then before I know it I'm wrapping my arms around her and she's squeezing me back, and I realise that this is the first time I've had any meaningful human contact in over a year.

I glance back at Christian, who is watching intently from a distance. When we pull apart I use my sleeve to dry her cheeks, before leading her gently away from the gate. She doesn't try to argue. Christian's lips pull up into a smile as we approach.

'Impressive,' he says.

Chapter Nine

86 Days Before the Murder

Norah

'Where the hell have you been?' My voice pulsates with anger as I barrel down the driveway towards Lacey and my neighbour. My tear-stained cheeks are now burning, heat rushing through me. I drop to my knees in front of Lacey and pull her face into my hands. 'Don't you ever do that to me again! I had all sorts of awful things going through my mind!'

'I'm sorry, Mum,' Lacey whimpers, her eyes trained on her lap. She looks suddenly much smaller and all the frustration and bitterness I've become accustomed to over the past few months has been replaced with remorse. I want to stay angry at her, but her tone pulls on my heartstrings and the tension in my body starts to dissipate. I return to standing, giving Lacey a squeeze on the shoulder.

'Go on. Get yourself inside.'

Lacey does as she's told, without argument, for the first time in weeks, disappearing into our house and leaving me with Jodie. I inspect her out the corner of my eye. She's watching after Lacey, and the look on her face is reminiscent of a mother watching her child disappear into the classroom on the first day of school. It sends a spark of alarm through me.

'Thank you so much, Miss Madison,' I manage, while the straggling neighbours start heading back to their own homes.

'Call me Jodie. Please. And no problem at all. I'm glad I could help.'

'Thank you, Jodie.' I dip my head by way of acknowledgement, then return my gaze to the house. 'Where did you find her?'

'Near the east gate, where you can see down to the school. She was asking me so many questions about school I just had a hunch.'

The words leave her mouth in such a carefree way, a flippant, off-hand remark that I'm sure doesn't mean anything, but I pick up on it like a bloodhound.

'How often do you talk to Lacey?' I ask, watching her closely. Something flashes across Jodie's face. Panic? Regret? It's gone before I can tell.

'Not often,' she says, waving her hand casually in the air. The muscles in her face twitch. She is attempting to backtrack. 'Just over the fence sometimes. When we're in our gardens. That sort of thing.'

I study her, my eyes shrinking into slits. There are many tells that someone is not being honest; they avoid eye contact, they begin to shuffle on the spot, they glance to the side as if the answer might be lying over in the bushes. Jodie is displaying all of them. It is now up to me to calculate whether to challenge her or not.

I let out a breath. 'You have to understand, things have been difficult lately. The older she gets the more she wants a normal life. She forgets how ill she is and . . .' I pause, satisfied that I have given enough by way of explanation for my daughter's behaviour.

'Look at me, taking up even more of your time. I'm sure you've got better things to be doing.'

An awkward silence passes between us. I can see the cogs ticking round in her brain. She's fighting the urge to ask me questions. I keep my gaze steady on her, a subtle yet effective signal that I am the one in control here. She smiles meekly and starts moving towards her house.

'Oh, and Jodie?' I call after her, and she turns to face me. 'I'd appreciate it if you didn't speak to my daughter without my knowing. She's very impressionable.'

She furrows her brow, taken aback. 'I was just being friendly.'

'And you think as a grown adult that you are an appropriate choice of friend, do you?'

For a moment I think that she is going to attempt to argue with me, but I have the moral high ground and she knows it. She shakes her head gently. 'You know what, it's none of my business. I'm glad she's safe.'

She continues heading back home, and this time when I say, 'Thank you, Miss Madison,' she doesn't turn back.

Lacey awaits me just inside our entrance hall, as instructed. When I return from outside, I expect her to stare up at me, anticipating my next command, but she doesn't. Her eyes are pinned to the floor, neck and shoulders visibly tense.

I can't tell if she's afraid of admonishment, or if she's angry she got caught out.

She had planned it well, timing her disappearance for my regular nap time. The downside to my stringent routines is predictability. But she was either careless, not paying enough attention to the time so as to return unnoticed, or she just didn't care.

'Take your jacket off.' The words are cold and harsh on my tongue, and my jaw aches as I realise how much I've been clenching it.

She leans forward and pulls at the sleeves of her jacket. It's denim with three-quarter-length sleeves. She begged me to buy it for her last summer and I've regretted ever since – it makes her look far too grown up. It is only when she removes it that I notice she's hiked her top up and tied it with a knot at the front, exposing her stomach. Her jeans have been rolled up at the ankles to reveal a beaded ankle bracelet with charms dangling from it. And on her toes, highlighted by the strappy sandals she's opted for, is a very pale pink polish that I'd have missed had I not looked closely. She must have gone through my wardrobe to find it.

'We're going to set out some house rules,' I say, placing my hand under her chin and bringing her face up to meet mine. Her eyes widen as she looks up at me – with alarm?

'You are not to leave this house unless I am with you. That includes the garden. I understand your need for independence, for freedom, but you are still only a child. And as much as you don't want to admit it, your illness makes you vulnerable.' I move my hand to her shoulder and purposefully soften my tone. 'You're not in trouble. I just want us to stop fighting against each other all the time, Lacey. I want us to go back to how we used to be. You and I against the world, remember?'

This appears to pacify her, as she breathes out a sigh and offers me a subdued smile.

'I'll tell you what. If you promise me you'll never pull anything like that again, what do you say to a trip to the beach tomorrow? Just the two of us.'

This achieves the goal of making compliance more attractive.

'Okay,' she nods, her voice still small but less despondent than before. Together we move into the living area and begin our afternoon routine as if nothing had ever happened, and though the flames of anger are still broiling in my gut, I push them aside, water them down. My daughter is drifting again, and I have to be purposeful with my approach. Trust must be re-established.

Chapter Ten

Emma
OMG, Norah! I just heard! Is she okay?

Norah
She's fine, thank you. Went out for some fresh air, didn't think to tell me. Kids these days.

Sally
Tell me about it. I can't keep Markus straight for love nor money. I think I've just accepted the fact that he'll never be home in time for dinner anymore.

Heidi
Thank goodness we live on such a safe estate.

Marisa
Still, anything could have happened. Lacey's not just any kid, is she . . .

Norah
Are you trying to say something, Marisa?

Marisa
Nada, no! Tone of voice never comes across on these things, does it? :(I just meant a lot of people know how vulnerable she is.

Sally
That's true. What with all the publicity. I take it everyone read the *Estate Reporter* this morning?

Norah
I was too caught up in everything. Why? What did it say?

Sally
Jodie's article about the fundraiser was in there. She called you compassionate and strong, Norah. And she called Lacey a brave yet tortured young soul. Very poetic.

Norah
Can you drop it round later, Sally? I'd like to read it.

Chapter Eleven

20 Days Before the Murder

Jodie

Two months. Two months this has been going on. Without meaning to, I have let one act of kindness develop into a routine. Most Monday evenings at 8 p.m., Lacey and I watch the quiz shows. Thursdays, it's Netflix, or whatever film is showing on the Freeview channel. Oftentimes it's a load of garbage that we then laugh about the following evening, but occasionally we come across a gem that will have us discussing the plot or the actors or the special effects well into the early hours of the morning. Her excitement at what she sees on the screen is infectious, and I find myself looking at things in a completely new way. To Lacey, the advert which shows a gleaming new car zipping along a cliff-edge road in the midst of snowy mountains is beautiful, breathtaking. It doesn't matter how many times it plays she is transfixed, marvelling at the bright blue of the sky and the way the snow reflects the sunlight.

Sometimes she doesn't appear. A slight change to Norah's routine will occasionally make it too risky, but as the weeks have gone on, our late-night frivolity has extended into the daytime too.

Lacey now actively seeks me out, calling to me from the window, waving over the fence, catching me outside when I'm on my way to the office. I've tried discouraging her, really I have. I've told her I don't think it's a good idea, that I'm worried she'll get in trouble if her mum finds out. But she's latched onto me, and though my gut is telling me to put a stop to it all before it gets out of hand, I can't help but feel a little happier when she's around. Once she opens up her personality shines, lights up the room. I keep having to remind myself daily that the reason I moved to Kensington Grove was to get away from the past. It unsettles me how Lacey has absorbed me into her life with such enthusiasm – and vice versa. She'll never replace you, I know that. She just dulls the pain, for a few hours, at least.

While watching *Tipping Point* last week – the latest quiz show to air during our 8 p.m. rendezvous – I heard more from Lacey than I have done in the entirety of our . . . whatever you want to call it. Friendship? Acquaintanceship? She was like a video that had been set to double speed. The 'stop' button had broken.

'Did you have lots of friends when you were my age?' she said, and then before I had a chance to respond, 'Wait, no. Tell me about your after-school clubs. Did they have an astronomy club at your school?'

I stuttered my way through the interrogation, my heart and my mind at odds with one another. The one thing I did not want to do when I arrived at this community was to answer questions about my past. Heidi has tried, Sally has tried, every resident at some point or other has asked me something about my life before the Grove. Each time I've expertly deflected, providing just enough information to satisfy them whilst knowing my secrets are safe.

But Lacey can't be satisfied. She wants every nugget, every tiny detail, and that makes my chest tighten. It's as if I'm wearing a corset that someone behind me is pulling the strings of each time Lacey asks a new question.

But then I think of Lacey's life, a montage of the inside of her house and doctors' offices, interspersed with the occasional fundraiser or television appearance, and I soften. *She's only asking because she's trying to imagine what it's like*, I tell myself.

So, I cobble together enough information to satisfy her, and we continue our evening TV binges, with Lacey growing more and more attached to me, and, though I hate to admit it, with me doing the same.

Today is one of those in-between days where the sun is still blaring through the autumn leaves but not quite enough to deter me from turning on the heating. It's cosy inside my house, especially where I've been wrapped up all morning in a fuzzy blanket while I drink my coffee, and the last thing I want to do is go to work. I briefly consider pulling a sicky, but I'm still not convinced Andrew likes me (even after my triumphant interview with Lacey) and I'd rather not rock the boat.

I grudgingly swap the blanket for my coat and open the front door, only to come face to face with none other than Dr Roth. His hand is raised as if he had been just about to knock, and I nearly crash straight into it.

'Hey,' he says, the corner of his lips quirking up at my perplexed expression.

'Dr Roth.' I flinch back and adjust my jacket. 'What are you doing here?'

'Please, call me Christian.' He flashes me a smile. It's crooked, with one side lifting higher than the other, but it suits his face. When I don't respond he says, 'I realised I never said "good work" finding Lacey that day. I guess being a reporter helps you figure things out,' he continues.

I bristle slightly. *Journalist, not reporter, thank you very much.* A beat passes between us and he rocks back and forth on the balls of his feet. 'Anyway, I was actually wondering if you fancied a drink some time but . . .' he looks me up and down, 'I can see I've caught you at an awkward moment.'

'Yes, I'm on my way to work.' I shuffle forward, making him take a step back so that I can close the door, and then realise what he said. 'Wait, you mean a date?'

'Yeah. I mean, if you want to.'

'Oh.'

That's all I can say? Oh? I turn and fumble with my keys, growing increasingly aware of my rising body temperature, and without looking at him I say, 'I really need to get to work.'

'Perhaps after work then?' he calls as I squeeze past him and head to my car.

'Yeah, maybe,' I call back, then duck into the relative safety of the driver's seat.

I curse myself for the entire journey. He now thinks of me as either insane or just plain rude. I'm not sure which would be better. There should be a rule against people dropping questions on others like that. Especially when they're not expecting it.

My day in the office is spent distracted, to say the least. Andrew thankfully doesn't notice, but I do. When I should be editing my latest column on the top five eco-friendly cosmetic brands (a ridiculous piece for me to have to write considering I haven't the first clue about make-up), my mind is instead turning over different potential responses I could give to Dr Roth. A polite 'thanks but no thanks'? Or something more likely to prevent future attempts such as 'I'm really sorry but my husband will be returning from prison in six months'? It's a delicate situation which has to be handled with care. I don't want to give the wrong impression, or invite unnecessary questions.

My response is ready and rehearsed in my head when, during my lunch break, I dial the number for his surgery and ask to speak to him. I'll explain that I've just got out of a serious relationship (not entirely a lie depending on how you define 'just'), and that I'm not on the dating scene right now. I twirl my instant noodles round my fork while I wait to be connected, the xylophone synth of Cisco's hold music grating at my ears.

I'm almost ready to hang up the line when Dr Roth's gravelly voice sounds through the receiver. 'Hello, Dr Roth speaking.'

'Hi,' I breathe, then cough to clear my throat and try again. 'It's me. Jodie.'

'Jodie, what a nice surprise. What can I do for you?'

I try to picture what his face is doing from the tone of his voice, but he offers up no clues. 'I can do after work,' I blurt. 'Meet at the Bear and Duck at six?'

'Sure. Sounds great. See you then.'

'See you then.'

I press the 'end call' button and gawk at the screen, the photo of you that serves as my wallpaper staring back at me, judging me.

I don't know why I've agreed to go with him. Dating is not high on my agenda. I'd much sooner curl up with a bottle of Pinot Grigio in the comfort of my dressing gown and slippers than actually put on real clothes and pay threefold for the pleasure. However, my intentional standoffishness has meant that in my three months of living at the Grove I have yet to have a proper conversation with anyone besides Lacey, and though I thought that was exactly what I wanted, I find myself craving adult company.

This is how I end up wandering into the Bear and Duck, the pub at the bottom of the hill, at ten past six, checking myself in the mirror at the entrance and promptly scolding myself for caring about what he thinks. I haven't bothered changing, have come straight from the office to the pub, but I've taken out my ponytail in an attempt to look a little less formal. Now, my hair has a huge kink where the hairband was, and I realise I would have been better off leaving it as it was.

Even at this early hour the air is thick with the smell of lager and ale, the occasional waft of cigarette smoke joining the mix each time the side door is opened. This is what I consider a 'real' pub, characterised by its garish carpets and dark wood beams, the old men hunched over the bar, and the dim lighting that tells anyone who enters that this is not a place for children. I became a regular at three pubs prior to this that had the same bitter, familiar stench, but they've all either been renovated into family-friendly – and therefore more profitable – restaurants, or they've gone under and are to spend the remainder of their lives boarded up until someone inevitably turns them into flats.

Feeling at home for the first time in months, I make my way to the bar and order a lager. I sit on one of the stools and nurse my drink while I look for Dr Roth. I spot him in the shadows of one of the pub's many dark corners, sitting at a round table for two, his legs stretched out underneath with one of his feet tapping to the Ariana Grande song pouring out of the speakers. My finger slides along the rim of my glass. I'm still not sure what I want out of this evening. I could still sneak back out without him noticing and pretend I was sick.

'Evening,' I say when I finally pluck up the courage to join him at his table. His gaze flicks up to me. Was that relief I just saw flash across his eyes?

'I thought you weren't coming.' He pushes out the empty chair with his foot and I settle into it.

'Work finished a little late.'

'How was it?'

'How was what?'

'Work. What kind of articles do you write, again?'

It's not exactly a riveting conversation. One of my least favourite parts of getting to know someone new is the inane pleasantries you have to get through first; work, the weather, how am I settling into town? He shares that he likes attending the theatre and visiting art galleries, and I share that I enjoy binge-watching Netflix and ordering takeout curries. Talking to him, I realise just how uncultured my life is. But even so, it doesn't bother me like it usually does. Just being in the presence of another adult who doesn't appear to be scrutinising my every move is comforting, and as the evening goes on the tension in my muscles relaxes.

'It's ironic really,' Dr Roth says as he takes a swig of his pint. 'Most of the families on the estate should be on *Jeremy Kyle*.'

I chuckle and lean my elbows on the table, choosing to ignore how sticky it is. 'How so?'

'Well, even in a place like Kensington Grove there are some dysfunctional families . . .'

I nod, wondering if he means Norah. From what I've gleaned so far, I wouldn't describe her as dysfunctional so much as hyper-protective. She's certainly got Lacey on a tight leash. But I say nothing, just let him go on, and soon the anecdotes start spilling out.

Apparently, Lucas Rotherman, the eldest of Emma's brood who can usually be found hanging around the recycling point sneaking a spliff, once drank a pint of oil from an engine pump for a bet. It cost him a kidney and his parents tried to cover it up, claiming he'd had sepsis. Not long after that, Marisa Diaz's sister moved to the Grove and became treasurer of the Residents' Association. 'Nicest lady ever,' Dr Roth says, leaning back in his chair so that two legs lift off the floor. 'But last I heard she's on trial for stealing around 20k from the Association fund.'

I press my lips together. I can just picture Marisa's reaction when she found out about the scandal, how she must have crumpled under the scrutiny. My toes curl at the thought of it.

'Marisa was mortified,' Dr Roth continues. 'She's one of the most honest people I've ever met. You could trust her with anything. So I think they gave her the role of treasurer at the fundraiser as a kind of chance to prove herself to the community. If anything, she plays too much by the rules, to make up for her sister, I suppose.'

I secretly hope there might be an interesting story about Heidi, but alas she seems to have done a pretty good job of keeping any of her skeletons well and truly in their closet.

By the time the bell rings to signal last orders, I've downed enough beer to be well beyond driving home, so I let the bartender know I'll be back in the morning to pick up my car and pull my coat around my shoulders ready for the chilly walk home. Since Dr

Roth – or Christian, as he continuously reminded me to call him throughout our date – didn't come by car, he says we can walk back together. Part of me wants to tell him that it isn't necessary, that I'm perfectly capable of getting myself home safely, but I know that isn't strictly true in my current state, so I smile agreeably instead.

We walk in silence for the most part, my muscles burning from our steep trek up the hill. The Grove looks out of place, nestled among the greenland like that. Boxy, man-made shapes that just don't suit the raw thicket of woodland surrounding it. From this angle and in the glow of the moonlight, it really does look like an old, abandoned hospital. If I was a little more intoxicated, I'd think the wind whistling through the trees was ghosts whispering to me. As we get closer to the main entrance the trees seem to grow in size and number, craning overhead, distorting. It never occurred to me before tonight, but it's the perfect cover for someone who wants to look into the houses.

When we get to the gates, I shake off uneasy thoughts and swipe my key card. I'm trying to decide if I had a good time this evening or not. There's something about Christian that comes across as arrogant. Perhaps it's the way he looks at me as if he knows exactly what I'm thinking, or maybe it was the way he winked at the waitress when she brought us our meat platter. Still, he's a welcome distraction. When we eventually reach my door and stand on the step under the moonlight, and I sway a little as I focus on his face, I allow him to plant a small kiss on my cheek.

In a happy, drunk daze – the best feeling as far as I'm concerned – I move into my living room, close the front door behind me and kick off my shoes. The house has been plunged into darkness, and whether it's the booze or the eerie sound of wind whistling outside, it all looks rather spooky. I circle the room closing the curtains, and as I reach the far side my eyes land on movement outside. At first, I think it's a cat sitting on the window ledge next door, but then my eyes focus.

'Lacey!' A heaviness expands in my core as I realise what time it is.

'Where were you?' is all Lacey says.

'I am so, so sorry. I completely forgot!' But before I can say anything else Lacey disappears into her bedroom and shuts her curtains, leaving me with a wrecked conscience and the stale taste of beer and acid on my tongue.

Chapter Twelve

19 Days Before the Murder

Norah

I'm starting to think I have two daughters. The one who accompanied me to the beach after her little excursion to the east gate, who squealed with excitement when she knocked £3.20 out of the coin pusher in the arcade, who begged me for a mint choc chip ice cream and looked once more like my little girl as she licked it and got a splodge of green on her nose. And then there's this other child, a moody stranger who inhabits my real daughter's bedroom more than I care to accept. I never know which one I'm going to have to deal with for the day, and each morning as I wake her up I get the distinct sense of standing on a thin sheet of glass. If I move too quickly it will shatter.

Yesterday I got moody Lacey. Difficult Lacey. Draining Lacey. It was as if in the time between her going to bed and waking up in the morning, any trace of joy or rationality had been sapped from her. She sulked and huffed and glowered all day, and when I tried to ask her what had her in such a foul mood she simply rolled her eyes and turned on her music. When did rolling your eyes at your mother become acceptable? I knew puberty would be an interesting time, but these teenage moods are far more intense than I expected.

Now, I'm running my finger along the rim of my mug of green tea and wondering who I'll get today. I could just not wake her up. I could leave her to her slumber and pretend for a few short hours that I'm a carefree singleton, not that I've ever really been carefree.

I smile at the thought as I tap at her door and peek round the corner. She's got funny with me just walking in recently, as if I don't have a right to check on my own daughter in my own house. To my surprise, she's already awake and sitting up in her bed. She starts as I enter and scrambles to hide what she's doing, like I can really be fooled that easily. I catch a glimpse of the corner of the notebook but pretend I haven't noticed, instead filing the information away in my mind for later.

'Morning, early riser,' I say in as chipper a voice as I can muster.

'Hey.'

Not the response I'd have liked, but not a total disregard for my existence. Maybe I'll get 'in-between Lacey' today. I eye the astronomy book, crumpled with use, lying on her desk beside her untouched homeschool workbooks.

'You're falling behind.' I nod towards them, attempting to mute the accusation in my tone.

She shrugs. 'I guess I prefer learning about astronomy.'

'But you've already read it so many times. Surely you can't be gaining anything new from that book.' I pick it up and flick through the pages, trying to understand just what makes it so riveting.

Lacey snatches it out of my hand. 'You just don't get it.'

She's right, I don't, but I don't want to argue, not about something so trivial. I'll sit down with her later at our usual time – 3 p.m. to 5 p.m. – and struggle through the homeschooling with her. At least she'll do it if I'm there. She used to be a good student, she enjoyed learning, but lately, as with everything else, she's been fighting me.

I move across to her bedside and pull her bronchodilator out of the wardrobe, handing it to her with a smile. A sudden urge to brush her cheek with my hand creeps through me and my fingers tingle, but before I can move our doorbell rings.

A pang of regret hits me at the missed moment. I leave Lacey to it and head to the front door, pausing to check through the peephole before I open it. I had expected a parcel delivery, or perhaps Heidi looking to unload her frustrations with her husband over a cup of tea. I had not expected my next-door neighbour.

'I've bought a present for Lacey,' she explains when I open the door, not bothering to hide my lack of enthusiasm over an uninvited visitor. I glimpse the bag in Jodie's hands, keeping my face as neutral as possible so as to disguise the alarm bells ringing in my head. My eyes linger on it, as if by staring at it long enough I might be able to see through the vivid green plastic.

'That's very kind.' I reach for the bag. 'I'll pass it on to her.'

She pulls back from me slightly. 'I don't suppose I could . . . give it to her myself?'

A familiar dread bubbles in the pit of my stomach, a dread I've felt only once before. My fingers tap against my door as I contemplate my options. I could tell her this is inappropriate, which it is. A present is an overtly familiar gesture, one that suggests to me this woman is a lot closer to my daughter than I thought. But if history is indeed repeating itself, it would do me well to know a little more about Miss Jodie Madison. After a moment of dithering, I open the door wider and allow her to pass through.

'Please, sit down. Would you like a cup of tea?' I ask, making a perfunctory gesture towards the living area. She nods and proceeds to select the armchair. I keep her firmly in my peripheral vision as I stand at the breakfast bar and prepare the tea. At first she leans back into the cushions, then changes her mind and sits forward with her elbows on her knees. Her eyes roam the space around her. Our house is minimal, free of clutter, an array of muted shades and dignified furniture selections. Everything has its place. Some find it intimidating, but it is a requirement for a home such as ours. Lacey needs space to manoeuvre her chair.

Once the tea is brewed I carry a mug to her and sit on the sofa opposite, crossing my legs and keeping my posture open. She needs to see that I am not daunted by her presence. She thanks me and sips it before resuming her scrutiny of my home. I wonder if she even realises she's doing it. This time her eyes move to the bookcase next to the bay window. The shelves are stacked with medical encyclopedias and reference texts. *Facing Cystic Fibrosis: A Guide For Parents and Their Families.* Below it, *Oxford Respiratory Medicine Library.* And next to that, *Standards for the Clinical Care of Children and Adults with Cystic Fibrosis in the UK.*

'Is Lacey here?' she asks, fidgeting. The reminder of Lacey's illness clearly makes her uncomfortable. The question is a redundant one; where would Lacey be without me? But I nod and answer it nonetheless.

'She's doing her airway clearance. It'll only take another few minutes.'

Jodie forces a smile and opens and closes her mouth, as if floundering for a response. When she can't find one she crosses her legs, uncrosses them, squirms in her seat, brushes a stray strand of hair from her eyes.

'So, Jodie, what brought you to Kensington Grove?' This is always the question I am most intrigued to learn about a person when they move here. Everyone else asks about career choices and family set-up, but for me nothing tells more about a person than their reasoning for choosing a gated community. It takes a particular sort of person to live in a place like this.

'Oh, I'm just a bit of a worrier. Since I live on my own I thought a gated community would help me to feel safer. Though I have to admit, the asylum memorabilia dotted around the place does freak me out a bit!' She laughs then, a little too loudly, and rubs at her forearm.

She's hiding something.

'Do you have any family nearby?'

'Nope, just plain old me.' She takes a long, drawn-out sip of tea, presumably to give herself an excuse to not talk, and starts looking around again. I can practically hear her willing Lacey to hurry up. I don't say anything else, rather enjoying watching her squirm instead.

'You're a very strong woman,' she says finally. 'To do everything you do for Lacey all on your own.'

I frown. I hadn't anticipated that remark, and am suddenly aware of my mouth growing dry. I say nothing, allowing the silence to linger, but then smile with humility. The moment of eye contact we share is brief, as she almost immediately lowers her eyes and runs a finger along the top of her bag, tracing the areas where the plastic has been fused together to create the handle. What I'd give to know what's inside.

She notices me staring and says, 'I just thought she'd like something to brighten her day a little.' Her eyes widen as she backtracks. 'Not that she's not already happy, of course. She's extremely cheerful for someone in her ... situation. You must do a good job of keeping her spirits up.'

'I'm sure she'll appreciate it.' My acknowledgement of her generosity, half-hearted as it is, has the desired calming effect and she stops rambling.

When Lacey eventually appears in the hallway, her chest still covered in her airway clearance machine – a blue vest with tubes trailing off it – Jodie leaps up from her seat with such vigour her shins smack against the marble-topped coffee table. Wincing, she picks up the bag and looks to me, presumably for approval. I nod and beckon Lacey over, not wanting to prolong Jodie's stay any more than is necessary.

'Hi, I bought you a present.' She lifts the bag and takes it to her. As she places the bag in Lacey's lap, I watch my daughter's chest puff out a little and a pink blush warm her cheeks. Her fingers drift over the items inside, pausing to inspect the contents. I arch my neck to spy packs of face masks, a terry cloth headband, a pot of coconut-scented hand cream.

'Thank you,' Lacey whispers, so quietly I almost miss it. A twinge of annoyance sparks through me, and it's all I can do to stop myself from charging across the room and snatching the bag from her hands. But I know that is not the way to handle this situation; that is, if I have any hope of seeing cheerful Lacey again tomorrow. So instead I offer another cup of tea – a token that conveys gratitude – which, as hoped, Jodie refuses. She is then walked to the door.

As she exits my home and crosses the lawn to her own, she

hesitates as if there is more to be said, perhaps to me or perhaps to Lacey. She doesn't return, though, instead shaking her head slightly and disappearing behind her own front door. My eyes narrow as my lips press together. Something tells me this is not the first meaningful interaction this woman has had with my daughter.

Chapter Thirteen

19 Days Before the Murder

Jodie

It's a relief to return home from next door. It felt overly sterile, though it should have occurred to me that that's what it would be like. Lacey is probably extremely vulnerable to germs. I was afraid to move or touch anything for fear of dirtying it. I couldn't live like that. Granted, I could do with sprucing up this place a little – dust settles on every untidy surface and the distinct smell of off milk permeates the air whenever I open the fridge – but cleaning is always one of those 'I'll do it later' situations. Norah's house is not a place I'll be eager to return to any time soon, but I did what I went there to do. All I cared about was apologising to Lacey in a way that let her know I truly was sorry, and I think I achieved that.

I make my way to the office and tap out my stories quietly confident that she'll be at her window tonight and things will go back to the way they were. Even a text from Christian – **Hey, been thinking about you. Let me know when you're free to get together again** – isn't enough to distract me. I've surprised myself in my eagerness to resume my evenings with Lacey. Looking at her hurts my heart. Speaking to her makes my stomach churn and my throat constrict. But I don't care. She gives me the same fuzzy warmth that comes from downing a bottle of vodka – yes, it has its downsides and after-effects, but you drink it nonetheless.

I finish work late. Andrew decided to drop a bunch of interview notes on my desk that needed transcribing five minutes before I was due to leave, and by the time I make my way out to the car park the sky has turned a dusty grey. The coolness of autumn has well and truly settled on England now, and I pull my coat tighter around me and find myself wishing I'd thought to pick up a scarf when I left this morning. I hesitate for a second – the car park is empty apart from my car and two others, and something about the dim open space and the ghostly silence seems almost threatening. I shake my head, telling myself I'm being silly, and set off towards my car.

'Where are we going?' you say.

I stop in my tracks, fear settling into me. A solid mass. You're not here. You're not with me. It's not far to walk to my car, but as I do a tingle runs down my neck and makes the fine hairs stand up, as if someone is watching me. I pick up my pace, my palms sweaty around my key fob, and open my car. Once in the driver's seat I grip the steering wheel and glance at myself in the rear-view mirror, attempting to steady my ragged breathing. My face is flushed with a glossy sheen running across my forehead. *Pull yourself together*, I think. *You're being stupid.*

The sense of foreboding lifts the closer I get to Kensington Grove, and by the time I've passed through the gates it has practically evaporated. For once the Grove's history doesn't feel quite so unnerving in comparison to the car park. I can definitely see the appeal of a place like this. It does feel safe as the gates close and lock out the world behind me. I should count myself lucky, really.

I glance at the clock on my dash. It's 7 p.m. Just enough time to bung a pasta bake into the microwave before my evening with Lacey. An odd excitement swells inside me at the prospect. But as I turn into my road and pull up to my driveway my stomach lurches. Norah is standing on the step outside my front door. Is it a coincidence that we've arrived at the same time, or has she been waiting for me?

It's only when I turn off the engine and pull myself out of the car that I notice the pharmacy bag clutched in her hand.

'You can have this stuff back,' she says as I approach, not even offering a greeting first. She pushes the bag into my chest so that I have no choice but to take it.

I stare at her, dumbfounded. 'Sorry, I don't understand?'

'It isn't an appropriate gift. She's fourteen. She's barely a teenager.'

A stray face mask falls out of the bag and lands on my shoe. Norah lowers her eyes, as if deeply regretful of what she's about to say. 'I want you to stay away from Lacey.'

I can't speak. My mouth just hangs open as I try to process what I'm hearing. I replay Norah's words in my head, trying to ascertain if I've misheard somehow. But Norah's face is deadly serious.

'I was just trying to be nice,' I finally manage.

'And that's appreciated, Miss Madison. But I'm her mother and I know what's best for her. And I trust you'll respect my wishes as her mother.' And with that, she turns her back on me and strides over to her house.

After taking a few moments to process the encounter, I make

my way, still totally bewildered, into my house. I drop the bag by the front door, plug my phone in to charge and pull all the curtains closed, except for the window I hope to see Lacey at. I don't take kindly to being told what to do. As soon as 8 p.m. rolls round I'll be positioning myself there in a metaphorical 'screw you' to Norah. Unfortunately, Lacey, it seems, feels otherwise. I sit eating my pasta bake and no one comes to join me at the window. She's probably received the same warning from her mother, or – and I really hope this isn't the case – maybe she's still mad at me.

There are so many unanswered questions floating around my head. Had I known that our most recent talk was to be our last, I would have pressed Lacey to tell me why she said what she said that day at the gate, why she felt Norah didn't want her anymore. Perhaps it was a throwaway comment. Perhaps Norah had simply lost her patience one day and said something she didn't mean; an understandable error when you look at how much the woman has to deal with. But if it wasn't, then I can't leave Lacey alone. I won't.

The phone ringing almost makes me choke on my pasta. Jeez. The mixture of my anxiety in the car park and the run-in with Norah has me on edge. I place the plastic container on the coffee table and trudge over to the TV unit, where my sad little landline sits flashing in its holder. I don't know why I even bothered to get a landline. No one calls me on it except for people trying to sell me things.

'Hello?' I say into the receiver, fully anticipating having to give a polite yet firm rejection to whatever the person on the other end of the line is offering.

'Jodie? Is that you?'

My shoulders curl forward. I clutch my shirt in my fist, feeling as if my chest is caving in on itself. I try to think calmly, logically. There's no way. There's no way she could possibly know where I am, let alone be able to figure out my number. But that voice is unmistakable.

I slam the phone down and stare at it, the glowing numbers displaying the time on the base blurring before my eyes. I rush to the front door and double, triple check that it's locked, and do the same with the back door. How did they find me? Who else knows where I am? For the first time in God knows how long I find myself wishing I didn't live alone. The house suddenly feels too big for me. It seems to balloon in size while I shrink.

I curl up on my bed and stare at the crack between the curtains, convincing myself that at any moment a face would appear through the glass. I replay Norah's words in my head. *I want you to stay away from Lacey.* And when I'm not thinking of Norah and Lacey, I'm thinking of the phone call, and when I'm not thinking of that, I'm thinking of you.

I fall asleep still in my work clothes.

Chapter Fourteen

18 Days Before the Murder

Norah

'Good grief, Heidi. Are you trying to choke me?' The thick mist of hairspray lingers around me to the point where I can barely see my reflection in the mirror. It's been a long-held tradition that Heidi comes round whenever I'm to appear on television and primps me. It's her area of expertise. And, to be honest, even if I was confident in doing my own hair and make-up, I'm sure she'd batter down my door before she'd let me exclude her.

'It needs a thick coating or you'll lose all the volume by the time the cameras start recording.'

The crew are pottering around, adjusting the lighting set-up for the fifth or sixth time. At this point I think they're just waiting for us, and Heidi's fussing is starting to get on my nerves. She's still got to do Lacey. Back when we first appeared on TV, I hadn't worried nearly as much about my appearance. But the years haven't been kind; my under-eyes are permanently shadowed, my lips are thin and beginning to look pinched, my skin is dry and uncared for. I don't need to see my tired face staring back at me on the screen.

'I think that's good,' I say, raising my hand to Heidi before she attempts to spray me again. 'I'll go and get Lacey.'

I smile apologetically at the crew, who assure me there's no rush. I imagine they're used to delays doing what they do. They're filming for the Children of Courage award. Before the awards are to be presented – by the prime minister, no less – a short VT is to be played showing each child's story. We've told our story so many times it's like reading from a script these days.

I push Lacey's door gently open, knocking as I do so. She's hunched over her desk, hand scribbling furiously on the drawing pad in front of her, and doesn't even glance up as I enter.

'It's time to get ready, darling. Let's get you dressed.' I unhook her outfit from the door – this time I opted for a velvet-effect dress in a gorgeous burgundy tone – and when Lacey still doesn't move I say, 'Come on, put that away now. You can draw later.'

'I don't want to do the interview.' She's so buried in what she's doing I barely hear the words and think I must be mistaken, but the look on her face confirms it. We're going to have one of those days.

I blink a few times, giving myself a moment to choose the best course of action.

'Look,' I say, moving towards her and pointedly laying the dress on the desk beside her drawing. 'I know you're still mad at me for taking that . . . gift bag away.' Her hand slows, but she doesn't stop. 'But there are far more appropriate gifts that I'm more than happy to get for you. Perhaps after this we could choose one together. Some new clothes perhaps? Or those expensive paints you wanted?'

Lacey's head lowers so close to her pad it's a wonder she can see what she's doing. 'There wasn't anything wrong with the gift Jodie got me.'

My lips pinch together and I can feel the layers of foundation that Heidi painted on my face cracking. *Don't take the bait. Don't take the bait.*

'Well, that's your opinion.' I can hear the tension in my own voice. Unwilling to get any further into this conversation, I yank the dress off the hanger and start unbuttoning the back.

'Jodie said I deserve a pamper session after all I've been through.'

I stop undoing the dress. For a moment, I think I stop breathing too. 'Miss Madison,' I pointedly don't use her first name, the words coming out stilted and sharp, 'does not know what's best for you. I'm your mother. She's just a random woman who's taken an unnatural interest in you.'

For the first time this morning Lacey looks up at me, her expression giving no hints as to what emotions might be playing behind her eyes.

'I'm starting to think maybe you don't know what's best for me.'

Anger churns inside me. How dare she? After everything I do for her, how dare she treat me with such contempt. She's fourteen years old, for Christ's sake. It takes every ounce of self-restraint I have not to storm out, slam the bedroom door and lock her in there until she's ready to apologise.

'You're tired,' I say eventually. 'Let's check your iron levels.'

'I'm not tired! Not everything is about my stupid illness, you know?'

My self-restraint slipping, I throw the dress down on the bed. 'Look, just because our next-door neighbour thinks it's appropriate to talk to a child for hours on end in the evenings,' I say, forcing my tone to remain steady, 'doesn't mean she understands what kind of care you need.'

I don't even realise what I've said until Lacey's face changes, her stoic façade cracking into widening eyes of disbelief.

'How do you know about that?' she whispers. Her voice is suddenly small, having lost all its confidence from before. My mind searches for a plausible answer, but she already knows.

If she hadn't panicked so much when I walked in the other day and tried to hide her diary from me I probably wouldn't have done it, but I know my daughter less and less these days. As I slipped it carefully out from under her while she slept last night, I justified it by telling myself it was the 'responsible parent' thing to do. I need to know what she's thinking, and if she refuses to tell me I regrettably have to resort to these measures.

As I read my fingers clenched, nausea thickening in my throat. Tears stung my eyes, blurring the words before me, but I forced them back.

> *Evenings with Jodie have felt like hanging out with the older sister I never had. Or a way more fun mum. She doesn't get bored of listening to me talking about space. She actually likes hearing the facts I tell her, which makes a nice change. I never feel like I have to shut up around her. I can't wait until tonight. I only wish Mum would go to bed earlier.*

Now, I can only watch as Lacey pushes her wheelchair away from the desk in a swift motion and rips her pillow off the bed. I never got the chance to return her diary last night. There is still the indent of the book in her bottom sheet.

'You read my diary?'

Her voice rips through the room and I'm suddenly very aware of the TV crew just a hallway away from us.

'We'll talk about this later,' I almost hiss, willing her to lower her volume even though I can see her physically shaking with resentment.

'Get out of my room!' she screams.

I flinch. She's never screamed at me before, not like this. Tears prick my eyes and my own body is descending into a trembling mess. I take a wary step toward her and attempt to put my arms around her but she pushes me away.

'Please, baby, I'm only trying to do what's best for you.'

'Get out! I hate you!' She hurls insults at me through floods of tears, her face reddening, the veins in her temple pulsing. It's terrifying.

And then I snap. 'Don't talk to me like that, you ungrateful little bitch!'

I immediately clasp my hand over my mouth as the room descends into silence, save for the muted sobbing coming from both of us. She stares at me and I stare back. Never, in all my years as a mother, have I ever sworn at Lacey. No matter how frustrated I've got with her I've always remained calm.

'Baby, I'm so sorry. I didn't mean that.' I drop to my knees and reach desperately for her arm. 'I'm just . . . I'm so stressed and so tired. I need you to cooperate with me.'

Lacey's face is soaked with tears, and her chest is rising and falling at an alarming rate. Getting so worked up isn't good for her. I reach over to the box of tissues and cautiously dab at her cheeks.

'Let's . . .' I struggle to get the words out because my voice is shaking so much. 'Let's get you cleaned up. We'll do this piece of filming, get rid of them and then do something nice together, hmm?'

Lacey places her hand over mine, and for a split second I think she's going to squeeze it and pull me into an embrace, but instead she jerks the tissue out of my grasp and throws it in the wastepaper basket.

'You're going to have to find some other sick kid to show off on TV.'

She turns her back on me and pulls her headphones over her ears. I stand there for a few moments, stunned into helplessness, my insides feeling empty as if she's just pulled out all my organs and left the shell of a person. And then, with nothing else to do or say, I back out of her room and close the door behind me.

My feet drag along the floor as I make my way to the living room. When I emerge, a sea of faces stare back at me. Heidi, whose complexion is paler than I've ever seen it as she stands there holding her hand to her heart, is the first to move. She rushes forward and places an arm around my shoulders.

'Are you okay? Is there anything I can do?'

'Just leave,' I croak, my voice hoarse even though Lacey was the one who did all the screaming.

Heidi's eyes dart from me to the crew. 'But—'

'Just leave. All of you. Please.'

The crew don't need as much convincing as Heidi. They pack up their things in half the time it took them to unload it all, avoiding my eye the whole time. Heidi attempts to offer me a cup of tea, saying she'll stay with me after the crew have gone, but even she eventually gets the hint that I want to be left alone.

When I finally close the door and turn back to my empty living room, it's all I can do to sink down to the cold floor and weep. How did we get here? Whatever happened to my lovely, smiley little girl who would dazzle the cameras with her upbeat personality, who won the hearts of all those people who have treated us so well since her diagnosis?

But, of course, I already know the answer, and have for some time now. Lacey has acted like this once before, back when she got close to our old neighbour Alison. The pulling away from me, the refusal to listen to reason, it's as if every time she engages with anyone other than me her behaviour just becomes unbearable. Last time, things very nearly came crashing down. Lacey nearly exposed our secret. I had to put a stop to it then, and if Lacey thinks I won't put a stop to it now, she is severely mistaken.

Chapter Fifteen

Sally

How did the filming go? You do lead such an exciting life, Norah. The closest I got to being on TV was getting caught in the background of a news broadcast once.

Emma

Bit poor taste, Sally.

Marisa

Yes, I'm sure she wouldn't choose her life.

Sally

Oh God, you know what I mean. Sorry, Norah, you know I didn't mean that the way it came out. Me and my big mouth, eh?

Emma

Think you've pissed her off.

Sally

Norah???

Heidi

She's probably busy, ladies. When I left she was sorting Lacey's medication. I'm sure she knows you didn't mean anything by it, Sally. I wouldn't worry.

Chapter Sixteen

17 Days Before the Murder

Jodie

Over breakfast, as I push remnants of stale granola around my bowl with my spoon and pick out the occasional raisin to suck on, I rack my brain for a way to get a message across to Lacey without Norah knowing. As I consider the possibility of taping a letter to her bedroom window, my phone flashes and my 'Bohemian Rhapsody' ringtone fills the silence. Christian.

I sigh and rub my temple. He's called me a couple of times since our date to suggest another one, and each time I've apologised and said I was busy with friends that evening. Of course, anyone who paid enough attention would know that was a lie – the closest to a friend I've got in the Grove is a fourteen-year-old who now isn't speaking to me. But each time he said, 'No worries, another night?' and I replied, 'Of course.' I know I can't put him off forever, and if I'm not planning on going out with him again I should just tell him straight so he can move on with his life. But even though I'm certain going out with him again is a bad idea, one that I'm sure to regret later down the line, I don't want to *not* go out with him again.

I let the call ring out, and once Queen has stopped blaring I pick up the phone and text him. I prefer texting to speaking on the phone. As an anti-social journalist saying words out loud has never been my strong suit. Far better to write it down and take a moment to think about what I want to say.

> Hey, sorry I missed your call. I'd love to go out again . . .

I type out, then watch the letters erase themselves under the firm press of my thumb on the delete button.

> Hey, sorry I missed your call. You free this evening? X

No, no kiss.

Just a few seconds later my phone buzzes.

> I am indeed. How about dinner at La Plaque d'Argent? Pick you up at 6?

> Sounds like a plan.

Christian picks me up at exactly five minutes to six. After a brief honk to alert me to his presence, I open the door to find him leaning against his car, one leg crossed over the other and his arms doing the same, a whisper of a smile touching his lips. God, he looks cocky. It's a bad idea, I remind myself. I know his type all too well. But the Williams house in my peripheral vision tells me I could do with the distraction, so I trudge over to the passenger side and settle myself in the seat.

La Plaque d'Argent looks more like a grandiose hotel. He had warned me it was a nice restaurant we were going to, and I hopped onto their website before getting ready to check the dress code and scope out the menu, but seeing it in person makes me realise just how much I don't fit into a place like this. Towering glass doors with intricate metal patterns serve as the entrance leading to a marbled lobby, complete with a forest of potted plants and a huge chandelier. Christian, dressed in a crisp, tailored suit, likely from one of the high-end London shops, looks right at home as he greets the maître d' with a nod and a handshake. I, meanwhile, am acutely aware of how underdressed I am, even though I'm wearing the nicest outfit I own.

'May I take your coat?' the maître d' asks, holding out his arm. I give him a forced smile and, grudgingly, hand him my coat, revealing the only dress I have that was even remotely suitable. It isn't bad; I purchased it for the twenty-fifth birthday party that Gabbie bullied me into, and have worn it to every wedding or semi-formal event I've been invited to since. You always said I looked lovely in it, but it sticks out like a sore thumb against the other ladies dining in diamonds and furs.

'I'm not sure I'm classy enough for this place,' I whisper as we're escorted to our table.

'You're a lady of Kensington Grove,' he says in an over-the-top posh accent. 'Of course you are.'

He winks at me, and I force a smile in return, appreciating his attempt to calm my nerves with humour. As we take our seats he leans across the table and places a gentle hand on my forearm. 'You look great. That dress really suits you.'

The next half an hour or so is surreal. Wine is served to us in real crystal glasses. The menu consists of a lot of words I don't understand, so I resort to the safe 'I'll have the same, please,' after Christian has ordered. Raw slabs of steak are presented to us on a wooden platter, which Christian explains is so that I can choose how I want it cooked. At one point a smash sounds from the kitchen, and instead of the guests roaring with laughter like I'm used to, the restaurant continues its soft chatter, and I wince as I think about how much the waiter who broke the glass would lose out of their tips.

We go through the usual light chit-chat while we await our meals. He tells me about his day at work, how he nearly ended up in an argument with a neurotic mother who didn't understand that there was no cure for a common cold and was refusing to leave until he prescribed her darling son antibiotics. I tell him about my day, how I edited a riveting article on the top ten diets of the year, guaranteed to make you lose at least ten pounds.

'What do you want to write?'

I shake my head. 'Whatever pays the bills, I guess.'

'But what do you actually want to write? What excites you?'

He breaks open a crusty roll and butters it, and I watch as the butter melts and the golden rivulets sink into the bread while I consider his question.

'I like to people watch,' I say after a moment. 'I think the most fascinating stories come from what happens behind closed doors.' I scan the room, and my eyes land on an elderly couple. He has an old-fashioned pocket watch, the dainty golden chain dangling from his suit pocket. She has a set of pearls that look as if they've faded and withered with age. Both of them have a look of pure adoration on their faces.

'Take that couple, for example,' I nod towards them. 'They could be an old married couple. Or they could be on their first date. Perhaps that pocket watch has a picture of his late wife inside, and it's taken him ten years to get to the point where he can find love again. Perhaps those pearls were given to her by her ex who broke her heart, but she can't quite bear to let them go.' My cheeks flush warm as I meet Christian's intent gaze, and I let out a self-deprecating laugh. 'Those are the stories that interest me, I guess. Real life.'

'You should write those stories, then,' he says. He makes it sound so simple. I lower my gaze, focus on the candle flickering on the table, watch the reflection of the flame in the liquid wax.

'Maybe one day I'll get back there.'

The steak that gets placed in front of me is by far the best thing I've ever tasted. I'd forgotten how good food can make you feel, and though I'm completely stuffed by the time I've finished, I wish there had been more. For a moment I consider ordering seconds, then I remember where I am. The food coupled with the company has been enough to pull my thoughts away from my predicament with Norah and Lacey, but as I pop the last broccoli floret into my mouth I find myself right back there. The whole situation is making my head spin. So much so that when Christian asks if I'm ready to make a move, I suggest we get another bottle instead.

'You're pretty arrogant, you know that, right?' I say after my fourth – or is it my fifth? – large glass of wine.

'What makes you say that?' One corner of his mouth turns up. Whether he's amused by my comment or my tipsy behaviour, I can't quite tell.

'You know, you're all ... Dr Roth. Doctor. I am ... the Doctor.'

'Perhaps I can show you my Tardis later,' he says, and I laugh a little too hard. Then, through the cloud of my drunkenness, a thought occurs to me.

'Did you ever treat Lacey?'

My vision is somewhat impaired, the tables behind Christian are starting to blur into one, but I'm sure I saw it; a slight tensing of his posture, a ripple of the muscle in his jaw.

'I can't talk about a specific patient. Doctor-patient confidentiality.' His face has gone from jovial to taut and caged in a matter of seconds, like a light has been switched off. His sudden desire to come across as professional is a stark contrast to the doctor who was quite happily gossiping about his patients, albeit anonymously, earlier.

'Of course.' I nod and glance down at the table, now uncomfortable. It holds the remnants of our meal – wrappers from the complimentary chocolates we were provided with, half-drunk glasses of wine, the untouched water jug thick with condensation. I pick it up and pour myself a glass. I've forgotten where I am. I really need to sober up.

For the duration of the journey home, Christian is unusually silent. I keep stealing glances at him, his stern expression highlighted every few seconds by the streetlights which cast abstract shadows across the crevices of his face.

'I'm sorry if I made you uncomfortable,' I finally say when I can't cope with the silence any longer. I've found that, despite my initial reluctance, there is a certain refreshment that comes with spending time with him, and I've surprised myself with how much I'd like to do it again. To my relief, the familiar self-assured smile creeps back onto his lips, but it's stretched thin at the edges. I don't think it's entirely sincere.

'Don't worry about it.'

We pull up to the main entrance and Christian rolls his window down. He jerks his hand out and clumsily rams his key card against the reader. The plastic bends, snaps.

'Shit,' he mumbles.

'Here, use mine.' I pull my card out and offer it to him. He's either tipsier than I thought, in which case I probably shouldn't have let him drive me home, or he's still bothered by my question from earlier.

By the time we've reached my front door any awkwardness seems to have dwindled. As he did the last time he dropped me home, he leans in and gives me a light peck on the cheek, though this time instead of pulling away afterwards he lingers by my face, his breath warm on my skin. I swallow hard. *Don't say it. Don't say it. Don't say it.*

'Would you . . . like to come in?'

Christian is the one who goes in for the full kiss, who stumbles into the house and shuts the door behind us, knocking over the umbrella stand as his hands roam my body. But, despite my better judgement, it's me who leads the way, still locked in a fumbling embrace, to the bedroom.

Afterwards, I lay awake with my head resting on Christian's chest, watching it rise and fall with each breath. The lights are off; I made sure we stayed in darkness so he wouldn't spy my unshaven legs, my wobbly bits or my scars, but I can still see him in the light of the moon peeking through the curtains. He's staring up at the ceiling, a thoughtful look on his face, and I feel like I should say something but I'm not quite sure what. My stomach turns over and over, partly due to physical activity that my body is far from used to, partly due to the booze and partly due to the threads of regret pulling at my insides. Sleeping with him was stupid. It's just made things complicated.

I tilt my head to look at him. 'Can't sleep?'

He smiles down at me, and a shiver runs down my spine. It's been a while since someone looked at me like that.

'I tend to have difficulties sleeping. I usually take sleeping pills but they're at home and, well, I wasn't expecting to not be there tonight.'

I wasn't expecting it either. Not saying a word, I shimmy out from beside him, trying and failing to cover myself with the duvet. It's one thing seeing each other's naked body when we're in the throes of drunken passion, it's quite another thing in the awkward aftermath. As quickly as I can I grab my dressing gown off the hook on the door and keep my back to him as I wrap it around myself, hoping the darkness is on my side. I then shuffle across the hall to the bathroom, grab a small bottle from the shelf and return to the bedroom.

'Here,' I say, throwing him the bottle.

He squints to read the label. 'Whoa, these are strong.'

'Yeah, well, I used to have trouble sleeping too, when . . .' I trail off, my breath catching in my throat. I almost said it. I almost mentioned you. I'm too drunk still, too caught off guard from the night's events, and it's making me careless.

Luckily, he doesn't seem to have noticed my almost-slip-up. He's too busy scrutinising the bottle, ever the doctor.

'I'm going to go grab a glass of water. Want one?'

The water hitting the bottom of my stomach makes me want to heave, and I clasp my hand around my mouth in an effort to stop myself chundering over the floor. As I gulp back the sour saliva gathering in my mouth, my eyes land on movement outside the window. Through the blackness I can just make out a figure, and for a moment it's like the entire world has stopped.

A dull ache pulses in my chest. Chills slink from the nape of my neck to my tailbone. I'm paralysed, trying to make sense of what I'm seeing. The moonlight highlights your hair, bouncing off the textured surface. I lift a hand, reaching out towards the window, willing you to turn around. I'm imagining things. The alcohol has messed with my mind. I blink a few times and try to focus, and then I realise what I'm seeing.

It's not you, doesn't look anything like you. Of course it isn't you. How could it be? It's Lacey in her bedroom, her curtains not yet drawn. She hasn't seen me. She's talking to someone, must be Norah. But after a second her eyes flick out the window and seem to land directly on me. Her lips move, but everything is so fuzzy I can't make out what she's saying. Not that I'm a master of lip-reading at the best of times, but the alcohol certainly isn't helping. I squeeze my eyes shut and massage my temple, willing my heart to stop racing. *Snap out of it, you idiot.*

The chills still haven't left my body. By the time I open my eyes again Lacey is gone. Clutching mine and Christian's water and swaying slightly, I return to the warmth of my bed. Only when I've pulled the duvet up to my chin and taken a few deep breaths do I properly think about what I've just seen. My eyes snap open again as the image plays over in my mind. No, I'm being ridiculous. Hell, I've just seen a ghost. Nothing I saw can count for anything in the state I'm in. But even so, if it hadn't been for the lack of lighting and my obscured perception, I could have sworn that Lacey said, 'Help me.'

By the time morning rolls around I'm both exhausted and hungover, a delectable concoction if ever there was one. I spent hours lying awake last night thinking about what I saw, to the point where I had to join Christian in popping a couple of sleeping pills. When I did eventually fall asleep, the image invaded my dreams. I startled myself awake more than once with bizarre illusions of someone standing over me, laughing at me while I remained pinned to the ground, unable to move.

I edge out to the kitchen, my mouth dry and sticky all at the same time, and a shirtless Christian gives me a double take. The dishevelled morning appearance looks good on him, the bastard. I dread to think what I look like.

'Good morning,' he nods, and I groan in response. He hands me a steaming cup of coffee, a nice gesture on any other day, but the smell of it only increases the sense of pressure building in my cranium.

'Put some clothes on.' His shirt is still hanging where it had been left – flung over the chair as we made our way to the bedroom. I pick it up and throw it to him. Seeing him without his clothes only serves as a reminder of my behaviour. I'm slightly annoyed at him too. I was too intoxicated to focus on it last night, but he had far too much to drink to then drive us home. I thought doctors were supposed to be responsible. He doesn't say anything as he gets himself dressed, but must have caught onto my wish to be alone in my misery, because he hands me a pack of paracetamol and heads to the door, his tie hanging undone around his neck.

'You coming to the residents' meeting?'

I give him a look that says 'I'd rather die', and he lets out a laugh.

'What about Heidi's Halloween party tonight?'

'Not really my scene,' I say, acutely aware of how uneager I sound to spend more time with him.

'Okay well . . . I'll see you soon?' There's a hopeful undertone to his voice.

I force a smile which makes my dry lips crack. 'Yeah, see you soon. I'll call you later.' And I do want to see him again, it's just clouded by little sleep and my need for a fry-up. Damn it, should have seen if he fancied making one.

'Christian?' I call to him just as he's about to open the front door, and he turns to look at me with a hopeful expression. He wants me to ask him to stay.

I bite my lip, feeling a tad bad for what I'm about to say. 'Can you . . . go out the back way? I don't want people talking.'

He raises an eyebrow but doesn't say anything. He should understand. He lives here too and knows what the people can be like.

'Sure,' he says, moving to the back door and stepping outside, causing a sudden rush of cold air to flood the living room and make my head spin. I sink further down into the sofa, hoping it might swallow me up, right down into the fibres of the cushions where I could pretend that last night didn't happen. As I sit here, my eyes keep flicking to the window against my will.

Spending my Saturday morning sitting in front of the blare of my laptop screen is not my idea of a hangover cure – if it had been any other day I'd have returned to bed and likely rolled out just in time to grab dinner – but I can't shake that niggle at the back of my mind. I'm not sure what to search for, or even what I'm looking for. In the end, after staring at the blinking cursor for goodness knows how long, I start with something simple: 'Lacey Williams cystic fibrosis'.

The first page of links are articles I've already read from when I was prepping for my interview with them. I'm just starting to give up on learning anything new when my mouse hovers over another link: LACEY'S ADVENTURE – A JOURNEY TO HEALING. At this point, I disappear down a rabbit hole. The blog, as I discover it is, dates back six years, written by Norah. Seemingly endless posts share details of Lacey's life and, more specifically, her illness. Each entry holds photos, some of Lacey in hospital, wires and tubes surrounding her, some of Lacey at home in a state of recovery. The thing that strikes me as I scroll through, is the amount of procedures that poor girl has endured. Countless scans, endoscopies, even surgery to have a feeding tube implanted. I don't think I'd have chosen to document it all in pictures. It seems wrong, inappropriate somehow.

And then I reach a post, written seven months ago, that makes my blood run cold.

Looking to the Future

Today we got the news we'd been fearing. Lacey isn't expected to live past forty. I knew this was going to be the case from my own research, but actually hearing the words was something else. A mummy shouldn't have to outlive her baby. It isn't natural. After hearing the prognosis I went into a bit of a spiral, even picked out her coffin.

At the sight of a picture of a coffin, pink with a huge 'L' printed on the lid, I close the laptop. What kind of a mother would post a picture of their child's coffin on a blog? This is too much for me, too raw. I've allowed myself to get close to a terminally ill child, and I just can't do it anymore. I haul myself up from the table, grab another glass of water, and go back to bed.

Chapter Seventeen

16 Days Before the Murder

Norah

Heidi scoots towards us, the tray in her hands piled high with scones, jam and cream. There are already two commercial-style tea dispensers on the fold-out table of the community centre, but Heidi is renowned for supplying her freshly baked scones and matching linen napkins. I wonder if she finds her existence as tiring as I find mine.

I wasn't sure I wanted to attend the residents' meeting this week. I usually enjoy the gossip, as long as I'm not the subject, of course. In fact, I look forward to it. It's the perfect distraction. The community centre events are one of the only things these days that put a smile on Lacey's face. I used to think she was just being polite, but as she's got older I realise that she genuinely enjoys the company of our fellow residents for some bizarre reason, even those who are not our nosy neighbours.

This week, however, it took all my might not to excuse myself. I haven't spoken to Heidi since the drama with the television crew, and the fact that she was there to hear every spiteful word that was screamed at me sends my cheeks and earlobes aflame. The only reason Lacey and I are here right now is because if we didn't show, she'd know it was because I'm embarrassed, and I think that would be worse.

'Have you seen Erica lately?' Sally says, helping herself to the largest scone and spreading a sizeable dollop of cream on top. 'She came back from holiday last week and, let's just say I'm pretty sure she had to purchase some bigger bras while she was out there.'

Sally conceals a laugh behind her hand. 'Well, she had to do something to keep that toy boy of hers. How long do you reckon before he realises his mistake and leaves her?'

'You know, you don't always have to pry into other people's relationships, Sally,' Heidi snaps suddenly. 'You're hardly a shining example with your three divorces.'

At this, everything seems to go very still and quiet, the chatter of the other residents far off. Marisa and I glance awkwardly between Heidi and Sally, not daring to comment and equally intrigued to see who will be the first to speak. As it turns out, neither of them do. Heidi just shakes her head, her dangly earrings jingling like sleigh bells, and heads to the bathroom.

'Well,' Sally says once Heidi is out of earshot. 'Someone got out the wrong side of the bed this morning.'

It's true, it is very unlike Heidi not to want to engage in the estate gossip. Her snipes are usually the best of the group.

I look down at Lacey, who is twiddling with her fingers, and squeeze her shoulder. 'Stay here with Sally and Marisa, okay? I'm just going to check on her.'

When I open the door to the ladies' I'm met with the sight of

Heidi leaning over the sink, staring at the mirror. She starts as I enter and swipes furiously at her face.

'Sorry, I'll be out in just a moment,' she says.

I take a step forward. 'Are you okay?'

'Yes, yes. Fine.' In true Heidi fashion she gives herself a little shake and a smile instantly appears on her face, though her red-rimmed eyes betray her. 'I'm just not feeling great today. I've had an awful headache all morning.'

I nod, knowing Heidi well enough to choose not to push the matter. 'Okay, well, you know where I am if you want to talk.'

She smiles gratefully and turns back to the mirror, pulling out a compact from her handbag and gently reapplying her make-up. I've known Heidi for a long time now, and she's the resident I've grown closest to over the years. When she's ready to talk, I'm sure she will.

I'm about to leave her be when she stops powdering her under-eyes. 'Norah, while I've got you alone, there is something I wanted to speak to you about.' She hesitates, not quite meeting my eye. 'I'm not sure if you know, or even care, but I saw Christian and our new girl in his car last night.'

My muscles stiffen.

'You mean Jodie? My neighbour?'

'Yes.' Her cheeks flush pink and she presses her lips together, wincing at me. 'Sorry, I wasn't sure if I should say anything or not.'

'It's fine,' I lie, 'I just . . . didn't realise they knew each other.'

When I return to Lacey, Marisa and Sally are already back deep into a gossip session. I zone out, instead allowing my eyes to roam the room in search of Christian. I eventually spot him;

he wanders in unusually late for him and heads straight for the coffee. I try to distance myself from the girls as discreetly as possible, nudging Lacey's shoulder and telling her to come with me to get a drink.

'Hi.' I force a smile and grab a cup, choosing to abandon my coffee hiatus.

He jerks his head back and gives me a double take. 'Hey.' There's a hint of surprise in his voice. He leans down towards Lacey. 'How you doing, kiddo?'

'I'm good,' Lacey grins. She's always liked Christian. He's good with children, I suppose because of his job. I realise, as I stand awkwardly next to him and spoon sugar into my cup, that I haven't spoken to him in a couple of months, not since he helped out looking for Lacey that day. Even then I barely said two sentences to him. He is clearly aware of how long it's been, because he's eyeing me expectantly.

'I just thought I'd say hi; catch up. It's been a while.'

'Sure has. How have you been?'

'Fine, we're doing good.' I glance over to the other end of the community centre that's been blocked off with a temporary mesh fence to ward off adventurous children. The hole that will soon become the swimming pool is deep now, an ominous void. The builders assured poor Heidi it will look better by the end of today since they'll be laying the pool floor and siding. I can see her physically itch every time she looks at it.

'The swimming pool's nearly finished,' I say. 'They're putting the water in next week.'

'Nice. Just in time for the winter, eh?'

'Yes, well, it's going to be heated and it's probably the most exciting thing that will happen to me for a while so I may even take a Christmas Day dip.' My throat is so dry it scratches when I talk. I take a swig of my coffee. 'How are you doing? You look tired.'

'Ouch.' He laughs but I can tell it's not genuine. We know each other too well.

'Still not sleeping well?'

He shrugs, his usual air of confidence giving way to a hint of vulnerability. 'You know. It is what it is.'

I nod, remembering the little bottle of sleeping pills he used to keep by his bedside. It's ironic, really, how some doctors self-medicate like that. *Do what I say, not what I do*, I suppose. I glance at Lacey, and find myself wishing I could be apart from her without having to worry. Having her permanently at my side tends to make adult conversations rather difficult. I choose my words carefully. 'What have you been up to? Do anything fun last night?'

His eyes narrow and his brow wrinkles. 'Not really, work keeps me busy, you know.'

I do know. I'm no stranger to the sound of his answering machine at the surgery, even during the times when I really could have done with him picking up the phone. I push the memories aside – I need to focus on why I'm here.

'Friday night. Don't you usually go to the pub?'

'Yes, as I said, it was just the same old.' He lowers his head and studies me, sending pinprick goosebumps crawling along my skin. I've purposefully avoided him for so long now, it feels wrong to be here talking to him like this.

'You're not seeing anyone?'

Christian regards me, a small smile creeping onto his lips. There is a horrifying moment when I realise he might think I'm still interested in him.

'No, no, no.'

I would have known he's lying even if Heidi hadn't said anything about Jodie being in his car. The overcompensation with the three 'no's and his nervous disposition give him away easily. It shouldn't bother me that much. After all, it's not like we're close anymore, but something about being lied to by Christian hits a nerve.

I lower my gaze, allowing the pause in the conversation to remind him who he's dealing with. 'Heidi said she saw you with...' I hesitate, glance down at Lacey. 'With someone in your car last night.'

He tilts his head to one side. 'Did she now? And what business is it of Heidi's who's in my car?'

'Ladies and gents, can I ask you to take your seats?' Paul's voice makes me jump, a few drops of coffee sloshing over the side of my cup and pooling on the side of my hand. I let out a hiss as my skin starts to throb.

Christian picks up his cup and makes a start towards the plastic chairs. I don't want him to go yet. I haven't said what I need to say. I fumble for something to keep him here. 'Are you going to Heidi's Halloween party later?'

'Uh, yeah. I'll probably drop in at some point.'

'Okay, I'll see you there.'

He nods, raising his hand to rub the back of his neck. I've made him uncomfortable.

'Nice catching up,' he says, then with twice the amount of life and warmth, 'See you later, Lacey.'

It doesn't matter who it is, Lacey is always shown a level of affection I doubt I'll ever experience. I used to, back when Lacey had her first few hospitalisations, but the sympathy for my plight has worn off after all these years. The benefits are shrinking.

Chapter Eighteen

16 Days Before the Murder

Jodie

I've decided to do something entirely out of character. I'm attending the Downhursts' annual Halloween party. When I first received the invitation, an ivory lace-rimmed card that looked more like a wedding invitation, I tossed it into the bin and went about my day without giving it a second thought. You would have thought I was crazy to miss out on a party, especially one as anticipated as Heidi's, but you know it's not really my scene. It was only when I glanced out the window to see Norah pushing Lacey into their van and driving off in the direction of Heidi's house, that I plucked the card back out from under a banana skin and a couple of tea bags, and reconsidered my attendance. It's not actually Halloween for another few days, but the Grove's strict noise level restrictions means parties are only permitted on Friday and Saturdays nights.

There's no mistaking which house the party is being held at. It seems every resident and their dog has chosen to turn up, since the street outside the Downhursts' driveway is packed with cars lined up in rows like sardines. At first, I wonder why Heidi chose to host the party at her house instead of the community centre, given how many people she's invited, but upon stepping through the threshold of the front door I realise lack of space is not something Heidi needs to worry about.

It doesn't look like any Halloween party I've ever been to. Granted, I've only been to a couple, back when I was a young teenager, and I spent most of those pressed into a dark corner hoping that no one would talk to me, but even so, I thought I'd have at least some idea of what to expect, and this certainly isn't it. The only hint that it's Halloween in Heidi's grand foyer is the huge bouquet sitting atop a polished round pedestal at the foot of the staircase, which, upon closer inspection, has little skulls-and-crossbones peppered amongst the lilies. Heidi clearly hasn't discovered the joys of IKEA. No, her home is an impressive amalgamation of antiques and designer furniture.

'Jodie, glad you could make it.' Paul saunters over to me, looking a little flushed from the collective body heat inside the house. 'Can I take your coat?'

'Oh, sure.' Slightly taken aback, I slide off my jacket and pass it to him.

'I'll pop it in the spare bedroom. Help yourself to food.'

I nod and shimmy into the dining room, where the majority of the partygoers are lingering. A huge buffet of dainty smoked salmon pinwheels and bite-sized sandwiches covers the long table, and a fruit platter in the shape of a pumpkin sits pride of place in the centre. Upon spotting that only the children are wearing costumes – the grand French doors open onto a bunch of Frankensteins and mummies running around and screaming – I offer a silent thanks to the gods of luck that I didn't choose to don the cat ears I've got tucked away at the back of my wardrobe.

Already uncomfortable, I make my way through the crowds and make a beeline for the huge punch bowls on the far end of the dining table, where I pour myself a large glass of the 'Haunted Graveyard', which smells unmistakably bourbon based. As I go to take a sip, hands appear around my waist.

'I thought you said you weren't coming?'

I spin around, choking on the cocktail. The bourbon stings the back of my throat and I cough, sending a light spray of whisky out of my mouth and onto Christian.

'You good?' he grins, wiping away the drips that have landed on his shirt.

'What are you doing?'

He lowers his eyebrows, then gives me an uncertain smile. 'Erm . . . okay. Sorry?'

The hurt look on his face gives me a tinge of guilt, and I loosen my posture. 'I just don't want to be the source of the next piece of town gossip, you know?'

He nods, but even though I'm sure he must understand – he lives in the Grove, too, and knows what it's like – his bearing remains somewhat stilted.

He takes a sip of his drink and smacks his lips. 'You want me to go stand on the other side of the room, or . . . ?'

'No, no. Of course not. Stay.' I can already feel the back of my neck getting warm. At the very least, having Christian here to talk to will save me from seeking conversation with the likes of Heidi.

'You know, you never called me,' he says after a moment.

'What?'

'You said you were going to call me today. I thought we might come here together.'

Damn, maybe Heidi would have been better. I drop my eyes to the floor and clear my throat, trying to remove the visions of him on top of me that are now infiltrating my brain. 'Yeah. I'm sorry, I've had a . . . really hectic afternoon.'

'Hey, I'm a big boy. It's fine, honestly. I just like to know if I'm wasting my time.'

Even with the roar of the chatter around us and the music pulsating through the floorboards, to me the entire room has fallen silent. Half of me is wondering if I'm just a horrible person, and the other half is wondering if Christian is being overly clingy. I'm not sure which possibility troubles me more. Either way, I regret entering into this conversation.

'So, *am* I?' he presses. 'Wasting my time?'

He doesn't give up, does he? I chew on the inside of my cheek, trying to think of what to say that would cause the least amount of awkwardness, but I sense we might have already passed that point.

'I'm all over the place right now, Christian,' I say finally, my voice raspy from the bourbon. 'I don't know what I want.'

His shoulders loosen as the tension ebbs.

'No worries. If you figure it out, you know my number. Enjoy the party.' With that, he turns and retreats into the crowds, and I wish the floorboards would disappear from beneath me. I have to remind myself that I didn't come to this town in search of romance. In fact, if someone had asked me when I first arrived what the specific things I was *not* looking for were, the top two on my list would probably have been romance and making friends with the kid next door. *Well done, Jodie, expertly executed as always.* I shake my head, hoping to dislodge the discomfort of our encounter, and set my sights on what I actually came to the party to do.

Norah is standing with one of the largest groups, commandeering the conversation as per usual, and Lacey is sitting next to her. I slide into the gap between Sally and her son Markus, and flash a smile at the group. I might be imagining things, but I'm sure I can feel the atmosphere physically shift as I join them.

'Afternoon,' I say, faking my best friendly neighbour routine.

'Jodie, what a nice surprise.' Sally's voice is unusually high, and I can't tell if she's being genuine or not. I don't much care. 'I didn't think this was really your scene.'

'Not usually, but you know what they say. Neighbours by chance, friends by choice.' I flash a smile at Norah, whose already pinched face tightens. Beside her, Lacey's eyes remain trained on the floor, as if she daren't look my way.

'So what's the deal with Halloween round here?' I say. 'Can I expect knocks on my door on the thirty-first?'

'Oh yes!' Sally nods with enthusiasm and gestures over to the kids. 'It's quite a spectacle each year. The children walk the estate in one huge group. You wait until you see it!'

I force myself to look enthusiastic, though inwardly I'm cringing at the thought.

'I tried to convince Markus to go,' Sally continues. 'Bought him a costume and everything. Apparently, he's too old for it now.'

'Mum, shut up.' Markus rolls his eyes beside her and digs his hands into his pockets. I realise in my three months living at the Grove this is the first time I've ever heard Markus speak.

I turn to the girl sitting in the wheelchair. 'Are you going to be joining them, Lacey?' This is the question that has been gnawing at me since I entered the party. I can't help but notice that while all the other kids play in the garden, Lacey is still attached to Norah's side. Lacey's eyes go wide and her mouth opens and closes like a goldfish, as if she hadn't realised anyone knew she was there.

Norah reaches down and pats her shoulder. 'It's not really Lacey's scene, is it?'

Lacey lowers her eyes and shakes her head. Just being in the same room as them is giving me a headache. I want to take Lacey to one side and ask her if she's okay, ask her if she wants to go hang out with the other kids. During our evenings together I saw a spark in Lacey, a fire behind her eyes, but it seems every time I see her these days that fire has dwindled a little more. Like it's being snuffed out.

I turn to Sally. 'Do you know where the ladies' is?' The room has suddenly become claustrophobic and I have the acute sensation of being smothered.

'Up the stairs, along the landing. There's a guest bathroom.'

Shooting her a thumbs-up, I force my way past the clusters of people. A sign hangs off the stair banister which reads: SHOES OFF, PLEASE. The small, childish voice inside of me tells me to see what would happen if I went up with my Timberlands still on. A vision of alarms sounding and lights flashing *Mission Impossible*-style makes me chuckle inwardly.

Upstairs, I find the small guest bathroom, which I'm about to use when curiosity gets the better of me. So, I wander along the hall, to the open door of Heidi and Paul's vast bedroom and spot their en-suite directly opposite me.

The en-suite is complete with fluffy towels, expensive hand soap and fruity moisturiser that smells disconcertingly similar to Heidi's perfume. The claustrophobic atmosphere of downstairs has given me a headache, so I pull open her medicine cabinet and rifle through the various boxes in search of paracetamol.

My hand knocks against one of them and they fall, in domino fashion, tumbling out into the sink.

'Shit,' I mumble as I pick them all up and try to remember where they all were. Knowing Heidi, she'll notice if anything is even slightly out of place. As I'm arranging them as neatly as I can, I can't help but notice a packet of condoms pushed right to the back, hidden in the dark corner. I check the use-by date. Not for another year. Weird. I suppose it's not totally strange for a married couple to have condoms in their medicine cabinet, but I'm sure I heard Heidi talking to Sally about wanting to start a family.

After shutting the cabinet, splashing my face with water and studying my reflection for a while – my mascara has already smudged and the little foundation I had applied is starting to gather in the fine lines of my forehead, yet another reason never to bother with the stuff – I go to head back downstairs when a wave of inspiration hits me. Giving a quick check to ensure no one is ascending the stairs, I begin opening doors. The first leads to an office, the second leads to an actual walk-in wardrobe complete with a velvet settee which sits arrogantly in the centre, and the third is the room I'm looking for.

The spare bedroom matches the downstairs of the house perfectly, with a huge four-poster queen bed, piled high with a leaning tower of coats, only taking up a small portion of the space. The lush cream carpet is so soft my toes sink into it like a pillow, and I understand why Heidi doesn't want shoes upstairs. It must have cost a fortune. My carpet is so thin I can practically feel the subfloor underfoot.

Eyeing the stairs one more time, I close the door behind me

and make my way over to the bed. I try to remember what Norah was wearing when she left the house. Most of the jackets look the same, as if every woman went to the same shop to purchase the same style. I'm not sure what I'm looking for, I just know I need to research my neighbour beyond what is readily available on the internet. After all, if anyone is going to find out if there is something untoward going on, it's going to be a journalist.

Finally, I recognise Norah's green parka, under a few other coats, and rummage about in her pockets. I pull out a purse. It's chocolate-brown leather, quite classy, and contains the usual stuff: a few receipts, loyalty cards, driver's licence, a debit and credit card. Nothing stands out as unordinary except for a folded piece of paper tucked right at the back, with messy handwriting scrawled over it. I squint to read it. It's a name, *Gareth Wilson*, and below it a number. The paper has crumpled corners and the ink has started to fade away, as if it's been forgotten about in the depths of the purse for months, maybe even years.

Footsteps sound from the stairs, accompanied by the unmistakable shriek of Heidi reacting to a joke. I grab my own coat, return the parka to the bed, stuff the purse in the back pocket of my jeans and dart out of the room, where I nearly crash straight into Heidi on the landing.

'Jodie! Are you leaving already?'

I swallow. 'Yes, sorry, I have a really important meeting at work on Monday that I need to prep for. Can't be out too late.'

I put on my coat, and go to make a start down the stairs, but Heidi's hand lands on my forearm to stop me and for a moment I'm sure she's got X-ray vision and knows about the purse.

'Jodie, before you go, I just wanted to warn you.'

I blink, taken aback. Is she about to tell me to stop poking around Norah's business? How much does she know?

'Warn me?'

'Yes. I saw you in Christian's car last night. I just wanted to give you some friendly advice. He has a certain . . . reputation with women. Probably best to steer clear.'

I'm not sure what I'd expected her to say, but it wasn't that. To be honest, all she's done is make me more intrigued to find out more about Christian. The petty, childish side of me that hates being told what to do decides here and now that I'll be seeing him again. Still, I don't want to be the source of gossip, so I force a smile.

'He was just giving me a lift,' I say, my mouth dry. 'Nothing more to it than that.'

I can't tell if she believes me, but I'm not going to stick around to find out. I've already begun to descend the stairs as I speak. 'It's been an amazing party, though. Thanks so much for inviting me.' By the time I've finished my sentence I've reached the bottom of the stairs, and with a quick wave to a perplexed Heidi who is staring down after me, I escape through the front door. Threads of anxiety pull at my insides as I hurry down the road. I definitely looked shifty as I left the room, and when Norah notices her purse is missing it wouldn't take a genius to put two and two together. There's nothing I can do about it now.

Chapter Nineteen

16 Days Before the Murder

Norah

'Have you seen Lacey?'

My breathing grows shallow as I whip round Heidi's house. Each person I ask shakes their head. 'No, sorry.'

I only went to the bathroom. I was gone for maybe five minutes, and she knew to stay put. She knows to always, always stay put. I hurry to the garden, frantically scan the array of Halloween costumes for a glimpse of her wheelchair, but she's nowhere to be seen.

'Everything okay, Norah?'

I spin around and nearly knock Heidi's glass straight out of her hand.

'I can't find Lacey,' I say, my voice coming out strained.

'Lacey? She's there.' Heidi nods towards the foyer and I follow her gaze. Sure enough, Lacey is sitting next to the flower arrangement, watching me. I storm forward, grip onto the tops of her shoulders.

'Where were you?'

Her cheeks flush bright pink. 'I just went outside for a moment.'

'Why would you do that?'

'I... I was starting to get a bit out of breath. I thought I should get some fresh air.'

I stare at her for a moment, trying to determine whether or not to believe her. Eventually my hold on her shoulders slackens.

'You must tell someone if you're doing that. I was worried sick.'

'I'm sorry.'

I close my eyes, my mouth dry. 'Okay. Come on, let's get going. It's late.'

The late-October air stings my nose and makes my eyes water as I push Lacey home. I've pulled my sleeves down over my hands in an effort to shield them from the biting chill. The skin between my fingers is already splitting open. It doesn't matter how many times I find my knuckles cracked and bleeding during the winter months, I never remember to wear gloves.

We've left earlier than the rest of the partygoers; mustn't miss Lacey's bedtime. I wasn't really in the party mood, anyway. As I trudge along the pavement, our shadows unfurling before me and stretching into the night, I find myself getting more and more frustrated. I can't shake the sense of dread that Jodie Madison instils in me. At first I thought I was simply being paranoid, but facts cannot be ignored. She has seeped into almost every area of my life. I have to see her daily, be it through the windows across our shared fence or out on our respective driveways, knowing that she has had conversations with my daughter I may never have. She knows her intimately, though the extent is still to be determined, and that unsettles me. And now she has started... what? Dating Christian? Sleeping with him?

I have to reason with myself. *He's just dating*. Of course, he'd find someone eventually, at some point I'm sure he intends to settle down. But it can't be her. Not a journalist. Not the woman who lives next door, who talks to my daughter for hours through the window, who tells her she needs to be in school, who buys her inappropriate gifts and pretends that she knows what's best for her.

I squeeze the bridge of my nose. A throbbing sensation is beginning to pulse behind my eye, the telltale sign of a migraine on its way. Just what I need. Luckily, the walk home isn't far. I pick up my pace. When we get home I'll do Lacey's medications, get her to bed and then spend some time allowing myself to rest and relax. Perhaps I'll curl up with a book. It's been some time since I've done that.

We don't get that far, though. As we pass the allotments my eye is drawn to an orange glow. The smell of wood smoke drifts through the air. It reminds me of an incense shop. I stare at the glow for a while, taken in by the beauty of the halo it has created in the evening sky. It's only when embers float into the breeze and Lacey shrieks that my body kicks into gear.

'Fire!' I shout, before scrambling for my phone. It's lodged in my pocket and my numb fingers struggle to free it.

'I've already called them,' a voice says behind me. I turn, stunned, to see Jodie staring beyond me at the fire. What is she doing here? She left the party hours ago. I want to ask her but the heat on my back draws my attention again to the carnage. In the distance sirens echo through the night. I wonder how much the gates having to be opened will slow them down.

I take a step towards the flames, which are now fully visible, licking their way through the old shed. It is eerily beautiful in its destruction. It's dancing for us, or so it seems, playing among the kindling like a child with a new toy, its blaze leaping in excitement. The three of us stand watching, part captivated and part horrified, as first the residents begin crowding, and finally the police and fire engines come hurtling down the road towards us.

Jodie could not know that I have purposefully positioned myself so that I can keep an eye on her in my peripheral vision. She couldn't know that I can see her as she tilts her head towards Lacey and offers her a reassuring smile. She couldn't know that I can see the ash on her fingertips, and that if anyone asks me who I think started the fire, I'll know exactly where to point them.

Chapter Twenty

16 Days Before the Murder

Jodie

The fire was enough to halt the party, much to the residents' annoyance. Instead of running around in Heidi's garden, an array of child-sized horror movie characters are now crowding around the allotment holding their parents' hands while the fire engines tackle the blaze, which had already started to die down by the time they arrived. It has consumed everything it can. The shed is practically a pile of ash, the pumpkin and beetroot patches closest have all suffered the same fate. There is nothing left to burn.

Police are in attendance, too, since there's suspicion of arson, and a tall, skinny policeman with a high-vis jacket interviews me. Constable Harris is stiff, his face rigid and stern, and he has a low, droning voice, as if he would much rather be elsewhere. He drawls through the initial questions – what's my name, where have I been, where was I when I spotted the fire – without once taking his eyes off his notepad, and I imagine I could quite easily swap places with another resident and he would be none the wiser.

'So, you called emergency services as soon as you saw it,' he repeats my words, his head bobbing up and down like one of those nodding dogs in souvenir shops. 'Did you see anyone in the area at all?'

I swallow and my eyes flick to the crowd. The truth is I did see someone. After I left the bustle of Heidi's party, the evening was silent and crisp, almost serene. My legs moved of their own accord as if in a trance, and before I knew it I found myself by the duck pond. How ironic that I'd end up there of all places given what day it is on Monday.

I stepped along the water's edge, one foot in front of the other, tracing the outskirts where the grass has turned to soggy mud. There weren't any ducks, not that I was expecting to see any that late into the evening. They were probably all tucked away in the reeds or the plants, turned in for a restful sleep. Only a crazy person would be out on the pond at that time of night.

I followed the stream all the way to the gates, where I proceeded to sit down and stretch out my legs in front of me. I didn't even care that the mud caked my jeans, seeping through the fabric and making my bum moist.

A fox, amber-eyed and pointy-eared, pulled me out of my thoughts and attracted my eyes to the gate. It hadn't seen me sitting there. Why would anyone be there? It ducked its head under the water, pushing itself through the gap at the bottom where the bars don't quite reach the bed of the stream, the white tip of its tail flicking up as its back arched.

It was then that I smelt the smoke. Panic had roared through me as I thought it might have been one of the houses, perhaps Heidi's, but it didn't take me long to spot the glow coming from the allotments. And then, behind the oranges and the reds, hiding in the shadow of the smoke, movement as Sally's son Markus darted out from next to the shed.

I vaulted to the side so that I was blocking his path and grabbed his arm. He hadn't seen me. His bulging eyes and cowering body told me that much. In an instant he seemed to grow younger right before me. No longer a strapping teenager but a little boy, trembling under the weight of what he had done. He didn't say anything, just watched me, waiting to see what I was going to do.

I wasn't sure what I was going to do, but before I could decide the choice was made for me. A groan sounded from the shed as it protested under the heat. The door toppled, snapping off its hinges. The impact of it hitting the ground sent fragments jumping up at us. One landed on my leg, biting through my jeans and searing my skin. I hissed through my teeth as the sting travelled from my hip to my toes, and by the time I'd shaken off the initial shock Markus was nowhere to be seen.

I can see him now, amongst the crowds, half covered by Sally. His head is bowed but his eyes are fixed on me, his face ashen, fingers picking at the skin around his nails. He still looks childlike.

'Did you see anyone, Ms Madison?' Constable Harris asks again.

I clear my throat. 'No, I didn't see anyone.' I'm not close enough to see Markus' expression of relief, but from my peripheral vision I see his stature loosen, as if he is a puppet whose strings have just been cut.

I'm not sure why I chose not to tell on Markus. Perhaps it's because in the likes of Sally Peters and Heidi Downhurst I can see my own 'fussy' mother, that constant desire to be better than the rest, to exceed the ordinary, and burning a shed down by way of rebellion is exactly the sort of thing I would have done at that age. Of course, the truth will come out eventually. But for now, at least, Markus can relax, and he offers me the briefest of nods of appreciation as PC Harris concludes his questions.

Once the fire is out and everyone has started dispersing to their own homes, I check my phone. Half eleven. I've been outside for nearly three hours. I didn't think I was at the lake that long, but I must have been. I pull my jacket tighter around me and start in the direction of my house, muddy water squelching between my toes. The chilling bottle of rosé in my fridge calls to me. Realistically, it is now far too late to crack it open, but I know I'm going to anyway. Though I won't allow myself to admit it, I half hope I might be able to drink enough to see you again, like I did in the living room that one time. It wasn't real. Of course it wasn't, I know that. You're gone. But it doesn't matter. My mind clearly isn't ready to move on, and all the time it still wants to conjure up visions of you alive and well, who am I to stop it?

Chapter Twenty-One

Heidi
Quick roll call to check everyone's okay after last night?

Marisa
We're fine.

Norah
All good.

Sally
Us too. Markus was walking scarily close to it when it all started. Thank God he had the common sense to come and find me.

Emma
I don't understand how a fire can just start like that.

Sally
It didn't. Someone obviously set it.

Heidi
Now now, let's not speculate.

Marisa

Did Markus see anything, Sally?

Sally

Unfortunately not.

Norah

I saw Jodie Madison there . . .

Chapter Twenty-Two

14 Days Before the Murder

Norah

My purse is missing. I'm almost certain I took it with me to the Halloween party, but Heidi says it's nowhere to be seen at her house and I've turned my own house upside down looking for it to no avail. I can't imagine anyone in the Grove is partial to petty theft, but then again, there's no knowing what people really get up to behind closed doors. So now I'm having to wait.

I've never been a huge fan of waiting. Back before the days of disabled queue-jumping rights, I refused to go anywhere that involved standing in a line. I never arrive for a train more than a couple of minutes early, never set foot inside an A&E if I can help it, and always check the reviews of restaurants to ensure 'long waiting times' aren't a common theme. So waiting to get through the rest of the weekend so that it can finally be Monday, and so that Jodie can finally go to work, has been unpleasant to say the least.

My rationale for what I'm about to do is weaker than I'd like. If I get caught, my response of 'I've just got a bad feeling' probably wouldn't hold up under questioning. But I do have reason not to trust Jodie. I'm convinced she took my purse out of my jacket at the party – Heidi said she saw her coming out of the bedroom looking flustered before rushing home early. And I'm convinced she set that fire – her motive is unclear but she was the only person there and her hands were covered in ash.

I spend my morning counting down the hours.

It is 6.51 a.m.

It's impossible to sit still without fidgeting, so I stand and stare out at my garden. What little grass we have left after the ramps were installed is now coated with a thin layer of frost. It looks like hundreds of tiny knives dancing in the breeze.

I begin to pace, collect a couple of dirty mugs, start the dishwasher, check the time again.

7.24 a.m.

I prepare Lacey's formula, all the while remaining in a position where I can clearly see through the front window to Jodie's driveway. She normally doesn't leave for work until around 8.30. I've likely still got over an hour of waiting to do, but I want to ensure I can see out just in case she's been called in early.

Lacey's feed is done. Now her inhaler. Her nebuliser. Her physiotherapy.

8.43 a.m.

Jodie should have left by now. I flip absentmindedly through the magazine on my coffee table. It is a travel magazine brimming with stunning photographs of far-off exotic locations. I've been compiling a list of potential spots for our next holiday. That reminds me, I still need to contact the travel agency in London that offered us a subsidised trip. I jot a note on my palm telling me to call them.

8.47 a.m.

There is movement outside, the sound of a car engine humming to life. She's finally gone.

I take a moment to check on Lacey. She is exactly where I thought she'd be, lying on her bed with her headphones covering her ears, a book propped up on her knees, and I'm quietly pleased to see it's a biology textbook as opposed to that blasted astronomy book. She doesn't even notice me peering in. She won't move until lunchtime.

I move to the kitchen and pull out the metal box from the back of our junk drawer. My fingers are trembling so much I struggle to roll the numbers on the combination lock. I take a slow, deliberate breath. My anxiety is ill-founded. The chances of getting caught are slim; Lacey is oblivious to the world, Jodie is gone, any nosy neighbours should theoretically be getting ready for work or wrestling their children into obedience on the school run. Perhaps I am nervous of what I might find. I silence these worries by assuring myself it is better to know.

The box creaks open, revealing an assortment of keys. They have been filed meticulously into alphabetical compartments. It looks like the work of Heidi Downhurst, but in actual fact there was a time when I used to pride myself on my organisational skills. It just goes to show how long it's been since this box was opened.

My finger runs along the letters until it reaches 'P'. Alison Peterson left me her key when she went on a cruise and I was requested to water her plants. It is such a shame about what happened to her. I liked her.

Stepping into Jodie's house is disorientating. The open floor plan is a replica of my own, as if I've walked in to discover someone else living in my home, replacing my furniture with theirs. I'm not sure what I expect to find here. My nightmares have pictured rooms wallpapered with photos of my daughter, taken through the windows, through the cracks in our fence.

Slowly and methodically, I make my way around her living room, opening the occasional cupboard and keeping an eye out for anything that might shed some light on my neighbour... and for my purse. Upon finding nothing of any consequence, I move to the master bedroom and investigate the contents of her bedside drawer. An unopened bottle of hand lotion. Contraceptive pills, nearly empty. A lighter – does she smoke? A smashed iPhone and what looks like a vibrator, though I've never used one and so can only hazard a guess that that's what it is.

A shrill ringing makes me recoil and slam the drawer shut, nearly trapping my fingers in the process. I wince, but move out of the bedroom, just as I hear the click of what I vaguely remember to be an answering machine picking up a call. How quaint, I think, then wonder why Jodie even has one. I thought journalists were welded to their mobiles? No one I know uses their landline anymore. Out of sheer curiosity, I move a little closer to the machine and listen for the message. There is silence for a moment, then two heavy breaths, and finally a woman's voice.

'Jodie, it's me. Please call me back. We're all worried about you. We just want to talk to you, make sure you're okay. I'm not sure if you've still got my number but here it is just in case. Please call.'

The woman rattles out her number and the answerphone beeps. I'm frozen to the spot. Part of me wants to run out of the house and pretend I never came here. It's not like I found anything incriminating. My niggles about Jodie may be completely unfounded. Maybe she is just trying to be a friend to Lacey, however inappropriate it might be. But that call. Why hasn't this woman got Jodie's mobile number? She sounded so frantic. So desperate. So worried. What is Jodie hiding?

My hand moves to the phone almost of its own accord. Without thinking I'm replaying the message and tapping the number into my mobile. It only rings once before it is answered.

'Hello?' The woman's voice rings in my ears again.

'Hi, this is Jodie's neighbour. I'm watering her plants while she's away.' I'm speaking without engaging my brain. What if this woman tells Jodie that she spoke to her neighbour? She'll know I was here. But the words continue to tumble out of me. 'Sorry I didn't quite make it to the phone in time. Can I help at all?'

'Oh, how has she been? Where has she gone on holiday?'

I purse my lips as I think of a credible lie. 'A caravan park, I believe. Apologies, I can't remember exactly where. But she seemed okay when she left. Would you like me to pass on a message when she returns?'

'I just really need to speak to her. Can you please ask her to call me as soon as she gets back?'

'Of course, who shall I say called?'

'Gabbie. Gabbie Chambers. Thank you.'

When the line goes dead I try to swallow. My mouth has completely dried up. An ache forms in my hand and I realise I've been squeezing the key so hard its ridges have left a pattern in my skin. I loosen my grip, hold down the 'delete message' button, and exit the house.

Chapter Twenty-Three

14 Days Before the Murder

Jodie

Despite my hangover, I turn my attention to the piece of paper I found in Norah's purse. Whilst slugging much needed filter coffee and forcing down mouthfuls of dry toast, I fiddle with the crumpled edge. It's likely nothing, of course. Another dead end, which, as a journalist, I'm no stranger to. Some stories I had to go down seemingly endless rabbit holes before arriving at the truth. Still, whoever this Gareth Wilson is might have some insights on Norah. She's either kept it tucked away in her purse because she's forgotten about it, or because it means something to her, and if it's the latter, that person might know a thing or two about her.

I abandon the toast as it's making my stomach churn, and instead chew on the skin around my thumbnail as I dial the number under the name – almost immediately the error tone comes up. It's not a valid number. I return the paper to the purse and slump back in my chair, feeling stupid. Of course it's not a phone number. It's too short. What does it mean then?

I plan to continue my hunt for Gareth Wilson once I arrive at the office, but have barely sat down and turned on my monitor before Andrew is breathing down my neck about the scintillating article I'm writing on the local gym expansion plans, currently half-finished on my screen. It's going to be harder than I thought to do research at work on things that even I can't blag are part of my remit.

I peer over my cubicle to see Andrew tucked away now in his glass-walled office. Perhaps if I approached him about writing a story on the Williams household, things would be easier. I'd be able to focus all my attention on it, resources would open up to me. But I can't bring myself to do it. Aside from anything, I have no proof. Other than a gut feeling that something is off, there's nothing to indicate that Norah has done anything wrong. Andrew is hardly going to put the newspaper's reputation on the line for my ill-founded hunch.

Maybe instead an anonymous tip is the way to go. There are people whose job it is to protect children. They're the ones who need to bother themselves with checking up on Norah, not me. I open up the website for the NSPCC and navigate to the 'What to do if you suspect child abuse' page. Child abuse is such a strong term. It sends an uneasy chill through my fingertips. Guilt nags at me as I tap through to the online report form.

Please describe what has made you suspect child abuse or neglect.

I lean back in my chair. What do I actually have to report? Her mum didn't want her to have face packs? She told the random neighbour who had taken a somewhat unhealthy interest in her daughter to stay away? Even as I type, then delete, then retype, then delete again I know it doesn't sound credible. If anything, it makes me sound like the lunatic. But surely they'll have to at least check, won't they?

In the end, I try a different tack.

> I'm concerned that Norah may not be coping with the strains of parenting a child with severe medical needs. She is a lone parent so all the stress is on her, and having visited the house and spoken to her on a few occasions I worry that things might be getting on top of her. A wellbeing check of some sort might be necessary.

I click 'send' before I can talk myself out of it and a sense of pride washes over me. As awful as it would be to have social services come knocking at the door, it's better for someone to notice you need help, in my opinion. I've done what's best for not only Lacey, but for Norah too.

A thought occurs to me. I pull open my drawer and rummage around the mess of highlighters, sticky note pads and rolls of sellotape that I threw in with the promise to myself that I'd tidy it all up later. A loose staple digs under my nail and I yank it back, sucking on my reddening fingertip as if that might stop it throbbing. Eyes watering, I continue combing through the contents with my other hand, more cautiously this time, until I find the memory stick I'm looking for.

I plug it in and the content of the drive flashes up on my screen. Video files from August. The month I interviewed Norah. Chewing on my lip, I pull out my headphones from my pocket and curse under my breath as I attempt to untangle them. Eventually I give up, making do with pressing just one bud to my ear, a mess of knotted wire dangling below my chin.

I haven't watched the interview since I first wrote the article, haven't even given it a thought in the couple of months since. I was right, though. Lacey definitely looked more alive, less haunted, back when I first met her. Her eyes were brighter, her smile genuine.

'Are you happy?' My voice echoes through the headphones, the question hauntingly poignant upon rewatching it.

I blink. I pause the video, drag the playbar back a few seconds, hit 'play'. I watch it again and again, zooming in a little closer each time, until I've watched it so many times my eyes begin to go fuzzy. But it's unmistakable. When I asked Lacey if she was happy, Norah discreetly yet purposefully squeezed Lacey's shoulder. It's as if . . . as if she was warning her not to say something she shouldn't.

My phone, jammed against my hip, buzzes with a message and I let out a small yelp. Apparently, using my work time to do non-work-related research has made me jumpy. I flick my monitor back over to the half-written article before pulling out my phone and opening up the notification.

It's just Heidi, asking if I want to go round to hers for a meal with her and Paul tomorrow evening. This is the third time she's asked me since I moved to the Grove. I roll my eyes. It's not that I don't appreciate the offer, I just don't particularly want to go for a meal in her posh house and sit there staring at her gallery wall of sickly romantic photos, drinking her overpriced wine from her Smeg fridge and listening to her and Paul reminding me how perfect their life is compared to mine.

Of course, I don't say that, just type out that I would love to but I already have plans. This is not an acceptable answer to Heidi though, who clearly isn't used to being turned down, certainly not three times in a row.

> Oh come on. Sally's coming too. And Paul's prepping a gorgeous piece of steak. You'd be crazy to miss it.

My grip tightens on the phone. I consider what my evening would look like otherwise. TV, wine, rotating thoughts about Lacey and, after the second bottle, you. And, please don't take this the wrong way, but tomorrow of all days I could really do without thinking about you.

I can't even invite Christian over. That bridge has been well and truly burned.

> Sounds good. What time?

If someone had said to me at the beginning of this week that I was going to be heading to Heidi Downhurst's place twice in one week I'd have told them to jog on, but here we are. I suppose it's better than spending the evening alone again. Ever since I got the feeling that someone was watching me in the car park that time, I've not liked being alone in the house.

I had thought, back when I told your dad he was going to be a father, that I'd never have to worry about living on my own. I'd imagined in my youthful naivety that we'd move in together, find a way to make both of our career ambitions come to fruition with a baby in tow and eventually get married. But he just got angry and threatened to sue the condom manufacturers.

My mum's knee-jerk reaction was to get embarrassed and turf me out onto the street. She came round to the idea of it eventually, when you were a toddler, but I think that might have been more because she found out she didn't have long to live and had some kind of end-of-life epiphany. And, if I'm honest, even though we made up to some extent before she died, I'll never forget she left me a single mum on my own at nineteen.

The only person who ever stood by me was your Aunty Gabbie, and I'm pretty sure that was just because she was secretly desperate to have a baby of her own. She even suggested 'forgetting' to take her pill a few times so that we could be bump buddies.

Steeling myself, I knock on the door, and Heidi's beaming face appears at the glass within seconds. As she opens the door, I notice that while she's still dressed in her usual pin-skirt and blazer, she's barefoot. I've never seen Heidi out of heels. It softens her, which is disconcerting.

She steps out and gives me a kiss on each cheek before leading me through to the dining room. The house looks even bigger now it isn't crammed with partygoers. Sally and Marisa are already sitting at the table, large glasses of red in hand, and the sound of meat sizzling suggests Paul is in the adjacent kitchen. I sit awkwardly next to Sally.

'Isn't this nice?' Heidi says as she flits about the room. 'Norah was supposed to be here too but had a headache, and Emma couldn't get anyone to watch the kids.'

I start to pick at the skin around my nails and take a big swig of wine. I wasn't sure whether to expect Norah to be here tonight or not, but I'm quietly relieved she isn't.

I can't figure out why I've been invited. Of all the people in the community, why me? Sally makes sense. Marisa makes sense. But me? Does Heidi consider me a friend? It feels as if a spotlight has picked me out of the shadows, and I'm not sure it's a good thing.

Before I can think too much into it, Paul emerges with a serving platter. Perhaps it's the heat of the kitchen, but he looks unusually flustered. Beads of sweat have gathered at his hairline. I pick up my fork and go to stab the piece of steak in front of me.

'Before we begin,' Heidi says, and my hand hovers in mid-air for a few seconds before setting the fork back on the table. 'Paul and I have a little announcement. I had hoped a couple more of the ladies would be here to join us for this but you two get to hear the news first. We're expecting!'

My heart seems to fold in on itself. My fingers tighten on the stem of the glass. Sally lets out a whooping noise and scurries around the table to embrace Heidi, but I can't move. My eyes are fixed on Heidi, picturing her holding a baby, feeding a baby, laying a baby down in its extravagant cot with plush bumpers and a chandelier mobile dangling overhead. Heidi and Paul. Paul and Heidi. The two of them represent everything I no longer have, and though I know it's unreasonable and selfish, I hate them for it.

Marisa has now joined Sally in fussing over Heidi, so that it's now only me and Paul sitting at the table. Our eyes meet and I know I have to say something.

'Congratulations,' I force out.

'Thanks.'

I frown. There's a distinct lack of enthusiasm in Paul's response.

Throughout dinner, I try to ensure I always have a mouthful of food to serve as an excuse for my quietness. In actual fact, I'm not listening in the slightest to the conversations that are occurring.

I'm completely focused on Heidi. As I watch her laughing at one of Sally's jokes and twirling a strand of hair around her fingers, it occurs to me that there is a definite pregnancy glow about her. I wonder how long that will last once she's up all hours of the night with a screaming baby. I can't quite picture Heidi in a cardigan and turned-up jeans, although, knowing Heidi, she'll probably make 'yummy mummy' look effortless.

As the plates are emptied and the glasses are refilled, I become gradually more intoxicated, but for once I'm not the most far gone of the group. By the time dinner is over Sally's eyes have taken on the cloudy sheen of someone who is on the verge of welling up. She swirls her wine round her glass, peering sorrowfully into it, a few drops sloshing over the edge. Heidi is quick to jump up and start blotting the red spill with some kind of homemade mixture. Of course she'd know exactly what to use. When I spilled red wine at my house I just moved the sofa over a couple of inches, and to this day the stain is still there.

'I don't know what to do with him,' Sally says. 'It's like I don't recognise my own son anymore.'

They've arrived at the topic of Markus after a painfully long discussion about what Heidi could expect from parenthood, and if Sally's intention is to get her excited for what lies before her, she's doing a crappy job. Apparently, she's the first parent ever to struggle with the likes of a rebellious teenager.

'Honestly, I don't think you can ever prepare for the teenage years,' Sally continues, her lip quivering like a child – oh woe is me. 'Sometimes I wish he'd just disappear.'

My stomach twists.

'No, you don't.' I don't even realise I've spoken. It's only when

Heidi, Sally and Paul all look up at me with widening eyes that I realise those words came from me.

'No, of course I don't really wish that. I just mean . . .' Sally's voice wobbles. I've never seen her so unsure of herself. 'I just mean sometimes it would be easier if he wasn't around.' She quickly tries to backtrack. 'Of course, I wouldn't really want him gone. I love him. I do. It's just the wine talking. Forget I said anything.'

But it's too late. My pulse is already quickening, heat flushing through my body, and though I'm trying not to let it show I can feel my self-control slipping. If I don't get out of this room, out of this house, I'm going to say something I regret.

Without another word, I step past Sally and leave the house.

Chapter Twenty-Four

13 Days Before the Murder

Norah

> Please come and have some drinks with us. You know Lacey is more than welcome too.

I twist my ring around my finger as I tap out another apology to Heidi. I just can't face it tonight. I'm not in the mood to paste a smile on my face and join in the mindless Grove chatter when I have so many more important things to be worried about. I do need a distraction, though. Sighing, I scroll to the rarely opened folder on my phone entitled 'Social Media'.

Apart from Instagram, I'm not one for social media. I have accounts for most of them but largely forget they exist. They are a requirement for a woman in my position. Friends and community members, strangers even, who have donated towards Lacey's fund expect updates. They expect to see where their money has gone, be it photos from our holidays or insights into our renovations, messages from beside her hospital bed. I post these things dutifully when required, a photo every now and again, a hastily written blog post that I then share to my various platforms, but otherwise tend to stay away from all the liking and sharing and tweeting.

I navigate to my Instagram profile, then type the name 'Gabbie Chambers' into the search bar. There are seven results, two of which are accounts set to private and three of which are women living in America and Australia. The Gabbie I spoke to had both an English accent and a UK phone number. The final two Gabbies could both be her, so I scroll through their feeds hoping that I might spot Jodie in one of the photos, and sure enough I do.

It isn't a particularly old photo, posted just over three years ago, but Jodie looks different. I can't quite put my finger on it. Her features seem somewhat softer, her face fuller, her smile wider. Her smile, in fact, is hypnotic, spreading right up to her eyes.

What happened to you? I wonder.

My finger swipes the screen, scrolling through the stream of photos, going back as far as I can in time. Gabbie is a lively woman, her feed brimming with cocktail-drinking selfies and bendy yoga poses with 'hashtag blessed' captions. It doesn't quite work in my head – Jodie beside this vibrant personality. I always imagined Jodie's life before the Grove to be similar to what it is now. Quiet, work-focused, aloof. But it seems my neighbour had quite the different life before she moved in next door to me.

There is a child in many of these photos. A pretty thing, with Gabbie's warm skin tone and textured hair. I certainly hadn't thought 'mother' when I first came to her profile, but I suppose not all mothers have to look as bedraggled and life-beaten as me. I scroll a little further, and my breath hitches in my throat.

There is a post dated three years ago, with a photo of Jodie in a hospital bed, a bundle wrapped up in her arms. My eyes drift to the caption.

> #TBT to this day eight years ago. There's not many gals I'd let break my hand while they push a baby out their lady parts, but I'd do it again any day for you, hun. Happy birthday, sweet girl, and happy eight years of being a mama, Jod. Love ya xxx

It is as if the walls are closing in on me, squeezing me until I can't breathe.

Jodie was a mother.

'Hello?'

As soon as Christian answers the phone my throat clamps up. I'm not sure how to properly articulate my worries, but I have to try. I have to get through to him, make him see how risky it is getting involved with Jodie.

I clear my throat. 'Hey. Sorry to call this late. I wanted to talk to you about . . .' I lower my voice. Lacey is asleep in her room, but I don't want to risk her hearing me. 'About Jodie.'

Christian's sigh is loud enough to carry over the line. 'What's Heidi said now?'

'This is nothing to do with Heidi. I have a right to be concerned, Christian.'

'Jeez, Norah.' He's starting to sound exasperated. 'What do you want from me? You told me to move on so that's what I'm trying to do.'

I wince, the memories of our break-up unwittingly filtering into my mind. He had begged me not to end our relationship, gripped onto my wrist and promised me we could work through our issues, that everything we'd been through together wasn't enough to break us. But it was. Every time we were together it was like a solid mass sitting between us, reminding me. It took a long time for us to be able to face each other, and even now, even though we've managed to reach a certain level of comfort when we bump into each other, I think I can still see the hurt in his eyes. The love. The anger.

I, at least, had Heidi to lean on. She was the only person I'd told about our relationship, and was my rock in those weeks after the break-up. But as far as I know he hasn't told anyone.

'Look, I'm not asking you not to move on. Nor am I trying to offer you relationship advice.'

'So what are you trying to say, Norah?' The tone of this call is not what I had wanted. There is a hostile undercurrent.

'She's a journalist,' I say. 'She researches people for a living, that's what she does.'

'So you think Jodie is, what, using me?' He lets out a small chuckle, as if we are schoolchildren talking about the girl who keeps pulling his hair because she's got a crush. Does he not understand the gravity of this situation? Does he not remember what's at stake?

I'm about to speak when what sounds like a doorbell ringing pierces across the phone.

'Bloody hell,' Christian says. 'Norah, I've got to go.'

'Wait, please.'

'I can't talk about this right now.'

An uneasy feeling settles in my stomach and I glance out of my window at the house next door. All Jodie's lights are off.

'She's there, isn't she?' I say.
'I'll call you tomorrow.'
'Christian!'
But before I can say anything else the line goes dead.

Chapter Twenty-Five

13 Days Before the Murder

Jodie

'Where are we going, Mummy?' Your voice rings in my ears. I've chosen not to return home after Heidi's shambles of a dinner party. All that awaits me at home is misery, tortured thoughts, reminders of what day it is. But apparently my mind is cruel enough to bring those memories with me as I trudge towards Christian's house. I know, of course, that you're not walking next to me. I know that your little hand clasped in mine is a figment of my imagination, my brain's attempt at coping. But that doesn't stop it from feeling beautifully, unbearably real.

My stomach turns over with every step, but as much as I've drunk tonight, I have a sneaky suspicion that isn't the only thing making me feel sick. Guilt tugs at my insides. I shouldn't have said what I said to Sally. I remember all too well what it's like to struggle, what it's like to feel unable to cope. I loved you unconditionally, but there were times when I couldn't even remember who I was before becoming a mum. Your world gets turned upside down, dismantled, remodelled into a life you don't recognise, one you've got absolutely no idea how to navigate. It's easy to say things you don't mean when in the middle of a tough spell. I make a mental note to pop round Sally's tomorrow and apologise to her.

When I arrive at Christian's I can see him through the window, having what looks like a rather intense phone conversation. When he spots me he takes a moment to end the call, then appears at the front door with his arms crossed and his eyebrows lowered. Not exactly the reaction I hoped for, but at least he hasn't stormed inside and slammed the door in my face.

'Hey,' I say, my mouth dry.

'Hey.'

There is a long, excruciating pause. I can smell his aftershave from here, spiced and woody.

'Can I come in?'

He runs his eyes over me as if appraising me, and I have to stop myself from telling him to forget it. After a few seconds, he steps to one side and disappears inside the house, leaving the door open. I take that as an invitation to go in. I give a quick glance back at the street before shutting the door. You're no longer there.

I'm not sure what I was expecting his house to look like. I always envisioned doctors' homes to look a little like hospitals, all white and sterile. Christian's isn't like that at all. It's lived in, with cozy throws on the sofas and bookshelves packed with classic fiction. I can't help but smile as I eye the novelty dog-ear slippers wedged under the coffee table.

'Can I make you a cup of tea?' Christian calls.

'Yes, please.' I hover in the hallway while he clatters around the kitchen, and allow my eyes to drift over the framed photos on the wall; a shot of him next to a camel, another of him diving in some very un-British ocean, all turquoise waters and brightly coloured coral. No photos of him with anyone else, I notice. I have an urge to ask him if he's ever been married – he's around my age, I figure, so it's not out of the question – but remind myself not to follow in my nosy neighbours' footsteps.

My heart nearly leaps into my throat as something touches my leg and I let out a small yelp. A small, furry brown-and-white face peers up at me.

'You have a cat?'

'Yeah, that's Toby,' Christian says from the kitchen. 'Don't worry, he's friendly.'

I let out a laugh as I bend down to pet the animal which is now winding itself around my legs. I hadn't pictured Christian as a cat person. I realise, as Christian emerges with two steaming mugs and gestures for me to take a seat in the living room, that I really don't know that much about him, considering we've shagged.

The tea scalds my lips but I sip it anyway, thankful for the warmth that spreads through my chest. It makes me feel better, less anxious. Christian watches me intently and I chew my lip, knowing I'll have to explain what I was thinking turning up at his door so late in the evening. I'm not even sure I know.

'I'm sorry,' I say after a moment, 'for messing you around. I'm not great at the whole . . . emotions thing. They kind of make me uncomfortable.'

He shakes his head. 'Don't worry about it. Really.'

Another silence. Great. I almost miss the mundane weather conversations.

'So is that what you came here to say?' Christian is trying to look serious, but Toby has now jumped up onto his lap and is proceeding to paw at his chin, which is a distraction, to say the least. I avert my eyes, not wanting to laugh at an inappropriate time, and clear my throat.

'I guess, I just wanted someone to talk to. It's kind of a tough day for me today and . . .' I sigh, wishing I could articulate myself better. Of all the useless crap you learn at school, they don't think to teach things that would come in handy like being able to speak without sounding like an idiot. 'I went to dinner at Heidi's . . . hung out with her, Marisa and Sally to take my mind off it.'

Christian raises an eyebrow at that, and the smallest of smirks appears at the side of his mouth. 'How did that go?'

'Not great.' Understatement of the year.

Christian's phone starts to ring, giving me a moment to figure out exactly what I want to say. He pulls it out of his pocket and swiftly declines, his politeness not wavering in the comfort of his own home. Pins and needles are starting to set in from how tightly I've been gripping the mug. I place it down on the table and stretch out my fingers. 'Do you know, you're the only person in this entire town who hasn't asked me about my life before I came here?'

Christian shrugs, using his free hand to stroke Toby and stop him from drinking his tea. 'I figured you'd tell me when you were ready. Of course, that was when I thought I'd be seeing you again.'

There is something quite touching about that remark. I like the fact that he respects my privacy, a trait that most in the Grove severely lack. It makes me want to give him a hug.

I look over at the steam rising from my mug, swirling patterns mixing with dust particles, almost hypnotic. I take a calming breath. 'Today would have been my daughter's birthday.'

Though he seems to try to hide his shock, I still notice Christian's lips parting and the tightening of his posture. 'I had no idea you had a daughter,' he says, gently, and I can see concern in his eyes.

That's all it takes. I close my eyes, and the whole sorry story pours out.

Christian's bedding is exceptionally soft, some kind of plush Egyptian cotton. I keep running my hands over it and wriggling about just so I can feel it brush against my skin. I like being here, in Christian's bed. I like being with him. When I told him about you, I waited for him to ask what everyone asks when they find out I was once a mother. But he didn't. He simply lifted his arm, beckoning me to come closer, and I shuffled along the sofa until my body was pressed up to his, his arm around me. Anyone else would have wanted all the details, would have seen my story as a hot piece of gossip, but not him. He's different to everyone else here. Christian makes me feel safe, like sharing things with him is completely on my terms.

'Keep still,' he murmurs, his voice drowsy from the couple of sleeping pills he downed.

'Sorry.' I'm not used to opening up like I have been tonight, and it's as if my body is recoiling against it. The feeling of vulnerability. I fix my eyes on the ceiling and concentrate on not moving, but then because my body hates me, I inevitably get an itch on my ankle, and the more I focus on not scratching it the more it itches. I need not to think about you for a moment. So I turn my attention elsewhere; to Lacey, to the video from the fundraiser. I wonder how long it will take after submitting a report of concern to the NSPCC for them to check out the Williams house, and what exactly they will be looking for.

'Christian?'

'Hmm?' He is clearly trying his hardest to go to sleep, but my brain won't switch off. I raise my thumb to my mouth and start chewing on my nail.

'What would you do if you suspected one of your patients was being abused?'

There is a long silence, and the pillow rustles as he tilts his head to the side. 'Why do you ask that?'

'Just hypothetically. Is there a process to follow?'

'Well, yes. There are agencies we have a duty to report concerns to.'

I nod and, having run out of nail to bite, start on the surrounding skin. Now that I'm headed down this road I've woken up even more. I sit up on my elbows and flick on the bedside lamp. Christian recoils from the light, blinking frantically and pulling the duvet up over his eyes.

'Jeez, Jodie. What are you doing?'

'I'm worried about Lacey.'

Christian lets out a long, deep sigh, the realisation that he isn't going to be allowed to sleep evident in his pained expression as he peeks out from under the duvet. 'Can we talk about this tomorrow?'

'I can't get it out of my head,' I say, ignoring his request. 'There's something wrong about them. The way Norah is with her. Like she's controlling her.'

Christian opens his mouth as if he's about to say something, then rolls out of bed, bending down to grab his shorts and pulling them up in jerky movements, tugging on the zip.

'What's wrong?' I ask, following him with my eyes.

He doesn't answer, just stalks off down the hallway. Baffled, I reach for my knickers and top and follow him.

To my surprise I find him sitting on the sofa with his feet up having opened a beer. Toby has taken advantage of the unexpected visitor and curled into a furry ball on his lap, purring happily. Christian doesn't even look my way as I approach.

'Are you annoyed?' I ask, feeling suddenly exposed in my lack of clothes. Still no response. I move to sit next to him. 'I know you're not allowed to talk about past patients, I understand that, but if you noticed anything at all that seemed odd when you treated her your testimony could be the thing that gets her help.'

'I barely treated her, okay?'

I've never heard his voice like that; pinched and sharp. He leans his head back and closes his eyes. 'I only saw her a few times and then Norah decided to take her somewhere else.'

'Why?'

'She wanted to take her to a specialist in London or something, I don't know. Why does it matter?'

I open my mouth for a sharp remark, but quieten myself. Tensions are already high, and my tendency to start mouthing off wouldn't do anything to calm the situation down. But he's not telling me everything, I'm sure of that much.

'I can't let it go, Christian,' I say. 'Until I know she's safe in that house I can't stop.'

I think again to that night when I mistook Lacey for you, when I thought I'd seen her mouth the words 'help me'. If only I could remember more clearly, if only I could be sure that was what she said.

Christian drops his legs from the coffee table, the sudden

movement startling Toby awake. 'Is that why you're here? Is that what you and I have been about?'

A shocked silence drops over the room like a weighted blanket. Does he really think I'm that cold as to sleep with someone purely for information? Christian isn't paying attention to my indignant face. He jumps to his feet, sending poor Toby scrambling off his lap.

'You need to drop this. Lacey isn't your daughter, Jodie. It sounds like you're . . . I don't know . . . projecting your grief onto her or something.'

It's like I've been punched right in the gut. Christian seems to immediately regret his words, his face twisting. 'Look, I'm . . . I'm sorry. I shouldn't have said that.'

But the damage has already been done. Any attempts at remaining calm were diminished with that one comment. A flame has been lit inside of me and is blazing through me. I stand up, nostrils flaring. 'How fucking dare you.'

It feels like the worst possible betrayal. The first person in the Grove I've told, the only time I've allowed myself to open up since I've been here, and he chooses to use it against me. I can't bear to look at him.

'I said I'm sorry,' Christian calls to me as I tear through the bedroom, grabbing my clothes and throwing them haphazardly onto my body. 'But don't turn this on me. You're the one who's been using me!'

'It's not like you needed any convincing to take my clothes off! You threw yourself at me, let's be honest!'

'Me? Who came to whose door at eleven at night?' It's a battle now – who can throw the most punches?

Once dressed – although my jacket is inside out and the label is hanging out the back of my jeans – I push past Christian and charge to the front door. 'Don't call me!' I shout as I step out into the freezing outside air and slam the door behind me.

Chapter Twenty-Six

13 Days Before the Murder

Norah

My unread message asking Christian to call me back straight away is staring at me, taunting me. He's playing with fire, the bastard. The minutes as I wait for it to say he's seen the message go by at a glacial pace, my pulse quickening with each tick of the clock.

I can't just sit here and do nothing, knowing that Jodie is there with him right this second. But I can't leave the house unless I wake up Lacey and bring her with me, and how would I explain going round to Christian's at this time of night? Before I can think, my hand is retrieving my phone from my pocket and calling him. It only rings twice before the engaged tone sounds. She's still there. She has to be, otherwise he'd have answered.

I grip onto the phone, blood pounding in my ears, my throat feeling as if someone has scraped a nail down it.

Why has Jodie chosen Christian of all people? What kind of twisted game is the universe playing on me that she'd end up with him? Unless, of course . . .

My breath grows shallow. Black spots dance across my vision

as I open up my WhatsApp thread with Christian once more and this time type out six terrifying words.

> I think she may already know.

I place my phone down in my lap and lean my head back, closing my eyes. If that's the case, if she's worked out what I did and is just trying to get evidence from Christian, then I have to do something. I have to stop her. But my throbbing head is stopping me from thinking clearly.

The phone buzzes on my leg and I wearily glance down at it. It's a message back from Christian. I sit up straight, my heart racing.

> I can't do this anymore. It's doing my head in. If she's as close as you think she is, we should confess before it's too late.

Chapter Twenty-Seven

Marisa

What's going on? Police just went past my window.

Sally

Doubt it. Sure you're not imagining things, Marisa?

Marisa

¡Qué hostias!

Sally

I don't know what that means.

Emma

Leave off, Sally. I saw them too. Anyone know what's happened?

Marisa

Someone must have called them if they've been let through the gates.

[Heidi added Jodie Madison to the conversation]

Emma

@Heidi? Know what's happening?

Marisa

@Heidi??

Heidi

Morning, ladies. I'm not sure of all the details yet but something has happened at Dr Roth's house.

Chapter Twenty-Eight

12 Days Before the Murder

Jodie

I wake to a sharp pain in my neck, the kind that sends cramp down your arm from sleeping in an awkward position. My phone is face down on my chest. I must have fallen asleep while scrolling. I pick it up and squint. The screen is dark because I forgot to charge it overnight; unreadable. Sighing, I roll over and plug it in and, after ten minutes or so of attempting to go back to sleep and failing, haul myself out of bed.

It's only when I sit down at the breakfast bar with my coffee and go to check the news that I remember to retrieve my phone from the bedroom, and it is only when I return with it and wipe the bleariness of the night away from my eyes that I see the stream of unread messages. I've been added to some kind of WhatsApp group by the looks of it. I frown. The last time I was added to a WhatsApp group was when you started at school and the other mothers thought it would be a good idea for us all to keep in contact. I lasted about two weeks before I lost my patience with the incessant mindless chatter and removed myself.

Bracing myself, I flick open the group and blink. The message from Heidi is all I need to see.

Something has happened at Dr Roth's house.

My legs seem to move of their own accord. Still pyjama-clad, I bolt out the front door and fiddle with the keys to my car. My hands are shaking so much I drop them twice, before I give up and run. It didn't take long to walk last night, ten minutes, maybe slightly longer.

By the time I reach Christian's road, my muscles are burning and I'm wheezing like a poorly tuned instrument. I can't see that well from the sweat stinging my eyes, but well enough to make out three police cars and an ambulance, lights flashing, outside his house. Christian's neighbours and other residents, even some who live right on the other side of the estate, are gathered around his house, tears staining their cheeks. And a gurney is being wheeled out, covered with a black sheet.

Jesus Christ. He's . . . dead?

In classic Kensington Grove spirit, a WhatsApp message pings up to say that tea has been organised at the community centre, but I don't go. Instead, I wander home, feeling sluggish and weak, watching my feet as they retrace the steps I took last night, along the pavements, into my street, up the steps leading to my front door. Once inside I lean back against the door frame and close my eyes. I was with him last night. I slept with him last night. My head can't process that it was him under that black sheet, nothing about it makes sense.

I become aware that my hands are wet and unfurl them. I've been digging my nails into my palms so hard they've made bloody crescents in my skin. Wincing, I move into the bathroom and run them under the tap. Then, without warning, I retch, vomit. Liquid splashes off the sink. I clutch the cold ceramic sides and cave in on myself, my eyes screwed shut.

I must have been standing here for some time because a knock sounds at my door. I rinse away the remaining vomit from the sink and wash out my mouth before moving back to the living room. The windows in my front door are frosted glass but I can already tell it's a couple of police officers. I fidget in place. My skin itches; I'm desperate for a shower.

'Would you like a cup of tea?' I ask once they've introduced themselves and we've gathered round the breakfast bar. One of them I recognise; PC Harris from the fire. The other has introduced herself as DS Wolfe.

'No, thank you,' DS Wolfe says, perching on one of the stools. She doesn't look like how I envisage police officers to look, especially not high-ranking officers. I had a perception of tired, caffeine-fuelled eyes, lines in the forehead that tell stories of all the terrible things they've seen. DS Wolfe is rather glamorous, with subtle make-up and a gentle wave to her red hair. I wonder what she thinks of me, with my holey pyjamas and 'I genuinely *did* wake up like this' hair. PC Harris remains standing, while I, mouth dry and stomach still churning, take a seat at the dining table.

'I'm sorry to tell you that Christian Roth passed away last night,' she says. 'I believe you knew him?'

I nod, though shock is still reverberating through me. I know she doesn't need me to confirm that I knew him. If she's here, particularly so soon after, it's because someone has seen us together.

'What happened?' The words come out strained, a feeble croak. I clear my throat and try again.

'It appears he may have taken his own life.'

I blink, take a moment to process. Acid curdles in my stomach and my hands begin to shake violently. I don't know what I'd expected them to say, but suicide was not it.

'How?' My voice is now so hoarse it's as if the news has aged me fifty years.

DS Wolfe's face stiffens, as if this was the last question she wanted to be asked. 'His neighbour noticed a hose leading from his car exhaust to his bedroom.' She doesn't need to say any more. The acid is returning to my mouth, a sharp metallic taste running through my saliva as I picture Christian's lungs filling up with carbon monoxide, and I place my hand over my mouth in an attempt to stop the sick spilling out again. 'Can I get a glass of water?' I croak.

'Of course.' She nods at PC Harris, who is quick to grab a glass from my drying rack and run the tap. He hands it to me and I sip it gratefully, my head spinning. It's too much of a coincidence. We row over Norah and then he turns up dead the very next morning?

'In these situations, Ms Madison,' DS Wolfe pulls out a notebook from her pocket, 'it helps if we can speak to those close to him. Try to build up a picture of his life. Why he might choose to end it.' She's trying to come across friendly, approachable, but I can see a hint of sternness in her face. She's not one to be messed with.

'We didn't know each other that well,' I say honestly. Right now, I feel as though I didn't know him at all. They say you can never tell what's going on inside someone's head, but Christian came across as confident, pleased with the direction his life had taken. If anyone was unhinged out of the two of us it was me.

It feels unnatural to talk about him in the past tense, harsh on the tongue.

DS Wolfe regards me. 'But you were in a relationship with Mr Roth, yes?'

'I wouldn't say ... We slept together a couple of times. Went on a few dates. I've only been round to his once and he's only been here once.'

'And you were at his house last night, correct?'

I frown, wondering how she could possibly know that. Did someone see me?

'Yes,' I say. 'Look, he didn't seem the type to take his own life.'

She scribbles in her notebook, and I crane my head in as subtle a way as possible to see what she's writing, but it's fruitless. I can sense PC Harris' eyes boring into the side of my head. 'Am I a suspect?'

DS Wolfe's eyes flick up to meet mine. That was probably a stupid thing to say. *Way to make yourself look like you've got something to hide, Jodie.*

'We currently have no reason to suspect that Mr Roth's death was suspicious, but we need to keep all options open for the time being. Can you tell me about last night?'

I run a hand through my hair and exhale slowly. I don't particularly want to think about last night. Tears are beginning to prickle beneath my eyelids which I desperately don't want to let free.

'I got to his about ... ten thirty, I guess. He made me a cup of tea. We chatted for a bit. We had sex and then I went.'

'What did you chat about?'

I swallow hard. Just how open and honest do I have to be in order for them to leave me alone? 'My daughter. It would have been her birthday yesterday. She passed away three years ago.'

'My condolences.'

I try to say 'thank you' but my voice won't engage. It's been so long since I've heard those words, and it's like a knife digging into my chest and twisting. Those words are exactly why I had to leave and come to Kensington Grove. I couldn't bear to listen to them anymore.

'How did the night end? Did he seem troubled at all when you left?'

I cast my mind back to the argument, to the pained look in his face when he accused me of using him, to how the last words I shouted at him was that he wasn't to call me. If I hadn't said that, would he have phoned me and asked for help, asked me to talk him out of it?

'We had an argument,' I say, thinking of Norah. Perhaps I should tell DS Wolfe what we argued about. Perhaps it's the police I should have been talking to about Lacey, not Christian.

'What about?'

And then, it's as if someone has pulled open the curtains and let the light stream into a dark, fuzzy room. 'Was it Norah Williams who told you I was there last night? Is she the one who called you?'

DS Wolfe tilts her head to the side. I've piqued her interest. 'I'm afraid I can't divulge that information.'

'Well, that's who we were arguing about. I filed an NSPCC report about it a couple of days ago. I'm convinced there's something going on with her. I don't think she's treating her daughter well. I don't know if it's abuse or neglect or what's going on but there's something.' The words are tumbling out of my mouth so fast I'm tripping over them, but I can't stop. It's everything I've wanted to say to the police but been too chicken shit to actually say. 'I tried talking to him about it a couple of times because he used to treat Lacey and I thought he might know something. Each time he'd clam up. He got really angry. It was like . . . like he was holding back or knew something he couldn't tell me.'

DS Wolfe is studying me, her eyes narrowed. I sigh, exasperated. I guess I'll have to spell it out. 'If she knew I was there last night, if she thought he might drop her in it . . .' I trail off, searching for the right words. 'I just think you need to look into her.'

When I finally stop speaking the room falls silent, and I can practically hear our three heartbeats. The metallic tang of blood fills my mouth as I realise I've bitten my tongue in my haste to get my theory out. I stare back at DS Wolfe and have an overwhelming urge to say, 'Well? What are you going to do about it?'

Eventually, she resumes scribbling on her notebook. She asks me what led me to these suspicions, if I have any proof, and I go through the signs I've spotted in as much detail as possible. I don't miss the slight rise of her eyebrow when I tell her I used to spend hours chatting to Lacey in the evenings. I realise it sounds odd, but I'd love to see what anyone else would do in my situation. Who would have it in their heart to refuse a sick girl who just wants to watch a bit of television?

Once we've gone through everything, DS Wolfe flips closed her notebook and hands me a card. 'Thank you for your time. We'll look into everything you've told us. In the meantime, if you think of anything else, please call me.'

PC Harris also hands me a pamphlet – *Help is at Hand. Support after someone may have died by suicide.* The pamphlet shows a picture of budding flowers arching towards the gleaming sunlight, soaking up its life-giving rays. It seems strangely incongruent with the subject matter. I accept both with a nod and a 'thank you' and open the door for them. As I do so, my eyes land on none other than Norah herself, pushing Lacey back home, coming from the direction of the community centre.

She spots me, sees the police leaving my house and returning to their car, quirks the corner of her mouth into a melancholy smile and waves. I don't smile. I don't wave back. I'm done pretending. Instead, I simply watch her and scrutinise her face, trying to spot any semblance of guilt. Hers is a tired face. But not, I think, an innocent face.

I tell myself this is all about Lacey, about Christian, about getting justice for the both of them, but deep inside I can tell it's something more than that. There's something about Norah, some sinister unease that stirs within me every time I see her. Closing the door, I find myself with a reignited sense of purpose. I'll make some calls, do some research, find out what I can.

Chapter Twenty-Nine

11 Days Before the Murder

Norah

Heidi lifts up the bottle of wine in her hand as I open the door.

'Thought you could use a friendly chat,' she says, her lips turned down in a sympathetic smile.

I don't say anything but step to one side to allow her in. I knew this visit was coming. She's been trying to reach me all of yesterday and today. Even Lacey seems to have picked up on my distress. She's been kind and warm towards me ever since the police left. She put herself to bed this evening early and with no fuss, as if she can tell I have little resolve to fight her right now. Of course, she doesn't know the guilt I'm carrying within me.

Heidi hangs her coat on the hook next to the front door while I grab two glasses and meet her on the sofa.

She lifts a hand. 'Actually, just water will do for me, thank you.'

I raise an eyebrow. I don't think Heidi has ever turned down a drink in all the time I've known her, and she's the one who brought the bottle. Seeing my expression, she lets out a half-laugh.

'I haven't had a chance to tell you yet. I'm pregnant.'

'Wow. Congratulations.' I blink, slightly taken aback. I want to be happy for her, I *am* happy for her, but with everything that's happened over the last twenty-four hours Heidi's news seems insensitive somehow. I pour myself a glass of wine – white, but I can't be fussy at the moment – and a glass of sparkling water for Heidi. There's a hint of irritation on her face; I suppose she was expecting me to jump around ecstatically, but I think even she knows today isn't all about her.

She takes a long, slow sip of her water and places a hand on my arm. 'How are you feeling?'

'Fine.'

'Paul spoke to Christian's mother earlier. It was awful. I could hear her crying down the phone.'

'Heidi, I don't mean to be rude but I really don't want to talk about Christian, if that's okay.'

The mere mention of his name has constricted my throat, as if someone is holding me by the neck and is shaking me.

Heidi's cheeks flush and she looks down at her lap. 'No, sorry.' A tense silence stretches between us before she says, 'How's Lacey doing?'

'She's okay. Upset, of course. She really liked Christian.'

Before I can go on, a light switching on next door captures my attention. The blinds are lowered so I can't see into Jodie's house, but I can make out her hovering silhouette. My free hand beside me curls into a fist, heat flushes across my neck and up into my face. This is all her fault. If it wasn't for her, Christian would be alive.

'Norah?' Heidi places a hand on my shoulder, making me jump. She is following my gaze out the window. 'Are you okay?'

I consider Heidi for a moment. Those concerned eyes. But no

matter how well-intentioned she may be in the moment, I know she's desperate for a strand of gossip, something to share. It's never occurred to me how easy it would be to get a story going with Heidi around.

I exhale softly, allowing the anticipation to build for what I am about to say. 'It's probably just in my imagination,' I start. I need to be seen as holding back. She needs to coax it out of me.

'What is?'

'Jodie next door. It's probably nothing but . . . I've noticed her acting strange a few times. One time I saw her leaning over the fence. I might have been mistaken.' I rub my fingers along my temple to demonstrate what a strain it is to remember. 'But she seemed to be watching us.'

Heidi's brow furrows. 'Maybe she was just trying to be friendly? Leaning over for a chat? That sort of thing.'

'There have been other things too.' I swallow hard, place my wine on the table and begin wringing my hands. This is hard to talk about. 'She's called the house a few times. And I've caught her talking to Lacey, through the windows, outside, basically any time I'm not with her.'

Heidi's eyes are fixed on mine, though they are blinking rapidly as she tries to process what I've said. She knows what happened with Alison. She is journeying down the path I have led her to. Just a few more turns.

'Do you know much about her?' I ask.

Heidi shakes her head. 'Not really. She's always been so . . . private.' A brief nod conveys my disappointment. There is a beat, and then, 'I'll do some digging. And I'll chat to Paul, see if he's got any information on her from before.'

I lower my gaze – to her, I am abashed, but in reality, I am a puppet master.

'Do you want to stay with us tonight?'

I shake my head and smile, ensuring to keep concern in my expression. 'No, Lacey's already asleep. I don't want to disturb her. Anyway, like I said, I'm probably imagining things.' I pick up my wine again. 'Can we talk about something else? How are you getting on with the Christmas market you're planning for the residents?'

Luckily, Heidi accepts my diversion of topic and starts listing off ideas for stalls, decorations that could be brought in, marketing techniques, but the seeds have been sown.

Now I just need to wait for the WhatsApp messages to roll in.

Chapter Thirty

10 Days Before the Murder

Jodie

My first step is to look into Norah's past. If there's anything I've learned over my years of researching family secrets, it's that behaviours don't just come out of nowhere. A cheat has almost always veered from their marriage in some form previously, whether it be getting a lap dance at a strip club or indulging in a regular dose of first-person porn. A drug problem can usually be traced back to the first, mostly innocent puff of weed, and previous to that, the first cigarette. If Norah has violent tendencies – of which, at this point, I've totally convinced myself – there'll be something in her past that steered her that way.

Unfortunately, my usual resource – the internet – isn't much good to me. I've already looked up everything there is to find online about Norah. Her name only brings up articles about Lacey, and when I searched the census a total of six women with the name Norah Williams appeared who could possibly be her, and without some more intimate details about her life before the Grove it was impossible to tell which one. I need to look closer to home.

Paul's office is situated by the front gate. It's the first building you see when you pass through. I've only been inside it once, when I first visited the Grove as a hopeful, uninformed potential tenant looking for a property where I could start my new life away from prying eyes. Paul had taken down my details that day; full name, date of birth, previous address, occupation and so on, and if he took mine I can only hope that he would have taken Norah's when she first moved to the Grove, too.

'Paul?' I knock gently on the door, pasting my best journalist's smile on my face. Warm and approachable, yet with the tiniest hint of intimidation so the subject feels almost compelled to share the information I require. The heating is on full whack and it hits me like a brick wall as I step from the drizzly outside into the entrance hall. Above the plush red sofa hang black-and-white photos of Kensington Grove from the past: images of beds lined up in crammed rows, barred windows, nurses unsmiling in their floor-length white aprons and matching hats. There are no patients in the photos. It seems a great injustice that these pieces of memorabilia have been displayed around the Grove as 'décor', and yet no one seems to want to acknowledge the poor people who were imprisoned here.

Nausea hitting me, I avert my eyes from the photos and instead focus on the receptionist beaming at me. She's in her late teens, one of the residents' kids, maybe. Working here until she escapes to university.

'Hi, is Paul around?' I ask in my mock-friendly tone.

'Jodie!' Paul appears at the door of his office before she has a chance to respond. 'What a nice surprise.'

He looks a bit flustered, like he's in the middle of something stressful, and I can't tell if I've come at a bad time or not.

'Are you busy? I can come back.' I hold my breath, praying he's not going to send me away. I don't have time to come back. Every second I waste is another second Lacey is stuck in that house. But I can't let him know how delicate the situation is.

'No, no, just doing some boring old paperwork. Please, come in.'

Taking a breath, I step through the glass door and settle myself in the plastic chair on the nearest side of his mahogany desk, while he pours me a glass of water and takes his seat opposite me in his wheeled leather armchair. My eyes briefly scan his desk; a couple of photos, a wire pen holder with a selection of biros, a three-ring binder. I didn't pay much attention to this room last time I was here, and it is surprisingly modest. I had expected grandiose decorations and expensive fountain pens worth more than my handbag. Perhaps it's only Heidi who likes to present herself as Kensington Grove royalty.

'I uh... I wanted to see how you were holding up anyway.' Paul rolls his pen under his fingertips, not meeting my eye. 'After... Dr Roth...'

My earlobes burn as the lump in my throat returns. He peeks up at me, sees my pinched expression and shrugs.

'Heidi told me about... I had no idea you two were close.'

Neither did Heidi, I think to myself, wondering just how far news of mine and Christian's relationship has spread since Norah lifted the lid on it. God, I hate the word 'relationship'. It sounds so official, so meaningful, and I know exactly what comes with that. Those looks. The ones I got after you died. The look Paul is giving me right now. Pity.

'He was a good man,' Paul is continuing, and I wish I could

slap him across the face to make him shut up. 'If you ever need someone to talk to...'

'I'm fine, thank you for asking.' I swallow hard and try to realign myself. I came into the office with a goal, my mind was set on it, and talk of Christian has knocked me off-kilter. I can't get emotional. I need to focus on what I'm here to do. 'That's not what I came to ask you about.'

Paul shakes his head. 'Of course. Of course. What can I do for you?'

'Well, as you know I work for the *Estate Reporter*.' I clear my throat in an attempt to get back into my journalist head. 'I'm running a story on Lacey.' An uneasy feeling settles in my stomach at that. Am I writing a story on Lacey? If my gut instinct is right, if there is something untoward going on inside the Williams house, will I take it to my boss? In all my years exposing affairs and seeking out the juicy secrets that families keep hidden, I have never once felt a pang of guilt at insinuating myself into other people's business. But Lacey is different. I've allowed myself to grow attached.

Paul raises an eyebrow and presses his lips flat, suspicion flashing in his eyes. 'Another one? I thought you already did an article on her. That one about the fundraiser?'

'Yes, this is different, it's a kind of in-depth look into her life.' Paul still doesn't look convinced, so I'm quick to add, 'Hopefully it will raise awareness and in turn raise more donations.'

His face softens and I smile inwardly. 'They've been through so much, I'd love to help get their story out there. Play my part, as it were.' I survey his expression, satisfied that I've laid on enough good nature to have a chance at winning him over. 'I was hoping you might be able to give me some insight into their lives before they came to the Grove? Do you know where they lived before here?'

'Somewhere in York, I believe. Forgive me, Norah and Lacey moved here a long time ago.'

I file this nugget away in my brain and take a sip of water. 'I don't suppose you've got an address? I'd love to take a trip down there, chat to some of her old neighbours. You keep files here, don't you?'

The suspicion returns to his eyes and I know I've pushed too far. He tilts his head. 'Wouldn't it be easier to ask Norah herself?'

'I didn't want to bother her. She's got so much on her plate already.' Plausible, but not entirely believable. I fidget, take another sip of my water, now gone lukewarm from the stifling room temperature.

A shrill buzz sounds and the receptionist's voice trills through the speaker on the desk.

'Mr Downhurst, you're needed at the pond. Some kind of mishap with the Christmas tree.'

Paul mutters under his breath. It's not quite discernible but I'm sure there's a couple of swear words in there.

'Excuse me for a moment.' His chair creaks as he stands, already tapping numbers forcefully into his phone. 'Phoebe, make Miss Madison a cup of tea, will you?'

He bustles out, his mobile pressed firmly to his ear. A few minutes later Phoebe places a steaming cup of tea in front of me – though with the heating on as high as it is, a hot drink is the last thing I want – and then I am alone.

The room is strangely quiet, the only sound the ticking of the clock on the wall. It's an old clock, antique-looking. I think I recognise it from one of the old photographs. For a moment it's as if my heart is beating in time with it. Everything seems to have slowed right down. The ticking is growing louder now, more urgent. A pounding beat that echoes through the room, hammers in my ears.

I'm up, circling the desk and settling myself in Paul's chair. Phoebe isn't paying attention. She's back at her own desk, head buried in what I can only assume is her phone. My hand reaches for the mouse, shuffles it to wake up the computer. I curse at myself as the password screen flashes up. Holding my breath, I tap in a few of the most obvious combinations; Kensington1, KensingtonGrove1!, Heidi1, password1. None of them work, and I lean back in the chair so far I have to grip the desk to stop it toppling over.

A paper trail, then. Growing less and less confident in my plan by the second, I move to the filing cabinets lined up against the wall and scan through the labels. 'W' is, unsurprisingly, at the far end of the cabinets, but Norah and Lacey aren't in there. 'Walker', 'White', but no 'Williams'.

I've just reached the next label, but only have a chance to skim it because the sound of the glass doors opening stops me in my tracks and sends me skitting over to the side, away from the cabinets. I position myself as nonchalantly as possible by the window. I haven't been doing anything, just decided to gaze out at the meadow on the other side of the gate while I waited for Paul's return. Now that the colder months are upon us the long grass glistens, thin strands of ice blowing in the wind.

'Sorry about that,' Paul says, and I turn to him, shake my head and smile in understanding. I don't trust myself to talk without the tremble of my voice giving me away. Paul sits himself in his chair and I hold my breath. Did I put the mouse back where it was? Will he notice the warmth of someone else sitting in his seat? If he does, he doesn't say anything.

'Where were we? Ah, yes, Norah's previous address. Look, I'd love to help you, Jodie, but I can't give away confidential data like that. Sorry. As I said, perhaps you could ask Norah herself?'

I purse my lips but smile through them. I'd been hoping Paul was less of a goody-two-shoes than Heidi, but I had anticipated some amount of opposition. 'Not to worry, I understand. Thank you for your time.'

I head back out of the office, out of the entrance hall and into what feels like being plunged into an ice pool after being baked alive inside. I straighten my jacket, confidence washing over me. That was certainly one of my sneakiest moves to date. I'm actually quite proud of how discreetly I unlocked his window while I looked out over the meadow. Of course, it would have been easier if he'd just given me the information I required, but a small part of me is rather excited by the prospect of playing thief in the night after everyone's gone to sleep.

I've been home for a couple of hours when the doorbell rings. I'm not sure who I was expecting to see, but it wasn't DS Wolfe. For a second my heart jumps and I peek round the side of the door, half hoping to see Norah being walked down the driveway with her wrists in cuffs. But aside from the sleek-haired DS and a disgruntled looking PC Harris a few inches behind her, there is no one to be seen.

'Hello, Miss Madison. May we come in?'

I nod and leave the door open as I pad over to the kitchen. 'Coffee?'

'No, thank you. We'll not be stopping long.' She perches at the breakfast bar, her eyes drifting over me. I hate the way she does that – like she's appraising me. 'This is just a quick visit to let you know we received the coroner's report and we're now closing the investigation into Mr Roth's death.'

'Dr Roth,' I correct on impulse, and DS Wolfe's eyebrows fly up.

'Yes, of course. It's been ruled that Dr Roth did indeed take his own life.'

I place my coffee cup down on the counter harder than I mean to, the clatter of ceramic against granite echoing through the room. 'Did you even look into Norah's past?'

'We did. There is no evidence to suggest that Norah Williams had any involvement in his death. Or that she is mistreating her daughter.'

My muscles quiver and heat rushes through my body. I want to ask exactly what they've looked into, how they've come to this conclusion, but I already know what the answer will be. They're not at liberty to discuss the details of the investigation.

DS Wolfe clocks my strained face. 'Miss Madison, is there an issue between yourself and Miss Williams?' Her question drips with accusation, and out of the corner of my eye I see PC Harris stiffen. My eyes flick between the two of them.

'You think I'm making all this up, don't you?'

'When we spoke to Miss Williams, she knew straight away that it was you who asked us to look into her. She said you'd had a disagreement a few months back. That she'd asked you to stay away from her daughter?'

'Yes, because she's hiding something!' The words blurt out before I can stop them. I need to calm down, to think about what I'm saying before I speak, but any filter I normally have is gone. I don't even need DS Wolfe to tell me what she's thinking. It's clear as day on her face.

'She suggested that you might have an unhealthy fixation with Lacey. Would she have any reason to believe that?'

My stomach twists as I get the sense that DS Wolfe might know far more than she's letting on. I want to grab her by the shoulders and shake her, scream into her face that she's looking into the wrong person. This isn't about me.

'Would you like me to repeat the question?'

My mouth gapes open as if it's searching for the words in the air. Eventually I croak out a reply. 'Are you going to arrest me for anything?'

'Not at this time, no.'

'Then I think we're done here,' I say, squaring my shoulders.

Our eyes lock, and I know I haven't seen the last of DS Wolfe. She nods and stands to leave.

'I suggest you steer clear of the Williams family,' she says as she and PC Harris make their way to the front door. 'We hope not to see you again.'

I don't say anything, keeping my expression as neutral as possible while they disappear through the door and have it closed firmly behind them. If they don't believe me, I'll have to find proof myself.

Chapter Thirty-One

10 Days Before the Murder

Norah

I wonder how my neighbour is spending her day. Is she running over the events of the other night, replaying her conversation with Christian, picturing his hands on her body?

The female police officer who interviewed me yesterday wasn't subtle. Asking far too many questions about Lacey, about our life here. It wouldn't have taken a genius to work out they were investigating more than Christian's death. They were investigating us. I can only imagine what Jodie must have said to them.

How dare she?

I successfully diverted them by talking about Jodie instead. About her obsession with Lacey. How she'd started dating Christian to find out more about us. The dark past she never talks about... The daughter she had, who – for whatever reason – no longer lives with her. Was she taken from her? Is she dead?

My leg jiggles as I check my watch. Lacey's CT scans usually take about twenty minutes, so she should be out soon. The waiting room has become a familiar sight for me now. It's nicer than the old hospital I used to take her to, where the age of the place was evident from the flaking paint showing the concrete beneath. This hospital is modern, and newly refurbished. The floor is a chipper yellow, I suppose because it's a children's ward, accompanied by clean magnolia walls, and the ceiling is a grid of polystyrene squares. I've made a habit of counting these squares, one, two, three, as a way of calming any lingering anxieties about what the doctors might come out and say to me. Seven, eight, nine.

'Norah?'

Jodie striding into the waiting room is a surprise, and not a pleasant one. If she hadn't said my name I'd have thought I was imagining things. But no, she's here, wearing a leather jacket and chunky boots that make her look just a touch intimidating. And I'm not easily intimidated.

She doesn't wait for me to respond, she simply comes and sits next to me; her mouth is drawn into a flat, thin line.

'What are you doing here, Miss Madison?' I ask, and I'm immediately annoyed with myself for how breathless I sound.

'I need to talk to you. About what you said to the police.'

'Did you follow us here?' I'm in such a state of shock I can't even bring myself to get angry. Approaching me, away from the Grove, where I'm alone, is her attempt at throwing me off balance. But it's going to take more than that.

I glance down at her hands, which she is wringing in her lap. She's trying to feign confidence, perhaps to unnerve me, but her body language gives her away. It is unclear what she hopes to gain – unless she's stupid enough to think tracking me to the hospital and cornering me is going to make me revoke what I said to the police. I must put a stop to this, immediately. Lacey will be out soon.

'I just...' She is faltering, searching for the words. You'd have thought before blundering in like this she'd have taken the time to collect her thoughts and rehearse what she wants to say. She's clearly not used to confrontation. 'I just want to know why. Why lie?'

I raise my eyebrows, blink at her. 'But I didn't lie,' I say simply.

She lets out a half-laugh and leans her elbows on her knees. 'You told them I have an unhealthy fixation with Lacey!' She sounds exasperated. My allegation has hit a nerve.

'Miss Madison, you spent hours in the evenings talking to my fourteen-year-old daughter through her bedroom window, without my permission. You purchased a gift for her. And now you've followed us to her hospital appointment. Please explain to me which part of what I said to the police was a lie.'

She visibly bristles; hesitates for a moment, no doubt realising just how incriminating that all sounds, before placing her head in her hands and massaging her temples.

'Look,' I say, placing my hand on her shoulder. She stiffens under my touch and pulls away. 'I'm not trying to cause trouble for you. Lord knows the last thing I need is added stress. But this isn't the first time Lacey has grown close to a neighbour. The woman who lived next to us before you was nice to her too, and Lacey sort of... latched onto her. It wasn't healthy.'

I watch the subtle cues as to what might be going on in her head; the twitch of the facial muscles, the nervous swallow, and there – the hitch in her breath. I've got her questioning herself, at least. For a moment, I consider revealing that I know she once had a daughter of her own, but I decide instead to keep that little nugget to myself, for now. It may prove useful later on. I pause, glance subtly up at movement in the hallway. 'I am concerned about your friendship with Lacey. I think any mother would be.'

'It's not a friendship, jeez.' Jodie's head snaps up and she folds her arms across her chest, her demeanour suddenly protective. 'I honestly don't want anything to do with her. Spending time with a kid is the last thing I want to be doing, trust me. I just felt sorry for her.'

'Thanks a lot.' Lacey's clipped voice echoes through the waiting room. The colour drains from Jodie's face. She flinches around, meeting Lacey's eyes.

'Lacey, I didn't mean that.'

But it's too late, the damage is done. Lacey wheels herself around the nurse whose eyes are flitting awkwardly between the three of us, and makes a start back down the hallway. I stand to go after her, pulling the leather strap of my handbag over my shoulder.

'You knew she was there, didn't you?' Jodie says.

I stop in my tracks, tucking a stray tendril of hair behind my ear. 'Of course I did,' I say, looking down at her ashen face and smiling. 'I'm her mother.'

Our house is dim and still, except for the gentle sobbing of Lacey crying into my shoulder. My fingers brush through her hair, stopping every few seconds to pat her comfortingly. This is the closest the two of us have been for months. Maybe even years.

'Why doesn't anyone ever want to spend time with me?' she whimpers, her voice muffled by the wool of my jumper. There is a growing wet patch which is irritating the skin underneath, but I don't care.

'This is why I try to set boundaries, darling.' I rest my chin on the top of her head, breathe in the scent of her hair. She still uses Johnson's Baby Shampoo, and every time I get close enough to sniff it I am immediately transported back to bathing her as a newborn. 'Especially after how heartbroken you were about Alison. This is why I've been so guarded against you getting close to another neighbour. I'm just trying to protect you from getting hurt. The only people we can ever trust are each other.'

My eyes flick up to the window. Next door, the rooms are plunged into darkness. Jodie hasn't returned home since our run-in at the hospital. I had half expected her to turn up at our door, hoping to apologise to Lacey, and was prepared with a swift rebuttal, but no one has disturbed us. It's just me and Lacey.

I don't know how long we sit together like this, but it must be some time because Lacey's hiccuping cries are eventually replaced by heavy breathing. A tingling sensation scampers down my arm like ants. I daren't move. I think the last time she fell asleep in my arms was when she was about five. The sense of relief is overwhelming. She is still mine.

Jodie Madison would do well to steer clear of us from now on. She has no idea who she's dealing with.

Chapter Thirty-Two

10 Days Before the Murder

Jodie

The sickly gurgling in my stomach still hasn't left even after twenty minutes of strolling through the Grove. I couldn't go home after the hospital. I couldn't bear the thought of running into Norah and Lacey. How could I have been so stupid as to follow them to the hospital? All I've done is add fuel to Norah's claims about me. Honestly, I wasn't even going to go in. My plan was simply to follow them and see where they were going, on the off chance I might see something that proves Norah isn't as innocent as everyone thinks she is. I even took my camera with me, hoping that if there was something untoward going on I might be able to capture some evidence from the safety of my car. Once I saw them go into the hospital I should have been satisfied and headed straight home, but the chance to talk to Norah alone, without Lacey there, was too tempting. Part of me also wanted to see what kind of care Lacey was getting. Something about how Norah approaches Lacey's illness just doesn't sit right with me. But now, if anything, all I've done is make her look like a victim and me like a crazy person. I played straight into her hands.

I had hoped the fresh air might clear my mind, but all it's done is given me some distraction-free time to think, which these days is just plain dangerous. I haven't been walking in any particular direction, I've just let my feet take me where they want to go, but I've ended up outside Christian's house.

The house looks almost back to normal. If I didn't know better, I'd guess that he was at his surgery, hence no lights being on and no sign of movement inside. But knowing what I know, it has the eerie atmosphere of a ghost house. A shiver goes through me. I don't believe in ghosts. Not really. Even when I see you, I know it's only a figment of my imagination. But standing on my own, in front of the house that played host to such a tragic loss of life, no amount of reasoning can curb the heebie-jeebies.

The feeling of something brushing against my leg makes me jump back and let out a scream. My nerves aren't exactly steady anyway; this is just about enough to make me descend into a puddle on the floor. I glance down and am relieved to see Toby winding through my legs like he did the last time I was here. I haven't even thought about the cat. He doesn't look particularly thin or malnourished. Someone must have been feeding him, though no one has said anything about taking him in.

He looks up at me with his big, almond-shaped eyes and my heart flutters. I'm not really a cat person. But Toby seems quite sweet, and before my brain can properly kick into gear I find myself bending over and picking him up, giving him a stroke on the head as he nuzzles into the crook of my arm, and taking him home with me.

When I look around my house I realise I have nothing to offer a cat. No cat food, no bowls, no bed, no toys. How old is Toby anyway? Surely I need to know that in order to get his food? It reminds me of being pregnant and looking around my scrawny flat and realising just how little space there was for baby equipment, and just how little money I had to pay for it.

Toby whines at me and I notice just how hard I'm stroking his head. I decide to improvise with the intention of taking him to the vet later for some advice.

I pull out two bowls from the cupboard, fill one with water which Toby happily laps up, and shred some ham into the other. I then fold up my soft sofa throw and create a makeshift bed on the floor, though I have a sneaky suspicion he'll end up in my bed, which I'm not mad about. It's as I'm folding up the blanket that I wonder if I should change his name. That would formalise him as my cat instead of the rescued pet of my dead lover. I run through options in my head. What's a good cat name? Fluffy? Whiskers? He's a tabby cat, I think, maybe just Tabby?

I shake my head – nothing suits him as well as Toby. I guess I'll just have to get used to living with the reminder. It's not like it's the name that reminds me of Christian anyway. The whole cat makes me think of that night, running it over in my head again and again, trying to figure out if I missed a sign that Christian might be ready to end his own life. Changing Toby's name won't help keep the thoughts out.

Changing his name. The words repeat in my head as Toby, dozy from being watered and fed, hops up onto my lap, droplets of water spilling from his wet little mouth and soaking through my leggings.

And then it comes to me. I didn't find Norah Williams in Paul's office. Every other resident was in there except Norah Williams, but if I can live as an alter-ego so can anyone. What if Norah Williams is not her real name?

I can't stop my eyes from darting to the clock every few minutes, as midnight draws closer. I've had all afternoon to obsess over my plan to break into Paul's office, all evening too, and the more I think about it the less exciting it seems. Now I'm filled with a heavy sense of dread, a realisation that if I get caught that will be it – I'll be out of Kensington Grove quicker than I can say 'sorry' and Lacey will have no one to look out for her. I reason with myself, tell myself that I should leave all this to the police, but what use have they been so far? A small, perhaps arrogant side of myself tells me that I need to be the one to expose Norah. I'm the only one who cares enough to do it.

The alarm on my phone buzzes as midnight rolls around. I'd set it with the expectation that I'd fall asleep as I waited for my chance, but it was completely unnecessary. I'm already standing by the door with my coat and shoes on. Toby mews at me, his head cocking inquisitively to the side.

'I won't be long,' I say, realising I've reached a level of loneliness where I'm now talking to a cat.

Outside, the temperature has dipped. Unusually cold for this time of year, and I can feel the frost, so I zip up my hoodie, shivering a little. I keep my head low as I move through the streets, staying to the shadows where I can. There are no lights on in any of the houses, but I can't be too careful. I make like a fox, stalking through the town. I'm about to commit my very first crime. I can't tell if I'm dismayed or thrilled by that prospect.

It's just gone twenty past when I reach the office building. In the dark it gives off a sense of foreboding, as if the nurses from yesteryear might run out the front door at any second, screaming at me to leave their hospital alone. My skin crawls, but, of course, nothing happens. All is still, deathly quiet. I go round the back – luckily the CCTV cameras are all trained on the gates as opposed to the rear of the office – and find the window. There is a horrid moment of panic as I tug on it and it doesn't move. Paul must have checked the windows before he locked up for the night. What do I do now? But after another tug there is the sound of ice crunching and I realise the window is simply frozen shut. All it takes is a few shimmies and it dislodges.

My heart is battering my ribcage as I haul myself through it. I feel as though I'm a fox in a chase, though whether I'm doing the hunting or being hunted is debatable. The office looks completely different in this light, a ghostly bluish tint under the moonlight which doesn't do any good for my anxiety. I try not to focus on my heart pounding and head straight for the filing cabinets. Unlike last time, I haven't got any direction of where to start, so I go right to the first cabinet, starting at the top and working my way down. Methodical enough so I don't miss any names, but still trying to work as swiftly as possible.

The first cabinet doesn't give me any clues – no names jump out at me. Same with the second and third cabinet. By the time I reach the fourth, I'm losing faith in my plan. Perhaps I am being obsessive over this? Perhaps I really am making something out of nothing. But then, in the fifth and final cabinet, as my finger reaches where 'Norah Williams' should be, I see the label behind it. I didn't properly get to read what it said last time, but just as I slide the folder out of its slot and let the cover flop open, taking in the top line again, the sound of keys jangling echoes through the silence, nearly making me jump out of my skin.

Someone is outside, letting themselves into the office. My first instinct is the window but there's no way I'll be able to squeeze back through the small gap in time. My only option for a hiding place is, much to my claustrophobic inner voice's dismay, the storage cupboard. So, squeezing my eyes shut and fighting past my already shaking limbs, I wedge myself inside and pull the door closed.

Sounds are muffled from inside the cupboard. There's a lot of shuffling around, the office door opens and closes, I think the blinds are being drawn. If I'm not mistaken someone's in here with Paul. I'm sure there are two sets of footfall. I lean towards the door. Heidi? I'm pretty sure any resident of Kensington Grove would love to be a fly on the wall while the Grove's 'it couple' have a gossip. I can only imagine the sort of conversations that go on behind closed doors. But they don't gossip. There is more shuffling around and then, to my horror, Paul lets out a moan.

I cringe, clasp my hands over my mouth, then change my mind and move them over my ears. Visions of Paul's sweaty body rubbing up against Heidi's Botox-infused skin are already filtering into my mind. Heidi is a dark horse, that's for sure. The two of them must get off on shagging in his office. I shake my head frantically and try to think of something else. Puppies. Work. The list of cleaning jobs I have to do at home. Anything!

Another moan sounds and a shudder travels down my spine, so hard that my elbow catches the folders on the shelf next to me. I watch, stomach roiling, as the folder knocks the next and the next and the next, all of them toppling like dominoes. I'm so focused on the folders I don't even realise the coital sounds have stopped until the door is flung open. I flinch, turn around, meet Paul's raging gaze. I can actually see the veins in his neck straining against his skin, the muscles pulsing in his temple. For a moment I wonder if he's actually going to kill me, his face is that twisted and explosive. And then, after what feels like hours of simply staring at each other, my eyes drift over to the other person in the room, still buttoning up their shirt.

It isn't Heidi. It's David Timson, the concierge from the main gate.

Neither of them has said a word to me and I can't take a second more of the silence.

'I'm . . . I'm sorry,' I stutter. When they still don't reply, I hand the file gingerly back to Paul and squeeze past him, my cheeks burning so hot I imagine my skin is probably just as red, if not redder, than Paul's. As I burst into the open air my forehead is soaked with sweat.

What mess have you got yourself into now, Jodie?

Chapter Thirty-Three

3 Days Before the Murder

Norah

'Lacey, darling, it's time to go.'

I move about the living room, picking up the random bits that Lacey's left lying around and placing them in their appropriate drawers or cupboards. I pull on the back of the sofa and its feet scratch against the parquet flooring as I shuffle it back a few inches. It does my head in if it isn't exactly in line with the rug.

I check the time, then position myself in front of the mirror. I've chosen to wear make-up today for the first time in weeks to counteract how pale an all-black ensemble makes me appear. A few dabs of concealer under the eyes and a sweeping of mascara have breathed new life into my face. A black, wide-brimmed hat sits atop my straightened hair, angled slightly to one side. The hat seems a bit over the top, but I remember Alison's funeral, and the ostentatious hats and netted fascinators on show, and decide it's all part of the Kensington Grove uniform.

'Lacey?'

We really need to make a move. When I left her room about

twenty minutes ago she just needed to brush her hair. She must be ready by now. I listen for a few seconds but there is no response. She probably has her headphones on.

The sight as I enter the room takes me a couple of minutes to register. Lacey is in her chair, gently moving herself forward and back, eyes glazed and staring out at nothing in particular as far as I can see. But what takes me aback is that she has changed out of her black clothes and is now wearing a set of pink pyjamas.

'What are you doing?' My voice comes out clipped and harsh. The instinct to grab her shoulders and shake her, to bellow in her face, is almost uncontrollable. This is not the day for her games. I take three long, measured breaths. 'We need to leave in a few minutes, why have you taken your clothes off?'

She blinks and starts a little as she looks at me, as if she's only just realised I'm in the room with her.

'I don't want to go,' she says, her voice trance-like.

I don't have time for this.

'What are you talking about? We have to go. It'd be incredibly disrespectful if we didn't go.'

My volume is intensifying with every word. My jaw clenching tighter. We are headed straight towards an argument. The cycle is unrelenting; in a minute Lacey will snap back at me that she's old enough to do what she wants and that if I really want to go that badly I should just leave her here alone, even though she knows, *she knows*, I can't do that. Every time we careen down this path I know what is coming and yet I am powerless to stop it.

But this time is different. She doesn't come at me with some snide remark. Instead, she looks up at me with tears lacing her lower eyelids.

'Please don't make me go.'

I am unsure what to do. This isn't what I was expecting. I have become so accustomed to facing off with an indignant teenager that this fragile child is practically a stranger to me.

'Why?'

She lowers her gaze to her lap as I take a step towards her, the movement causing one of the tears to break free and splash onto her thigh. I crouch beside her so that I can see her face, half hidden behind her hair. My hand hesitantly raises to tuck the strands behind her ear.

'Lacey?' I prompt. 'You can talk to me, you know.'

She presses her lips together in a tight, thin line, and then, 'One day it's going to be me.'

My stomach hardens. Suddenly I find it impossible to look at her. A sickening sense of guilt consumes me, sitting heavy on my chest like a block of ice. No child should have to think about their own funeral.

I drop to my knees and, still unable to meet her gaze, take her hand in mine and hold it tight.

Chapter Thirty-Four

3 Days Before the Murder

Jodie

When I arrive at the cemetery the hearse is already there surrounded by a large group. I recognise some of them; there are at least twenty residents of the Grove lingering outside the chapel. Heidi is there wearing a black pencil dress and one of those hats with the lace you pull down over your face. It makes her look like a fifties glamour model. It's amazing how someone can keep up a façade like that. Now I know that her perfect life is a total sham.

I can't see Norah or Lacey anywhere yet.

The coffin is still inside the hearse, adorned with elaborate flower arrangements which I can't help but think don't suit Christian. His house was cosy, sure. Homely in an earthy sort of way, but not fussy or overpowering. He certainly wasn't one for decoration. Still, I doubt he'd care. Before I climb out of my car I pause a moment to take my grief and bury it deep down where no one will see it. I didn't get the chance to show much affection to Christian in life. In death it will be no different.

I pull myself out of my car and walk briskly, head bowed so as not to catch the eye of anyone I know, least of all the Downhursts. I've purposefully avoided them this last week since my run-in with Paul. I stand several feet behind the other mourners. Despite the fact that we're in the grip of autumn, the sun is shining through the trees and glinting against the car side mirrors. It's offensively bright and cheerful.

I'd worked myself up into such a mess, convinced the family would tell me I had no right to be here – his dirty little fling – but as it turns out they don't care. I'm an unknown. A nobody. I'm ignored, exactly as I had hoped I would be, throughout the entire service. And what a service it is. The momentum reminds me of a tour bus, taking just as many diversions. Everyone has a favourite memory to share, a poem to read, a hymn to sing. By the halfway point several of the elderly ladies in the front rows are swaying and I begin to wonder if we'll have more to bury than just Christian. Still, as much as I can't stand long funeral services, it is interesting to learn more about Christian's life. He had two sisters. He lived not far from me when he was a kid. He enjoyed skiing and other winter sports. It's strange how you can be so intimate with someone, can allow them to share your bed and touch your body, and yet you still haven't got to know much about them.

A shiver runs down my spine as we depart the chapel. I stay behind while the woman I've ascertained is Christian's mother leads the rest of the mourners towards the grave plot. It's amongst the shiny black headstones, all aligned in formation, perfectly measured gaps between each one. It reminds me of Kensington Grove itself with its uniformity, which sets my teeth on edge. I tear my eyes away and focus instead on the older section of the cemetery, where it looks as if someone picked up the headstones in their hand and threw them up in the air to see where they'd land, like leaves in the wind. It's been so long, too long, since I visited your grave. I loathe myself every time I think about it, but it's painful to go there and even more excruciating to leave.

'Not going to watch the committal?'

I jump so hard at the sound of Paul's voice behind me my heart nearly ends up in my throat. I whip around to see him, thick scarf wrapped around his chin so that he looks as if he has no neck, shuffling towards me. There's no sign of Heidi. I'm pretty sure I saw her go with the others.

'Oh, erm, no.' I give myself a little shake, which I expertly disguise as a shiver. 'I don't do graveyards.'

He nods and smiles but doesn't speak. Oh joy, it's going to be another one of those conversations.

'Shouldn't you be with Heidi?' I say, unable to help the hint of accusation lacing my tone. He flinches at this, but for the most part keeps his calm demeanour. I don't like the way he's just standing there. For a moment I wonder if he's reported me breaking into his office and is trying to keep me in one place while the police arrive, but I don't think he's the sort of person to create a scene at a funeral. Heidi probably would, but not Paul.

'Heidi probably hasn't even noticed I'm gone,' he says eventually. 'She's too busy trying to make today about her.'

My eyebrows flick up. I think that's the first negative comment, subtle as it was, I've ever heard made about Heidi. She comes across like an untouchable queen, so revered by her subjects that no one would dare tarnish her name, but, of course, I can't be the only one to think she's a little, well, fake and self-absorbed. I just wasn't expecting it to come from Paul. It actually makes me feel a little bad for Heidi. With everything Paul's been getting up to, he's kind of lost the right to snipe at her.

I tilt my head to the side and study his face. His smile hasn't quite met his eyes.

He notices me watching him and lowers his gaze to the ground. He clears his throat and says, 'Anyway, I wanted to talk to you.'

Every hair on my arms stands to attention, and I try to tell myself it's because of the gust of wind that accompanied him speaking, not because I'm bloody terrified of what he's about to say. I picture my house back at the Grove, all my bits that took so long to pack up into boxes and even longer to unpack. I really don't want to have to do all that again.

I give myself a little shake and remind myself that I'm not in as vulnerable a position as I think. I'm not the only one harbouring secrets. Paul is too. There might be a different way I can play this.

'Oh?' I say, my voice cracking slightly.

'Yes.' His eyes are still trained on the ground, on his feet as he shuffles them back and forth in the gravel. 'Have you . . .' His skin starts reddening, starting at his earlobes and creeping inwards. 'Have you told anyone what you saw last week?'

'No,' I say after a moment. My mouth is dry, my lips splitting in the chill. 'And I wasn't planning to, either.'

He looks up at me hopefully. He looks so turned in on himself, a far cry from the confident half of Kensington Grove's 'it couple'; a broken little mouse with a stooped posture and pained gaze. I have a sudden urge to give him a cuddle. That would be weird, though, so instead I say, 'I'll forget what I saw, if you'll forget what you saw?'

My heart rate quickens as I wait for his response. I could have just made things ten times worse. Finally, he nods and forces a smile, his bottom lip trembling.

'I can do that.'

A long silence stretches between us, eventually broken by him burying his hands into his pockets and turning to me. 'I should get back to Heidi in case she wonders where I am.'

'Paul?' I say, and he brings his eyes to meet mine for the first time today. He looks as if he's about to cry. I can't stand it when men cry.

'I won't say anything to Heidi,' I repeat, 'but you should.'

His half-smile contorts into a grimace. 'I . . . don't know how to . . .'

'It's none of my business. But she deserves to know. Especially since she's carrying your baby.' I can practically hear my conscience prodding me, saying 'you're one to talk'. It's true, I have no leg to stand on, no right to advise anyone what they should or shouldn't tell people. But even if I can't follow my own advice, the deep, thoughtful expression on Paul's face tells me that he might just be considering it.

We stand in silence for a good five minutes or more, and before I know it the congregation shuffles back towards the chapel and their respective cars.

'You going to the wake?' Paul asks. He opens up his order of service from the ceremony and checks where it's taking place. I should have guessed which pub it would be held at – it's the only one around here, unless you head into the city. I can't bring myself to stand in the place where Christian and I had our first date.

'I don't think so.'

'Okay, well, I'd better get going.'

Paul buttons up his jacket and heads towards Heidi, who is

shooting daggers at both of us. I can't hear what she says to Paul, but let's just say I'm glad I'm not on the receiving end of it. I avert my eyes and head towards my car, relieved to have got through the day with my dignity mostly intact.

Just as that thought crosses my mind, my ears prick up at the mention of Norah's name.

'I can't believe Norah didn't show up,' Heidi mutters to Paul, barely audible. 'After everything the two of them went through.'

My stomach roils. I whip around to listen in to their conversation, trip, stumble into my car door. The slam causes the alarm to go off and wail through the cemetery, and all eyes turn to stare at me as I fumble with my keys. As I silence the alarm I slink into the driver's seat and grip onto the steering wheel, trying to process what I overheard. Why is it such a big deal that Norah isn't here? Who was she to Christian?

The second I return home from the funeral I draw all the curtains, shutting out the sunlight and plunging my house into darkness, and bury myself under my duvet. Toby jumps up and curls appreciatively into the nook I've created by hunching myself over, his little head pressed into my stomach. Right now, the good people of Kensington Grove will be piling into the pub for the wake, taking advantage of the free sandwich platters and cups of tea, as if they don't get enough of that at the community centre each week. Small estate, small pleasures.

It seems odd to be home knowing that the houses around me are mostly empty right now, as if I've got the Grove all to myself, my own little gated retreat. But, of course, I don't think everyone is at the wake. Norah and Lacey didn't show for the funeral, so I doubt they'd turn up at the pub afterwards. The questions swirl round in my head again, blurring with visions of Norah and the look of distaste as she handed my gift back, of Lacey and the hurt on her face at the hospital. And finally, I see you.

Come, get into bed with me. Curl up in my arms like you used to after you had a nightmare. Let's sleep the day away.

I wake to the sound of my doorbell and groan. Rolling over, I pull my pillow over my head and try to block out the noise, clinging onto my ability to fall back to sleep but feeling it drift away by the second. Typical, even without having to haul myself into the office I can't have a nap. I've taken a couple of days off work claiming a migraine. The doorbell rings again and this time is accompanied by the rough texture of Toby's tongue on my cheek. Sleep has officially evaded me. Body aching, I pull myself out of the warmth of my bed and shuffle downstairs.

My vision is still blurry as I answer the door, and I squint against the outside light. It's still daytime – I obviously didn't sleep that long – but the sun has disappeared behind a wall of early afternoon cloud. It takes a second for my eyes to adjust and when they do they land on Heidi. She seems . . . well, a bit frazzled, if I'm honest. She's changed out of her funeral blacks and into a pair of white jeans and an expensive-looking beige jumper. Her hair is piled on top of her head in a knot and there is a distinct lack of make-up on her face. She looks practically casual. Maybe the strain on her marriage is causing a crack in her flawless exterior after all.

'Can I come in?' she says, and I barely get the chance to respond before she's slipping past me. In my still half-asleep state I can't think of anything to do other than to close the door and follow her to the living room, flicking on the overhead light as I do so.

'How was the wake?' I rub a finger along my lashes, suddenly aware that I didn't take my mascara off before I crawled into bed and I'm probably sporting some rather fabulous panda eyes.

'We left early. Not as early as you, mind.'

She tilts her head to one side, her lips pressed together so hard they've completely disappeared, her eyes boring into me. There's no fake smile, no swish of hair or fluttering of eyelashes. All the normal Heidi-isms have been replaced by something else. Something threatening. I have a brief moment of praying Toby will stay in the bedroom; Heidi will no doubt recognise him as Christian's cat, and I imagine animal theft would raise a few eyebrows in the WhatsApp group.

'Why are you here, Heidi?'

Her nostrils flare as she takes a step towards me. 'To tell you to mind your own business,' she hisses, the words punctuated.

My eyes widen. 'What are you talking about?'

'You know exactly what I'm talking about.' Her voice is barely a whisper, but still somehow comes across as intimidating. 'How dare you get involved in our personal life. Paul and I were fine. We were fine. And now you've screwed everything up!'

'Wait, this is about Paul?' I shake my head, confused. I'm not awake enough for this. My temple is pulsing and an ache is forming at the back of my eyes. I am overwhelmed with the urge to grab the bottle of wine that's sitting on the breakfast bar and take a swig. 'What's Paul said?'

'What's he said?' She throws back her head and lets out a forced laugh, her white teeth shining. 'Well, let's see. I asked him what you and he were talking about after the ceremony, and he wouldn't tell me. All he said was that he thinks we need some time apart. He needs to figure out what he wants.' She says the words in a mocking tone, lifting her fingers in air quotations.

'We were fine,' she repeats, her voice wobbling a little, on the verge of crying. 'I was okay with him doing what he wanted. I was okay with turning a blind eye. As long as he came back to me at the end of the day. He always . . . *always* came back to me.'

Then, to my horror, the tears she has been holding back break forth, spilling down her cheeks and making her look unrecognisable.

'You knew?' is all I can say.

'Of course. He had no idea I did. Thinks he's a genius for pulling the wool over my eyes for so long. But I knew what he was doing.'

She slumps down onto my sofa, defeated. Around us, the room has fallen silent and still. I take a step toward her, feel a flicker of remorse as I stare at the broken woman in front of me. It's crap timing, that's for sure. Having your husband leave you is never going to be pleasant, but just after you've found out you're expecting? Brutal. I wonder if I should say anything about the baby, but I don't particularly want to bring the subject up.

'You can't have been happy,' I venture, wondering if I should try to place my hand on her shoulder but deciding against it. 'I know how hard it is to accept when a relationship is over, but isn't it better this way for everyone?'

Her head snaps towards me, her eyes flashing with rage once more, as if I have just poured fuel onto a fire inside of her. 'Don't you tell me what I feel! Paul is all I have. All I have in this entire world.'

She stands now, hands scrunched into fists at her sides. I can practically see a pulse throbbing in her neck. Part of me wants to back away, hands raised in a protective stance, and attempt to reason with her, to calm her down. But another part of me wants to slap her right across the face. All she's got? She's going to have a baby in about seven months, for Christ's sake. She's got the fanciest house on the estate, the nicest clothes, the looks, the popularity. She has everything, and she has the nerve to stand in front of me and act like I've ruined her very existence by suggesting – shock horror – that her husband should live his life true to his sexuality. Yes, how dare I propose something so outrageous.

'He'd have left at some point whether I said anything or not,' I say carefully, attempting to keep my voice steady, forcing her eyes to meet mine. 'If all it took was a five-minute conversation with someone he barely knows to make him come to this decision, I'd say he was nearly there already.'

I wait for her response. I'm not sure what she wants from me. Does she want me to call Paul and tell him to change his mind? Tell him I offered him bad advice, that he should stay tethered in a loveless marriage? Or maybe she just wants me to grovel, fall to my knees and apologise, beg not to be kicked out of the elite Ladies of Kensington Grove WhatsApp Group. She'll be waiting a bloody long time.

She takes a step closer to me so that her overpowering perfume wafts into my nostrils, and bile rises in my throat. I swallow it down.

'He told me, you know? How you were rifling around his office after hours. Looking through confidential files. I should call the police on you.'

This sends my anxiety peaking, blood rushing in my ears. Thanks a lot, Paul. So she knows I was after Norah's file. My breath grows ragged and I press my palm to my chest, forcing myself to inhale slowly through my nose and out through my mouth. If only I could reach that bottle.

'I'm just trying to do the right thing,' I say.

The corners of Heidi's mouth turn up, a strange, bitter smile. 'The right thing? By sabotaging a marriage? By hounding a woman and her daughter who have been to hell and back?'

'I know you think you know her, but...' My words trail off. I can't accuse Norah of anything to Heidi, not without concrete evidence. They've been friends for years. Instead, I say, 'I overheard some women at the funeral. They used to date, didn't they? Christian and Norah?'

Heidi's eyes narrow. 'What's it to you?'

'I just... do the police know that?'

For a moment she studies me, her gaze drifting from my eyes all the way down to my shoes and up again. Then she shakes her head. 'Is that what this is all about? Jealousy because she had him first?'

'No!' I protest a little too loudly and my cheeks instantly start burning. I can't help but look away from Heidi, knowing full well how mortified I must appear. Why did I have to give her that sort of satisfaction?

I take a moment to compose myself before straightening my posture. 'Did you know she changed her name? She wasn't always Norah Williams.'

Heidi's eyes widen for just a second, a flash of understanding, and then the smile returns. 'Yes. I do know.'

'Why?' My heartbeat is thudding in my ears now as Heidi scans my face, her lips pinched as if she's trying to decide whether or not to play along. I'm treading a painfully thin wire. I'm hardly one to suggest a name change is a hint at something sinister going on. But maybe Heidi, with all her Grove wisdom and years of gossip under her belt, might hold the answer to one of my many, many questions.

'She changed it so that her husband wouldn't find her.'

'Lacey's dad?'

'Yes. He was a violent drunk and she got away from him. Got Lacey away from him. Moved to a gated community and changed her name to keep her daughter safe.' These last four words are punctuated, spittle flying from Heidi's lips as she says them. 'You have no idea what that woman has been through. Leave her alone. And leave us alone.'

Her shoulder collides with mine as she pushes past me, and the slam of the front door echoes through the room. My fingers twitch, and I only manage a few seconds of telling myself not to before I'm grabbing for the bottle of wine. No idea what Norah's been through? They've got no idea what *I've* been through, or what tomorrow is.

Chapter Thirty-Five

Sally
Where the heck is everyone? Am I the only person at the wake?

Emma
Soz, I had to get back to the kids.

Marisa
I promised I'd be back in work this afternoon.

Sally
Great. I'm sat here like a loser eating finger sandwiches on my own. @Heidi? @Jodie? You still here?

Emma
Is Markus not with you?

Sally
. . . no

Norah
Has anyone heard from Heidi? She's gone quiet on me.

Marisa
> Norah! Are you okay? Is Lacey okay? We didn't see you at the funeral.

Norah
> We're fine, thank you. Has anyone heard from Heidi?

Marisa
> No sorry.

Emma
> Nope.

Sally
> Oh, I'm fine by the way, guys. Thanks for the concern.

Chapter Thirty-Six

3 Days Before the Murder

Norah

I've spent most of today trying to distract myself from the fact that I've missed Christian's funeral. Part of me is riddled with guilt, but I just couldn't do it to Lacey.

Instead, I have made do with a running commentary from Heidi. At just gone eleven she reported that the hearse had arrived and they'd shortly be entering the chapel. About fifteen minutes later I listened to the service over a call, which didn't work quite as well as we'd hoped in theory, but made me feel better about my absence nonetheless. And then, after a few messages about the grave, how pretty the headstone is, how Christian's mother sends her warm regards, Heidi went quiet. The last message I sent to her was at 12.18, where I asked if she fancied popping in for a cup of tea once she's home, but no response. Most unlike Heidi.

Everything changes at 1.30.

This is when Jodie's front door slams so loud it makes me glance up from my crossword and, upon peering out of the window with curiosity, I spot Heidi tearing down the driveway away from Jodie's house. Instinctively I jump up from my seat and pull open my own front door. I call to her but she either doesn't hear me or completely ignores me, instead ducking into the driver's seat of her polished Range Rover and speeding off with an uncharacteristic screech of the tyres. I stare after her, taken aback. I'm sure she must have heard me.

My first instinct is to grab my phone and begin tapping out another message to her, but upon seeing my unread messages I decide against it.

'Lacey, darling,' I call. 'We're going to pop round Heidi's, okay?'

It takes a good twenty minutes to fend off Lacey's various complaints and insistence that she's old enough to stay home by herself before I get her into the van. It's not a bad thing, though. It will have given Heidi a chance to get home and cool down from whatever angered her at Jodie's, and I imagine by now she'll be desperate to air her grievances to the first willing ear.

My finger presses on Heidi's doorbell and the familiar chiming sounds from inside. The air has turned bitter in the last half hour, my breath turning to a cloud of steam in front of me, and I shuffle on the doorstep in an attempt to get my circulation pumping.

Lacey whines beside me. 'Why are we here? What's going on?'

'We won't be long,' I say, hoping that's true.

Heidi is definitely home – her car has been parked rather haphazardly in front of her garage – but there is no sign of life from inside the house. I press the doorbell again.

'Heidi? It's me, Norah.'

A small, whining sound comes from Lacey. 'Mum, I'm cold. Can we just go home?'

Ignoring her, I pull out my phone to call Heidi. I've known the woman for nearly eight years, and of all the residents of Kensington Grove she has never once strayed from her punctual, proper, overly friendly persona. Something is wrong.

The phone only rings twice before the door creaks open. The woman standing before me is unrecognisable. Her under-eyes are puffy and her cheeks are dotted with red splotches.

'Heidi...' I say, not quite sure what to do now that I'm face to face with her. I hadn't anticipated her appearance and now my usual 'how are you doing?' seems insensitive, somehow. In the end I settle with, 'What happened?'

She glowers at me, a stream of snot escaping her nostrils and threatening to touch her lip. Then she wipes her nose with her sleeve, sniffs, and glances at Lacey shivering beside me.

'Do you want to go and watch TV, sweetie?' Even her voice is different, flat and monotone.

Lacey doesn't seem to notice. She nods, peeking at me out of the corner of her eye. I have to bite my lip to stop myself from saying that she isn't allowed to watch TV. Right now talking to Heidi is more important. I help Lacey over the threshold, and as she disappears into the living room, Heidi moves to the dining area and falls into one of the chairs, leaning her elbows onto the mahogany table and scrunching her hair in her hands. I tentatively take a seat next to her.

For a moment, neither of us speaks. She stares straight ahead, scratching against the table finish, flecks of brown splintering under her nail. I want to grab her hand, remind her how much pride she holds in her home and her possessions, but I'm not sure how to deal with this version of Heidi.

After what feels like an eternity, she lifts her gaze to meet mine. 'I know what you did.'

Chapter Thirty-Seven

2 Days Before the Murder

Jodie

As soon as I open my eyes I wonder if it's acceptable to crack open a bottle, to drink enough that I can see you again. It seems only fair. Every other mother gets to see their child on their birthday. Why shouldn't I get to see you on the anniversary of your death?

I pull on my hoodie and yoga pants – which I wear solely for comfort as I've never done a yoga class in my entire life – and head to the corner shop, where I load up a basket with the items I'll require to make it through today. One bottle of Glenfiddich, two of the Blossom Hill rosé wine, a flimsy packet of pre-made Sex on the Beach cocktail (which looks like it will taste utterly vile but it's cheap and I like the packaging), a sharing bag of crisps that I don't intend on sharing, and a big old tub of Ben and Jerry's. The lady at the till grins at the contents of my basket and makes a comment about how she can tell I'm throwing a party tonight, and I try not to let my smile crack under the weight of the tears that are already pricking my lids.

I start drinking at a record 11 a.m. and I'm not even sorry. I switch on the TV so that I can have something mindless playing in the background while I sip my tumbler, hoping that the answer to moving on might be at the bottom of each glass. *Moving on . . .* what a ridiculous concept. How on earth is anyone meant to move on from losing their own child? I've heard it so many times it's become a sort of private joke that only I understand.

The thing with grief, I've discovered, is that there is a time limit to how long you're allowed to grieve. Right at the start, when it first happens, it's perfectly acceptable. I even had bouts of people encouraging it. 'It's normal to cry, healthy even,' they'd say. I think if I hadn't cried in those first few weeks they'd have all thought I was crazy. There's a ludicrous theory that says grief follows a specific pattern; the denial, the anger, whatever else they claim you have to go through before you finally reach that magical acceptance stage. It's meant to stay neatly in lines, methodical, structured. There's nothing methodical about a child dying before their parent. After a couple of months, you're still treading the thin line between trying not to look as if you're happy, which would seem heartless, and not being so depressed that you start to bring others down. And then the one-year mark rolls around, and by that point everyone is tired of your grief. They're bored with stepping on eggshells, of feeling uncomfortable in your presence. 'You need to start moving on,' they say, as if you've lost a mobile phone and need to give up looking for it in favour of upgrading to a newer model.

I can't see you yet, even with most of the bottle of Glenfiddich gone. Why aren't you here? It's still not even midday, though it looks as though it's early evening with the rain clouds lurking overhead, so I switch to a glass of wine and head into the bathroom where I run myself a bath. I hate baths, always have. I fail to see how you can possibly get clean when you're just lying there stewing in the grime you've washed off. Today, however, I'll make an exception. I wait until it's hot enough to scald me, my lowered inhibitions dulling my common sense, and gingerly step in. My skin has faded scars from the strains of bearing a child, stretch marks extending across my stomach. I slide down, letting the water rush into my ears and block out the world around me with a heavy rumble. My head sinks so that the water laps over my face. I want to be there with you, feel you. I wish the bath would swell and stretch until it's big enough to go swimming in, like I used to with your dad in the woods back when we were young and careless.

Even though I can't see you yet, I'm picturing your face perfectly. Even now, after all this time, I can still smell your soft hair, strands of textured ebony not yet rubbed bald from lying in your Moses basket. I can still remember how you peered up at me through brand-new eyes, how your tiny hand wrapped around my finger, how your cheeks glowed with a tinge of rose under your tawny skin; the perfect mix of me and Ty. His jawline, my dimples. His nose with the tip turned up, my cupid's-bow mouth.

I take another breath and lower myself further under the water, opening my eyes as my head rests on the bottom of the bath. The ceiling swirls in glistening patterns above me. The water distorts everything in such a beautiful way, softening edges and curving corners. Is that what you saw that day? Did the trees and clouds above you twist into an abstract painting while strands of your hair floated gently across the scene, catching in the sunlight? I like to pretend that's how it was ... peaceful. But, of course, that's not how it really happened. I can remember all too well.

No. I don't want to.

I lurch up to sitting, an involuntary gasp sending the water flooding into my mouth and up my nostrils. I grip onto the sides of the bath as I splutter, soaking the tiles beneath me. The water is cold now. I must have fallen asleep.

Grabbing the towel off the radiator I haul myself out of the tub, shivering and still coughing. As I pad out into the hallway I leave wet footprints along the parquet flooring. Must make a mental note to wipe them up before I go flying. Wrapped in my towel I make a beeline for the wine that I left on the side, half drunk. My fingers grip the stem of the glass like a clenched fist and I down it before filling it up again, almost to the rim.

The light on my landline blinks in my peripheral vision. There's no more space on the answer machine. Now, when someone rings me and I don't answer, they just get cut off. I can practically hear Gabbie's words. 'No point letting these things build up,' she'd say. 'Best to just get it out of the way before the job becomes too overwhelming.' I rub my fingers along my forehead as I click through message by message, letting it play just long enough for me to be able to delete it but not long enough for me to hear any of it. I don't need to hear them. I know they're all from her. Gabbie. Asking me to call her, begging me to let her know I'm okay.

I do miss her.

Humans aren't meant to live in solitude. Your Aunt Gabbie was my safe space. I don't know if I ever told you this, but when I had you six weeks early your dad wasn't there. I tried to call him, then again and again, then his parents. I tried to call my mum. No one came. I laboured in isolation until Gabbie burst through the hospital doors, crouched by my bed, gripped my hand and kept me going. My only friend in the whole world.

My fingers have dialled the number before I've even had a chance to think about what I'm doing. I don't have it saved anymore, haven't got it written down anywhere, but I don't need to. I know it off by heart, and as much as I've tried to forget it's burned into my memory. I press the phone to my ear and listen to the low drone, my breath catching with every ring. I'm not even sure why I'm calling. I just need to hear her voice. Gabbie was always the one I went to when I was struggling, the one who got me through the toughest situations, and in saying goodbye to my old life I said goodbye to her. Maybe I was wrong.

But she doesn't answer.

'Hello?' a gruff, deep voice mutters on the other end of the line. I recognise it immediately. It's your dad. Ty. My throat clamps up. It's like someone has me by the neck and is squeezing the life out of me.

'Hello? Who's there? I can hear you breathing.' I clamp my hand over my mouth, my fingers digging into the phone so hard I fear they might burst straight through the glass. My entire body has gone unresponsive.

'Jodie . . . is that you?'

I launch the phone across the room. I didn't even think to hang up the call, but it doesn't matter because it smashes into three pieces upon impact with the wall and the battery bounces along the floorboards. I descend into a fit of shakes, every limb trembling, my gasps for breath punctuated by ugly, snot-ridden sobs.

Why, why, why did I ring them? I've built a life here. I've managed to cling onto some semblance of normality, but hearing his voice has just dragged me straight back to that place. I don't know what to do. I can't breathe. I want to get back into the bath but I can't face it. I want to see you. I just want to see you again. Why aren't you here?

Before I know it I'm up, grabbing what's left of the bottle of wine and wandering out of the house. It's dark. The day has escaped me, disappeared into an alcohol-infused abyss. The streetlights glare at me, bouncing off the rain as I walk in a daze through the fallen leaves. It sends black spots dancing across my vision.

I fall to my knees at the edge of the pond, the rain battering against my face. I can't stop the mental images from coming: the treeline leaning in like ominous shadows, your empty expression, your fingers slipping through mine. As the images play in my head my fingers dig into the damp mud of the bank. I lean forward, see my reddened, blotchy face in the distorted reflection of the water's rippling surface. I want to lie down in it, submerge myself like I did with the bath.

'Jodie?'

Someone is calling me.

'What are you doing?'

A hand appears beside me. It grips my wrist and yanks it up. The mix of rain and tears in my eyes have made everything go blurry. I blink and try to focus on the person beside me. It's Heidi.

'You're bleeding,' she says. I follow her gaze to my hand. At some point I must have broken the bottle of wine, because a long angry gash stretches across my palm and the shattered remnants of the bottle lie on the grass beside me. Heidi takes one look at my face, shakes her head, then hooks her hand under my armpit. 'Come on, inside.'

I don't want to go with her. I want to stay here, near the water, where I can feel closer to you. But I have no energy to fight her off so I allow her to haul me up and lead me away from the pond. Little footsteps crunch beside me. You're here with me, finally.

'Where are we going, Mummy?' you say.

Chapter Thirty-Eight

2 Days Before the Murder

Norah

I've felt sick all morning, to the point where I've decided to lie down for my daily nap a whole hour early. Even Lacey asked if I was okay. Not once in all my years living at Kensington Grove has Heidi looked at me the way she did yesterday. I suppose I can't really blame her. If I found out she'd known about my husband's infidelity for years, not said anything and had been blackmailing him, I'd probably hate her too.

Blackmail is such an ugly word. That's not how it started. Not intentionally, anyway. When Lacey first got attached to Alison, I became so scared that she'd end up knowing too much. You can never tell who to trust when you're in my situation, you see. For all I knew she was sent to Kensington Grove to spy on us. So I had to protect what we've built here, and that's when I went to pay Paul a visit, just to make sure both he and Heidi were still on the same page regarding keeping my change of name a secret from all of the residents.

It's a stupid place to conduct an affair: your office. Clichéd and predictable, and ridiculously easy to get caught out. The first time I saw Paul and David together, I also saw an opportunity. So yes, perhaps I was in the wrong to tell him if my name change ever got out I'd share my discovery with Heidi, and possibly the other residents of Kensington Grove. Perhaps it was blackmail. But I preferred to think of it as two friends keeping each other's secrets.

Apparently, that's not how Heidi sees it.

I've sent her three messages this morning. I wish WhatsApp didn't have that blasted double blue tick to tell you when the person's seen the message. I'd prefer to think she just hasn't looked at her phone than to know she's read it and chosen not to respond. I need to know what's going on in that house, the conversations she and Paul have been having. Now she knows I was blackmailing Paul, I have nothing to hold over him anymore. My carefully constructed web of lies is crumbling.

I flip my phone around a few times in my hand, then bury it under the cushion and force my eyes shut. I had felt tired when I chose to take my nap early, but now that I'm trying to fall asleep my brain won't shut off. I've been lying here awake for exactly twenty-three minutes. I know, because I've been checking my phone every couple of minutes to see if Heidi has responded and I've somehow missed the notification.

This is pointless.

Groaning, I pull myself up from the sofa and head to Lacey's room to tell her she's free to come out. I rub my eyes as I walk, a dull ache starting to develop behind the sockets. There's an uneasy feeling in the pit of my stomach, like a sense of foreboding. I had thought it was because of the argument with Heidi, but now I'm not so sure.

In my drowsy, frustrated state I completely forget to knock on Lacey's door. She yelps as I enter, and her startle sends something small and heavy flying out of her hand. It lands beside the bed with a clatter.

For a moment, I just stare at it, unsure I'm seeing things correctly. Lacey doesn't have a mobile. It's a strict rule in this house. She is not to have a mobile until she's eighteen, and to be honest I'm not even sure I'll be comfortable with lifting the rule then. It can't be a mobile phone that I'm seeing on the floor, flashing up at me. But it is.

'Mum . . .' Lacey starts, her voice wobbling, but she is clearly as lost for words as I am because she doesn't say anything else.

I take a few steps forward and hunch down to pick up the phone. It's warm in my hands. *Lacey has a mobile phone.* I repeat the words in my head to attempt to make them make sense, but nothing about this makes sense. I look at my daughter, at her small, delicate face which seems to have gone about four shades paler since I entered the room.

'Where did you get this?' is all I can muster.

Tears pool in Lacey's eyes. She knows exactly what she's done. This isn't just an act of rebellion like the time she left the house and went and sat overlooking the school. This is a betrayal of the trust that we've spent months rebuilding, shattered to dust in an instant.

'Lacey, I'm going to ask you one more time. Where did you get this?'

She lowers her gaze from mine, as if maintaining eye contact is too difficult, and begins fiddling with the loose thread on her duvet. 'Markus,' she says.

My initial reaction is one of relief. I had been sure she was going to say Jodie. My legs were already gearing up for storming to her house and battering her front door until it caved in. But her actual response has me more confused than angry. Markus? As in Sally's Markus?

Lacey must see my perplexed expression because she continues, 'He gave it to me at the Halloween party. We were meant to hang out that night.'

The Halloween party. The fire. It was only last month but feels like years ago. It turned out that Markus was responsible for the fire. The week after, Sally found a lighter and a can of petrol under his bed, and after forcing him to apologise to the Kensington Grove Horticultural Society he became the hot gossip. The story evolved from 'Did you hear that Markus Peters was the one who burned down that shed?' to 'Did you hear that Markus Peters tried to burn the whole estate down?', and even at one point, 'Did you hear that Markus Peters killed someone and burned the body to hide the evidence?'

Suddenly, I can't see my daughter sitting in front of me anymore. I see a stranger, someone I do not know at all. 'Did you have anything to do with that fire?' The words feel bizarre on my tongue and I can't believe I'm actually having to ask it.

'It was only meant to be a small one.' Lacey's voice is cracking now, the tears no longer constrained to her eyelids but running down her cheeks and splashing onto her duvet. 'It was meant to act as a distraction so I could sneak away. He felt sorry for me. I told him I wanted to have some adventure for once. He was only trying to be nice. It's not his fault. Please don't blame him.'

Memories of the sheer panic I felt when I couldn't find her at the party, the sheepish look on her face when she emerged from outside, come flooding back to my mind. The information is coming too quickly for me to process. I'm starting to think I did actually manage to fall asleep on the sofa and this is all some strange, weirdly realistic dream.

'I didn't know you even spoke to him. I've never seen you with him.' I can't believe I'm not shouting and screaming. I want to. It's there, broiling away in my gut, but it's as if I can't muster the energy.

The thread snaps off Lacey's duvet and hangs limply from her fingers. 'I didn't think you'd let me be friends with him. You never let me have any friends.'

I blink twice, Lacey's words slicing through me. A retort forms in the back of my throat but I swallow it down. Instead, I turn away from her and over my shoulder say, 'I'll get you a new duvet cover tomorrow,' before closing the door on her.

Chapter Thirty-Nine

1 Day Before the Murder

Jodie

Heidi's blanket smells of her perfume. Tangerines. She must have matched her fabric softener to her perfume and hand wash. That's a real Heidi thing to do. Where I generally find it overpowering, I find it comforting now. I pull it closer to me, tucking it under my chin as I sit huddled up cross-legged on her sofa. There's a bucket next to me. I tried to assure Heidi I wouldn't be sick but she insisted. There is also a glass of water, a plate of buttered toast and my second cup of tea of the morning. I'm not sure what's brought about this sudden change of attitude, but I'm glad she seems to be in a better mood than the last time I saw her.

I bring my hand to my head and start massaging my temple. Heidi's in the kitchen unloading her dishwasher, by the sounds of it, and I'm trying to decide how long I should sit here in my warm nook before making the trek home. I get the distinct feeling that she wouldn't mind one bit if I wanted to stay. She'd probably start putting chocolates on my pillow and taking my order for tomorrow's breakfast. But as much as the thought of it is tempting, I know

I'll regret it when my pride returns. Besides, there's a nagging feeling at the back of my mind that I've forgotten something and it's driving me crazy.

'Do you need anything?' Heidi appears at the doorway, her own cup of tea in hand.

'No, thank you. I'll probably get going once I've drunk this.' I take a sip.

Heidi settles in the armchair opposite me. The atmosphere between us is thick and stagnant. I haven't spoken to the woman, aside from drunkenly insisting that I was fine to walk home on my own and didn't need a babysitter last night, since she came at me for speaking to Paul at the funeral. Where is Paul, come to think of it? I haven't seen him since I arrived here. I assume, even with their marriage deteriorating, that he has to stay in the Grove due to his job.

'I didn't realise you and Christian had got so close,' Heidi says, and I frown. She shakes her head. 'I'm sorry, I assumed that was why you were drinking last night. I know you two were... an item.'

I let out a small, humourless laugh and look down at my tea. 'I really didn't know Christian that well. As harsh as it sounds, last night wasn't about him.'

I mentally scold myself for saying that. Way to prompt uninvited questions. I chew on the inside of my cheek and glance up at Heidi. The desperation to pry is practically bleeding out of her, but I'll give it to her, she's managing to contain it.

'I had an unexpected phone call,' I say eventually, figuring I should give her at least something. 'I'm not sure how they got my number and it just... freaked me out, I guess.'

It's then, looking at Heidi, that I remember. I was so keen to get the paperwork over and done with when I agreed my tenancy, that I put Gabbie's number down as my emergency contact out of sheer habit. I guess I didn't think it would be used unless something bad happened to me.

'When I moved here and I filled out all my paperwork, I had to put an emergency contact number down. There's no reason Paul would have phoned that number is there?'

Heidi frowns. 'Well, yes, he always checks the person is happy to be contacted in the case of an emergency.'

A flicker of anger pulses through me that Paul would have contacted her without my permission, but there is a sense of relief, too. Gabbie didn't come looking for me until she got the call from Paul. She might even have thought I didn't mind her contacting me. She wasn't crossing any boundaries.

I nod at Heidi, and my mind drifts to another subject.

'Can I ask you a question?' I say, running my finger along the edge of my cup. 'What happened? Between Christian and Norah?'

She regards me for a moment, narrows her eyes slightly. I can see she's fighting between the urge to divulge all the dirty details and the desire to stay loyal to her friend.

'It was just a very messy break-up,' she replies eventually, crossing her legs. 'They were together for some time. No one else knew about it, just me and Paul. Apparently, Norah suspected he was getting ready to ask her to make it official, to not have it be a secret anymore. But before he had a chance she just . . . broke it off. I've never been able to get a reason out of her.'

I'm not sure what to say in response, so I just nod and look down at my lap. I can't believe I didn't know they were involved, let alone how serious they were. I'd have never gone near him if I'd known.

'I am sorry,' I say, to which Heidi cocks her head to one side. I tighten my grip on the cup even though it's still hot enough to burn my hands. 'I realised I never actually apologised for what happened with Paul.'

Heidi nods slowly, then places her cup down on the coffee table. 'Thank you.'

I had kind of expected an apology back from her for storming into my house the way she did, but I don't say anything. I suppose if I was in her shoes I'd have done the same thing.

'I should probably get going.' I take a large sip of tea so that my departure before finishing it doesn't come across as quite so rude, and go to stand. 'Thank you for your hospitality.'

'You were right, you know.'

Her words stop me so that my bum is hovering over the sofa cushion. I swallow hard then gingerly lower myself back down.

'Right?'

'About Paul. About me. Neither of us has been happy for a long time.'

'I'm sorry.' It seems such a clichéd thing to say, but it's true. I am sorry. Despite the stories I've written for the newspaper over the years, I've never taken pleasure in seeing a marriage fall apart. Even when I don't know the people, the dysfunction and emotional scars are hard to watch. It occurs to me, as I look at Heidi now, free of the filtered lens through which she usually presents herself, that she's been battling with this for a long time. I wonder how news of the baby was received when she told Paul.

And then, before I can stop myself, I find myself saying the most ridiculous thing. 'If you need any help . . . with the baby . . . I'm happy to babysit. I know how hard it can be to be a single parent.'

I immediately regret saying it. No way do I want to babysit her kid. I don't want to be anywhere near a baby. Not only that, but I've just good as dropped myself in it and am now going to have to explain how I can know how hard it is when, as far as Heidi knows, I've never had kids of my own.

I'm just rattling through the various excuses in my head – my mum was a single parent, I helped my friends out when they had kids – when Heidi's expression stops me. Her lips tremble and squeeze together, and she sucks in a shaky breath.

'I lost the baby a couple of weeks ago. I didn't know how to tell people.'

My body goes numb. I shake my head, unable to form any words.

'You don't have to say anything,' she whispers, seeing me struggle to come up with a response. 'We'd been trying for years. This was our third and final round of IVF.' Her eyes are red and raw. She bows her shoulders slightly so that she looks small and frail, like the entire world is sitting on her neck, weighing her down. 'So when I said that Paul leaving meant I had nothing . . . I wasn't being melodramatic.'

I suddenly become aware of a terrible ache in my core, like a vast emptiness where my insides should be. There is nothing like losing a child. Because you're not just losing a baby, or an embryo, or a sweet, sweet twelve-year-old. You're losing everything they could be. Everything they should be. The life you had planned out and all the future memories you were hoping to enjoy with them.

Part of me wants to tell Heidi about you. Hearing her secret, I'm suddenly desperate to share mine. But I can't. The words are still stuck there, chained to the back of my throat. So I simply say, 'Believe it or not, I do know how you feel.'

Her eyes shine as she looks at me. We don't hug. It kind of feels like we should, but we don't. Instead, I give her a small nod, she does the same, and we sit for some time in comfortable, understanding silence.

'Shit! The cat!'

I leap up from the sofa. I knew I'd forgotten something.

Heidi jumps up too. 'Cat? You have a cat?' Her eyes are wide, darting around the room. I think I startled her with my sudden outburst.

'Uh . . . yeah. It's a new addition.'

I scramble to find my shoes and coat, then try to figure out if I had my purse or phone with me when I ventured out last night. It's all a blur. My hands flap as if that's going to magically produce my coat in front of me.

'Your things are in the spare room upstairs,' Heidi says, gesturing to the hall. 'I put them on the dryer in there last night. They were soaked through.'

I smile gratefully at her through my panic and race up the stairs, taking them two steps at a time. I remember which door leads to the spare room from last time. Sure enough my coat is hanging off a standing electric clothes horse, and my shoes are balanced on top upside down. They're toasty as I slip my feet into them, cosy just like the rest of Heidi's house, and the urge not to leave deepens. No, I need to get back to Toby. I'll stick my duvet in the tumble dryer when I get home. It's not like Heidi has bagsied cosiness.

I'm putting my coat on when something stirs inside me. The last time I was in this room was when I found Norah's purse and the bit of paper inside it. I never did figure out if the man who left his name and a number on it meant anything to Norah. I dig my hands into my pockets. Luckily, I have a bad habit of never cleaning them out. In them there is an array of discarded objects – old tissues, wrappers containing chewed gum, parking tickets, and, underneath two hair bands, Norah's purse.

I pull out the scribbled slip of paper and stare at it for a moment. What with the drama of discovering Paul and David in his office, I'd somehow forgotten the name on that last file I'd opened before it all kicked off. It had been there in the top line. Wilson. Norah Wilson. She had changed her name to get away from her drunk of a husband.

Gareth Wilson is Lacey's dad.

Chapter Forty

1 Day Before the Murder

Norah

The noise of the drill rips through the house. It's been so quiet in here since yesterday – with Lacey avoiding me at all costs and not daring to talk to me while I administer her medication and feed – that the sudden noise as I replace her bedroom door handle with a locking system hurts my ears. My whole body seems to vibrate along with the drill, making my loose flesh wobble. Though, there is less of it these days. As my anxiety has grown I've taken to eating less, and these last couple of days I've definitely noticed a difference in the mirror. A perk, I suppose.

As the drilling ceases, I swipe my forehead with the back of my hand and take a step back to admire my handiwork. Luckily my father took it upon himself to make me help him with all the little jobs around the house when I was a child, so I'm no stranger to a bit of DIY. I slide the key into the keyhole, twist it round and give the handle a sharp tug to ensure it's solid. Lacey is whimpering inside her room, short bursts that quite frankly sound fake. When I said I was going to buy a lock for her door I think she assumed it was an empty threat. I've always been so adamant that she is to keep her door open so that I can see in, she didn't seem to believe that I thought the circumstances were extreme enough to break my own rule. She certainly hadn't expected me to be so efficient about it. Thank goodness for Amazon Prime.

Pleased with my work, I unlock the door and open it a few inches.

'I'm all done,' I say, my voice devoid of any inflection. I've said barely ten words to my daughter in the past twenty-four hours, but all of them have been flat and emotionless. I can only see the side of Lacey's face, just enough to know she's scowling at her new duvet in front of her. No tears, as I suspected. 'It's only a precaution, remember. I'm hoping not to have to use it.'

She doesn't respond and I can't be bothered to try to get anything out of her – I'm not even sure I want her to say anything to me – so I retreat from the door and slump back down onto the sofa. The mobile presses into my leg, taunting me. I don't want to look at it again. I've looked at it so many times already today the mere thought of it is making me nauseated. But I can't help myself. I reach into my jeans pocket and pull out the phone, then begin the sorry process of scrolling through the messages again.

She had put a passcode on it but wasn't particularly clever about it. It only took me a few attempts to figure out that it was the year man first walked on the moon. There is only one contact in the phone – an unknown number but it's easy to tell it is indeed Markus Peters. The messages go back to the evening of the Halloween party, just as Lacey had said. Some are relatively harmless; a few how are you today's, some talk about TV show characters and music, a whole stream of Would you rather . . . texts. Then there are some that are completely, devastatingly heartbreaking.

> My mum doesn't really care about me. She just likes having me around because of all the free stuff she can get.
>
> That sucks. I'd be so out of there if I was you.
>
> Try running away in this place. There's nowhere to even go :(
>
> You can live in our basement, Mum never goes down there LMAO.
>
> Don't tempt me.

I remember the day I woke up from my nap to see her gone, the sheer panic that ripped through me as I tore from room to room screaming her name. My grip tightens on the phone as I scroll down.

> Hey, Markus, you there?
>
> Yeah, what's up?
>
> Just needed someone to talk to. Mum and I had another argument.
>
> What happened?
>
> Same old. I don't get why she won't let me have any freedom. Am I just never supposed to have a life away from her?

> She's nuts, your mum. Absolutely nuts.
>
> Can I tell you a secret?
>
> Of course.
>
> After we had the argument I went to the bathroom and picked up one of Mum's razors. I really considered using it.
>
> . . . Lacey, do you want me to call you?
>
> Not now. Mum will be going to bed soon. I'll call you once she's asleep.

Those were the messages that had me frantically scrolling through Amazon looking for a door lock. Lacey protested, of course, screamed at me that it was a violation of her human rights, but I wasn't prepared to even talk about it. My daughter has lost her way. She's been lost for a long time, and I haven't noticed. I thought she was getting better, I thought our relationship was on the mend. How could I have got things so wrong? I scroll a little further.

> I love talking to you. The only other person I feel like I can talk to round here is Jodie.
>
> Jodie?
>
> Yeah, our neighbour. She's cool.

Oh yeah, she's all right. She saw me that night, ya know? She knew I'd set the fire but didn't say nothing.

I'm not surprised. She's not the type to snitch. I wish she was my mum instead. I reckon she'd make a great mum.

Before I can stop myself I'm hitting 'reply' on Markus' latest message and typing, my fingers jamming at the keys too hard. I type so quickly the message is littered with typos but I don't stop. I keep going until my thumbs start to ache and I can't type anymore. Then, hands trembling, I screenshot it, all the things I desperately want to say to Markus fucking Peters and delete the message.

I angrily switch off the screen, squeezing the phone's casing as hard as I can until the structure begins to creak under the pressure. I want to destroy it, throw it onto the floor and crush it underneath the heel of my shoe, incinerate the remnants, but I also can't stop looking at it. I've read those messages at least ten times by now. It's like a drug that is slowly destroying me from the inside, but I keep going back to it again and again.

I reckon Jodie would make a great mum. The words circle my mind and make my stomach turn. What a joke. People like Jodie, Heidi, Sally, Markus, none of them understand what I have to deal with. Although . . . Jodie was a mum once, and something obviously happened to change that.

The hurt from Lacey's message fuels me as I scroll back through my call log and find the unknown number that I dialled a couple of weeks back. My finger briefly hovers over the 'call' button before pressing it and holding my phone a few inches from my ear, as if I'm afraid if I let it touch my face it'll burn me. With each ring I tell myself to hang up but my brain has apparently disengaged with my hands. Finally, the ringing stops and a scuffling noise sounds on the other end of the line. My breathing grows raspy.

'Hello?'

Say something. Anything.

'Hello? Is there anyone there?'

I cough to give myself an extra second to think. I need to force out some words or she'll hang up and will undoubtedly block my number if I attempt to ring her again.

'Hi,' I breathe. A sharp shake of my body helps me to focus on what I'm doing, and I clear my throat once more and try again. 'Hi, Gabbie, isn't it? We spoke a couple of weeks ago. I'm Jodie's neighbour.'

'Oh!' There is definite shock in the woman's exclamation, but I can't tell if it's excitement or dismay. 'Hi, how can I help you? Is Jodie okay?'

'Well, I'm not sure.' I look around the room aimlessly, hoping for some random stroke of inspiration to hit me. I should have taken some time to plan out what I was going to say before phoning. 'She's been acting a little strangely over the last couple of months. Especially around one of the young girls who lives on the estate. She's become a little... I'm not sure of the word. Fixated, I suppose.'

'I see.' Gabbie doesn't sound in the least bit surprised.

'I just thought I should chat to someone who knew her before she moved here. I'm so worried about her, you see. She's become a good friend of mine.' The words taste like acid on my tongue but I force my way through them. Gabbie can't know how I really feel about Jodie or she'll never talk to me.

For a moment I wonder if she's going to hang up because

everything has gone very quiet, but eventually I hear the sound of a heavy exhalation.

'Has she been drinking at all?' she asks.

I blink. I hadn't expected that question, but it's clearly significant. 'Yes,' I say. 'Yes, she has. Why?'

'Bloody hell. I knew it.' There's a sharp intake of breath, then Gabbie says, 'I hoped she'd get help, wherever it was she was moving to. She only went to a couple of AA meetings before she left.'

The sickly feeling in my stomach subsides slightly as this latest information sinks in. 'I imagine it all stems from what happened with her daughter.'

'Yeah. That's when it all started.'

'She doesn't talk about it that much. She's only told me the basic details.' I grip onto the hem of my shirt and scrunch it between my fingers. 'What exactly happened?'

Chapter Forty-One

1 Day Before the Murder

Jodie

When I arrived home just after lunch, Toby practically leaped at me, filling me with guilt. He was fine, though, and after a bowl of cat food and a drink resumed his usual routine of curling up on my lap. He's acted like a little hot water bottle while I conduct my investigation at the kitchen table. The vibrations of his purrs have proved a great source of comfort.

I have let my grief distract me from trying to help Lacey. I've wasted two days drinking and regretting drinking, two days that I could have been pushing forward with this theory of mine. No, it's more than a theory. Of two things I am absolutely certain.

One: Norah never lets Lacey out of her sight, restricts the media she is exposed to, blogs about her illness and is financially supported by an array of charities and government funds.

Two: Norah and Christian used to be in a relationship.

My suspicions are more varied, but all branch off those two facts. I am especially caught up in the revelation that Norah and Christian were together, not because of jealousy, as Heidi assumed, but because I've realised more than ever that I really didn't know him at all. All the jumpy behaviour when I asked him about Lacey, constantly changing the subject, deflecting . . . it's all starting to make sense.

Maybe he never stopped loving Norah.

That bit of paper with Gareth Wilson's name on it has renewed my focus.

I'm sorry, my darling. Oh, God, I'm so sorry. But I can't think about you right now. I can't keep drinking in the hopes that I'll see you next to me. I can't keep searching for ghosts. Lacey is here, alive, in this world. I can't do anything to help you, but I can help her.

So I've spent the past couple of hours trying to figure out where Gareth Wilson is.

Heidi said Lacey's dad was a drunk. I briefly considered messaging a couple of people from my old AA group, but there's no point. They wouldn't be allowed to say anything even if they did by some bizarre coincidence know him.

It's late, just gone 11 p.m. I've skipped dinner entirely and really should be thinking about going to bed soon, but there's no way I'll sleep, not until I find Gareth Wilson. This is the first time in months I've not felt in the least bit tired. I googled him up to a point, back when I first found the bit of paper, but I didn't try Facebook profiles, so that's where I start this time. There are dozens of potential Gareth Wilsons on Facebook, though; trying to narrow them down is next to impossible. Besides, what would I even say if I were to find him on here? *Hi, I'm sorry if this sounds completely random and creepy but by any chance did you used to be married to a woman called Norah?*

I sit and think, then start typing 'Gareth Wilson Norah' into the search bar to see what that throws up. But before anything loads, an incoming message flashes up on the Facebook tab I've still got open.

It's from someone called 'Jane Smith' and there's an accompanying friend request. I glance at the profile photo; it's one of those avatars, no hints as to what this person actually looks like. It's probably someone trying to sign me up to some kind of multi-level marketing scheme. I get those kinds of message sometimes. I click into it.

> Hi. It's Lacey.

I stare at the message, questions flooding me.

Lacey? Is this a trick? What if it's Norah? My hand moves over my keyboard but I don't type anything. I have absolutely no idea how to respond. I want a glass of wine. No. I need to keep my thoughts clear.

Jane Smith is typing again. Those three dots are dancing along the bottom of the message and I hold my breath as I wait for something to pop up.

> Mum's asleep so I'm using her laptop. It's the only way I could think of contacting you. She's taken my phone.

My fingers drum along the table and Toby stirs in my lap. Finally, I swallow down the lump in my throat and begin to tap out a reply.

> How are you?

I have to assume it is really her. If she's contacting me it might be because she's going to ask me to help her. But I also need to keep in mind that I might be talking to Norah right now, so anything I say needs to be well thought out. I need to make sure I don't drop Lacey in anything, or give her more fuel to say I've got an obsession.

> Not great. I'm in a lot of trouble . . .

The three dots start dancing again, then disappear only to reappear a few seconds later. This happens again and again, as if the message being typed keeps getting deleted and reworded. I chew on the inside of my cheek and start rearranging the fruit in the bowl in front of me out of a sheer need to occupy my hands with something. Is she going to tell me everything? Is that why she's struggling to figure out how to word it?

A thought occurs to me and I jump up from my seat. I pull open the kitchen drawer closest to me. It jams and I have to shake it to get it open properly. It's my junk drawer, home to many a receipt, torch, box of paperclips and other miscellaneous objects that don't belong anywhere else. I dig around in the mess until I find what I'm looking for: DS Wolfe's card. If Lacey is about to incriminate Norah I need to be prepared to take screenshots and get them over to the police as quickly as possible.

I return to the table expecting to see a new message from Jane Smith, but there isn't one and the three dots have disappeared. My stomach drops, quickly accompanied by a sickening sense of dread. Has Norah caught Lacey on her laptop?

> Are you still there? I type.

I wring my hands in my lap, twisting my fingers until they grow sore. The throb of my heartbeat pounds in my ears as I wait. I glance at the time in the corner of the screen. If she doesn't respond within five minutes I'll go and knock on their door. If all is well I'll have to come up with some excuse for why I'm bothering them in the middle of the night, and I doubt Norah will believe whatever story I come up with, but that's a risk I'll have to take.

There are two minutes left on my self-imposed timer and I'm sure my blood pressure is at an all-time high when finally the dots reappear, and this time they only jump around for a few seconds before a new message flashes up.

> Sorry, I thought I heard her moving about. She's still fast asleep. We're good.

I let out a half-laugh, half-cry and slump back in my chair, pressing my palms together in front of my face. It takes me a good few minutes of just focusing on my breathing for the lightheadedness to subside. Once it does I give myself a shake and begin to type.

> You know I'm here for you. If you ever need anything all you've got to do is message me.

> Thank you. Why are you so nice to me?

I take a moment to consider my response before I reply.

> You remind me a lot of my little girl. She was only a little bit younger than you when she died.

Before I can think any more into it I hit 'send' and release a long, slow breath. I stare at the words on the screen, unable to believe I've actually said it. I had expected instantaneous regret, a desperation to retrieve the message and pretend I'd never sent it, but that doesn't happen. Instead, a sense of relief washes over me, and when Lacey's inevitable questions come flooding in I find the act of finally talking about you to her liberating.

We talk for just over half an hour before Lacey messages to say she'd better log off in case her mum gets up to pee and sees the light of the laptop. A pang of disappointment hits me. It's been so long since I've had a chance to speak to Lacey and I haven't even got to any of the things I wanted to ask her.

> Before you go, I type before she has a chance to go offline, can I ask you a question?

> Sure.

I press my lips together as I try to decide what's the most important question to ask. An almost overwhelming urge to ask about Norah's involvement with Christian nags at me, but I know deep down that's just my personal connection to him talking. I'll want to know that side of things at some point, but right now there's a more important lead to follow.

> Do you have any contact with your dad?

There is a pause, and the ticking of my clock on the wall seems to slowly amplify, filling the space around me.

No. He's in prison.

Prison? I know Heidi said he was a violent drunk but she never mentioned he was in prison. Frowning, I start tapping out my reply.

Do you know which one?

Chapter Forty-Two

1 Day Before the Murder

Norah

The sound of a door creaking infiltrates my dreams. I'm standing in a hedge maze, just like the one Lacey and I wandered round in LA that time. But Lacey isn't with me this time. I'm alone.

'Lacey!' I cry out to her. 'Lacey, where are you?'

The leaves surrounding me bristle under the wind. 'She's over there,' they say. 'With her.'

But I can't see which way the hedges are pointing. So I wander down random paths, marvelling at the way the leaves are changing shape and colour before my very eyes. The creaking noise startles me and I spin around, readying myself to fight off whoever is coming through the door behind me, but there is no door. Just hedges. What would a door be doing in a hedge maze anyway?

Creak.

My eyes flick open. Someone is in my room. I blink rapidly, pulling myself out of my dream-fuelled haze, and listen. Silence. I allow my eyes to dart around the room, trying to keep my head and body as still as possible so that my intruder won't know I'm awake. My empty bedroom stares back at me. For one terrifying moment I think whoever it is has managed to shimmy themselves under my bed, and I have visions of sharp spears jutting up through the mattress and piercing my heart, or of hands reaching up and grabbing my ankles, dragging me off the bed and down onto the cold floor.

I squirm at the thought and tell myself not to be so silly. I've been awoken at an awkward stage of my sleep cycle and it's causing irrational flights of the imagination. I sit up and, steeling myself, plant my feet firmly on the floor. No one grabs my ankles. There's no one there. Of course there isn't. But I swear I heard someone open and close a door.

Lacey. It was Lacey's door creaking. I've been meaning to put some WD-40 on it for weeks. She probably needed the bathroom. I twist my ankles round in a propeller-like motion, allowing them to click a few times, before standing and making my way out to the hallway. I'm just about to pass Lacey's room and head to the kitchen to get myself a glass of water when another noise stops me in my tracks. A light *tap, tap, tapping*. Only for a moment. All is silent now.

I freeze and hold my breath. The sound has definitely stopped. Maybe I imagined it altogether. But something else is off too. I glance down at the floor, at the crack under Lacey's door. A jolt of alarm powers through me. There is the tiniest hint of a blue glow.

Movement from inside the room sends me backing up as quietly as possible and retreating to my bedroom. I bury myself under my duvet just as the creak of Lacey's door sounds again. I squeeze my eyes shut.

'Mum?'

She's at my door, I can sense her there. I don't respond, keep my eyelids glued together, focus on keeping my breath steady and heavy enough to signal sleep. If I'm to find out what she's up to she has to believe I'm dead to the world. I need to induce a false sense of safety so that she lowers her guard and resumes her actions. There are a few beats of silence before she exhales and returns to her room, shutting the door after her.

Now all there is to do is wait.

Chapter Forty-Three

The Day of the Murder

Jodie

Fuelled by three espressos and just a couple of hours of disturbed sleep, I make my way through the entrance of Ridgemoor prison. Of all the things I'd thought the number represented on that bit of paper, a prison's number was not something I'd considered.

After some brief hesitation, Lacey had supplied me with the name of the prison. I would have found out where he was myself, with just a bit more digging. I had been almost there when she'd messaged me, after all. But I didn't want to keep any secrets from Lacey. Involving her, up to a point, would make her know she could trust me. Transparency is so often the best strategy. Again, not always my forte, but maybe that would change. I am so tired of pretending.

As soon as the birds started chirping I was on the phone to their visitor booking line, ensuring to use Norah's name. I didn't think some random journalist would be allowed to visit a prisoner, but his ex-wife surely would. The journey took three long hours and I didn't even stop to pee or stretch my legs.

Now, I'm somewhat regretting that as I can feel my muscles cramping up. Am I really doing this? According to the hurried research I did this morning before leaving, Gareth is in for murder. He's been incarcerated for twelve years already, with thirteen more before he can even apply for parole. And here I am heading out for a chat with him as if we're old friends catching up over tea. I'm not exactly sure what I'm going to say to Gareth when I see him, or even what information I'm hoping to get out of him. All I know is this man knew Norah before any of them; before Heidi, before Christian, even before Lacey. If anyone is going to know what kind of skeletons she's hiding in her closet, it's going to be him.

I place the only possessions I brought with me – my shiny new Android phone and Norah's purse – into a plastic tray as I pass through security. The uniformed woman instructs me to spread my arms and legs and I do so, trying to appear as calm and collected as possible as she pats me down. For a moment I panic that I'm going to be asked for a full body search in the buff, but to my relief the woman simply scans me with a metal detector before returning the purse to me. As I predicted they ask for my ID and I can't help but flash a triumphant smile as I whip out Norah's driving licence from the purse. It's not a perfect match – if anyone scrutinised the photo on the licence too hard they'd probably be able to see past the fact that I've done my hair and make-up to look as close to Norah as possible – but it's enough.

'No mobile phones,' the woman says, picking up my new phone out of the tray and giving it to the man in charge of the visitor sign-in sheet. 'You can collect it on your way out.'

I nod, though inwardly I'm cursing. Lacey sent me a photo of her dad last night, one of the only photos she could find in Norah's collection. The photo is old, Lacey must only be about two years old in it. Gareth is crouched down with Lacey balancing on his knee, and he appears in every way a doting father. He certainly doesn't look like a violent drunk, but then I know better than anyone that looks can be deceiving. I had hoped I'd be able to use the photo as a reference so I'd be able to spot him easily, but now I'll have to make do with my memory.

I proceed through the doors, down the hallway and through another set of doors. The visiting room is bleak; a vast open space with grey floors and walls. A few water fountains, bins and the white tables and chairs bolted to the floor are the only items in the room to break the monotony. I lower myself into one of the chairs and fix my eyes on the door where the prisoners will emerge, trying to picture Gareth's face in my mind. Of course, he's going to realise quite quickly that I'm not his expected ex-wife, but I'm relying on curiosity getting the better of him so he'll talk to me anyway. I can't imagine prison life is particularly riveting. A mysterious visitor might be the excitement he needs in his days.

It's easy to spot Gareth. He's aged well in the years since the photo was taken and looks mostly the same, save a few additional lines and grey hairs. Besides, if I had any doubt it vanishes as soon as he steps under the harsh glow of the suspended fluorescent lights. There is a striking resemblance between him and Lacey. Everything from the nose up has been inherited.

I wave and beckon him over, offering him one of my friendliest smiles. Confusion flashes across his face and his eyes scan the room before returning to mine and moving to sit opposite me. He leans back in the seat as if he's worried I might lunge at him.

'Hi, Mr Wilson, my name is Jodie. I live next door to your ex-wife.'

His eyes narrow. 'I was told my ex-wife was going to be here. What? She chickened out and sent you instead?'

'No...'

'Tell her if she's got something to say she needs to come here and say it to my face.'

'Mr Wilson, you don't understand. I'm not a friend of Norah's.'

This stops him in his tracks. He crosses his arms and looks me up and down. 'Why're you here then?'

'I've been talking to your daughter,' I say carefully, and his reaction is instant. A paling of the face, a widening of the eyes, and I'm sure the corners of his mouth quirk up just the tiniest bit. 'She's a wonderful girl.'

He breaks eye contact and fixes his glare on his lap, his hands which he's rested on the plastic table top bunching into fists. 'I wouldn't know,' he mumbles.

I shake my head. How awful, to know your child is out there somewhere but never to be able to see her. Even talk to her on the phone or see a recent picture of her. Even though I know he's a murderer and probably deserves everything he's had to endure, my maternal side can't help but feel sorry for him.

A long, quiet moment passes between us, and when Gareth looks up again the suspicion seems to have disappeared and been replaced by a pained expression, one of deep regret.

My feet cross and uncross beneath the table. I mustn't let him see how intimidated I feel. I had my questions all planned out, but actually sitting opposite a convicted murderer has knocked my professionalism. I need a moment to think and collect myself. Forcing my posture to remain confident, I eye the water fountains.

'I'm going to grab a cup of water. Want one?'

He shakes his head. As I stand and head to the fountain I expel a quiet sigh of relief. Despite my moment of fluster, I'd say things are going well. I got through security with no issues. Gareth didn't run back to his cell when he saw me sitting there instead of Norah. I just need to keep my cool for a little bit longer.

Gareth watches me expectantly as I return to the table with my plastic cup. 'So, Miss...'

'Madison,' I say, then flinch and check around me to ensure none of the staff heard me using a different name.

'Miss Madison. You still haven't told me what you came here for.'

There's no point in mincing my words any more than I already have. I'm on a clock. I bow my head slightly and lower my voice. 'Right. I have some... concerns about Lacey. I take it you know about her illness?'

'I know she's got cystic fibrosis, but I don't really know any details.' Gareth fidgets in his seat and I wait for him to continue, hanging on his every word. 'I didn't have much to do with the doctors treating her. Norah insisted on doing all that alone; her appointments, medication and whatnot. Honestly, I never thought it was as bad as it was until the doctors agreed with her.'

A shiver races down my spine. I clear my throat.

'I wondered if you could tell me what Norah was like when you knew her?'

Gareth leans forward, bringing his fingers to a steeple and resting his chin on his thumbs. He seems to be studying every inch of my face, taking me in. It's unnerving and part of me wants to run back out that door and drive as fast as I can away from this prison. But I'm too far into it now. I stay rooted to the spot while I await his response.

After what feels like an eternity he lets out a half-chuckle. 'I could have got a shorter term, you know? Fifteen years was the number my lawyer gave me. You know why I got twenty-five?'

I nod, remembering the article I found documenting his trial. 'Because you pleaded innocent.'

'That's right.'

My eyebrows involuntarily flick up at this. 'Are you?'

For the first time since I sat down, I take a moment to study his face as he has done mine. Usually, it's one of the first things I do when I interview someone for work. The face can tell a whole other story that words never could. It's one of our greatest tools. I've let the fact that this man is serving a murder sentence lower my journalistic perception, but now I can see it. His smile isn't quite reaching his eyes.

'Yeah,' he says, and as soon as he does his barriers drop. Information pours out of him in a gush. 'Mum never liked Norah. Didn't trust her. When she got sick she came to live with us, back when Lacey was just a young 'un crawling around on all fours. One day she accused Norah of cheating on me with some doctor.'

I lean forward, hanging onto his every word.

'Anyway, turns out Mum was right,' he continues. 'We started divorce proceedings and Mum, being Mum, started saying we should fight for custody. That it ain't fair the woman always gets the child and that she'd die before she let some cheating slag take her grandchild away. That night she fell down the stairs.'

Here, Gareth trails off, and a pang of sympathy hits me. If he really is innocent, he's not only missed out on so many years of his own life, but of his daughter's too. Part of me wants to get up and thank him for his time, stop forcing him to relive these painful memories, but I stop myself by remembering why I came.

Gareth clears his throat before continuing. 'At first I thought it was just an accident. But then, when the police came knocking, Norah started making up all this crap about me beating her.'

'Did they not check for bruises?' I find myself saying.

'Oh yeah. Wouldn't surprise me if the nut-job had given them to herself to make it look like I did it. And because I was a drinker they believed her. Mum's death was declared a murder, and with my history of violent tendencies, I took the fall.'

I lean closer, matching Gareth's stance. 'Do you think she killed your mother?'

There is a long pause. Then: 'Yeah. She killed her all right.'

Chapter Forty-Four

The Day of the Murder

Norah

My daughter is a liar. She lies and she hides and she betrays, leaving me with more messes to clean up as she continues her oblivious existence. I've tried telling her to appreciate everything I do for her. I've tried reminding her what I've sacrificed to get us here. But she doesn't care. It's about Lacey. It's always all about Lacey.

I choose not to wake her up this morning. Her medications can wait. I want to delay facing her for as long as possible. When she emerges from her room I'm hit with a flutter of annoyance at just how normal she looks. With the level of betrayal she's been living with, you'd think she'd be nervous, uneasy, jittery. But instead, she flashes me a carefree smile as she manoeuvres her wheelchair around the furniture.

'Morning. How come you didn't wake me up?'

Without responding I shuffle over a few inches to the next sofa cushion, revealing the thin black laptop open on the coffee table, the profile of Jane Smith staring back at us. She lets out a gasp.

Ah, there it is. The crack in that confident demeanour.

She sits there frozen, the only movement being her rapid blinking as she tries to process what she's seeing.

'What's the matter, darling?' I say, my voice flat. 'Did you think I wouldn't be able to guess the password to your secret Facebook profile?'

She blanches, not taking her eyes off the laptop.

'Come here.' I lift my hand and beckon her over. The movement makes my arm ache. I am so, so tired.

Lacey doesn't move, just stays suspended near the hallway, as if she might make a break for the front door at any second. She puffs out her chest and crosses her arms, her young face dropping into one of her sullen scowls.

'It's none of your business,' she says.

'Excuse me?'

'What I talk about with my friends. It's none of your business!'

It's strange. Sometimes, like last night when I waited for Lacey to fall asleep and commandeered the laptop to see what she was using it for, she can truly shock me. But other times she can be so predictable. I have spent the morning, while I waited for Lacey to wake up, planning out how this conversation will go. Her throwing the blame back onto me was step one. Now for step two.

'Come here,' I say again, more forcefully this time.

She hesitates for a moment and I can see the cogs turning in her brain as she tries to think of an excuse. It doesn't take long for her to resign herself to the fact that there are no excuses, not anymore, and her shoulders slump as she moves closer to me. I wait for her wheelchair to be mere inches away from my knee before I speak.

'Read for me.' I gesture to the screen and Lacey recoils.

'What?'

'Please don't make me ask a second time.'

She looks utterly dumbfounded, as if I've just asked her to recite a foreign language. She presses herself against the backrest of her wheelchair, inching further away from me. Her hands fiddle with her pyjama bottoms, pinching and stretching the fabric.

'Lacey, darling, we don't have all day,' I prompt. 'From here, please.'

'Okay . . .' She leans forward slightly, her brow set in a frown as she begins to read from where I've placed the flashing cursor. *'The prison is called Ridge something. I can't quite remember. Mum told me years ago when I asked about him, but we never really talk about him. He's allowed visitors I think but we've never gone. Mum says a prison is no place for me.'*

She glances up at me through her lashes, silently asking if she should continue. I hold up a hand to signal that she can stop, then allow what she's just read to permeate the air.

'Do you remember why we moved here?' I ask.

Lacey nods, her lower lip quivering, but doesn't say anything. I look at the screen, reread the words one more time, though I practically know them by heart I've read them so many times this morning. My face is reflected back to me in the screen. I look like a completely different woman.

'Do you think it was wise . . . telling a total stranger about your father?'

'Jodie's not a stranger.'

My stomach constricts at how immediately Lacey jumps to Jodie's defence, but I won't let her see the effect her words have on me. They're her sharpest weapon and my greatest weakness.

'We are going to move again.' At my words Lacey's head jerks up, but before she can speak I continue. 'Kensington Grove is not safe for us anymore. I'm having a phone call with an estate agent later today to arrange a valuation on our house. We will start again somewhere else.'

'No, Mum, please. I don't want to move. I've finally made friends.'

'Friends?' I stand suddenly, my knees smacking against the coffee table and sending the laptop sliding backwards. 'You mean the arsonist and the alcoholic? Yes, I can see why you wouldn't want to leave them.'

I swallow hard and smooth out my top with my hands. I've lost my composure. I must take a few seconds to regain it.

Lacey's resentment is tangible in the air. I can sense it swelling, attempting to suffocate me. She remains perfectly still for a moment, then her face twists and distorts. 'I'm not going anywhere! You can't make me! I won't do what you tell me to do anymore!'

She lifts a fist as if she's preparing to hit me, but I'd been anticipating her outrage. I grab her wrist and hold it steady, lowering my face so that it's level with hers. 'You *will* do as I say because I am your mother and you are a child!' The words tumble out of me in a waterfall, spittle flying from my lips. 'Jodie, Markus, Alison – this obsession with other people coming to your rescue and this unfounded hatred towards me . . . it all stops. Today.'

Tears form in Lacey's eyes as she rips her hand out of my grasp. 'I'll hurt myself! I'll go into the bathroom and slit my wrists! I'd rather that than be cooped up with you a moment longer!'

This I hadn't anticipated, though I probably should have, given her messages to Markus. I don't know if she's being serious or hoping her threats will be enough to disarm me, but I won't risk it either way. If this is the route she's going to go down then I will phone the hospital myself and get her sectioned. I don't care about how things will look anymore, I don't care about the cameras and the journalists that will undoubtedly claw onto this like rabid dogs, I will not let Lacey ruin our lives.

She screams as I move her to her bedroom. She writhes and scratches at my arm in an attempt to stop me, leaving an angry red mark tinged with blood. She batters against the door as I close it, she calls me obscenities, she wails like an injured animal. When the key is finally turned in the lock I press my back to the door and slide down it until I'm a hunched-up ball on the floor. I bring my knees into my chest and I sob.

I will get my daughter out of here. We will start again. And until we can, I'm going to make sure that the woman next door doesn't get anywhere near her.

Chapter Forty-Five

Sally
Police just went past my house again. Not another suicide, surely. There'll be none of us left at this rate.

Emma
Have a little tact, Sally.

Marisa
Agreed. We really shouldn't joke about it.

Sally
Jeez, you can't say anything these days.

Heidi
Feel free to remove yourself, Sally.

Sally
What's got your knickers in a twist?

Marisa
Ay yi yi, come on, ladies. We're all friends here.

Emma
> So back to the topic at hand. Any ideas where the police were headed? Blue lights?

Sally
> No blue lights so assuming it's not a suicide. Tragic as that would be, of course.

Emma
> FFS. You really are something else.

Chapter Forty-Six

The Day of the Murder

Jodie

I've left the prison with more questions than answers. Chatting to Gareth has only increased my suspicion of Norah. In fact, no. Suspicion is the wrong word. At this point I am positive that Norah is a psycho. She does what she wants to get what she wants, including – and this is my latest theory thanks to Gareth's admission of doubt – pretending her daughter is ill to garner ... what? Money? Attention? Sympathy? Fancy holidays and paid-for swimming pools? If she isn't making it up I'm convinced she's at least stretching it, making more of it than it is, pushing the doctors to perform surgeries she really doesn't need. All the while keeping Lacey contained – the never letting her make friends or go to school, it's all because she's terrified Lacey will catch on to what she's doing and drop her in it. I've heard of it happening before. Some woman a few years ago claimed thousands in benefits by pretending her kid had cancer before being found out. Maybe Gareth's mum started suspecting her too. Apparently, Norah is more than happy to 'deal with' whoever tries to stop her.

A slight shiver runs down my spine at that thought. She knows I'm onto her. Should I be worried? I shake the thought, telling myself that I could beat her in a fight no problem, but in the back of my mind I make a mental note to double check the locks on all the windows and doors tonight.

I suck in a sharp breath as I pass the gates, my mind going a million miles per hour. Knowing what kind of a person Norah is isn't enough. I need proof. I need to be able to show the police that Lacey isn't safe with Norah. My fingers drum along the steering wheel as I run through what I've discovered so far and try to pick out any loose strand that I've not yet thoroughly investigated.

There's an uneasy thought that's been gnawing on my stomach for days, clamouring for my attention. I've pushed it away thus far, but as I pass Christian's house it hits me like a bolt of lightning. What if Christian, in his misguided love for Norah, filed a false patient report which exaggerated, or even completely fabricated, Lacey's illness? What if that's why Norah killed him? It all makes perfect, terrible sense. I shudder and squirm in my seat. If he did do that, I don't think I'll ever be able to forgive myself for sleeping with him. The thought of his hands on me makes me feel unclean, contaminated.

As I make my way through the Grove I can sense something wrong. There are quite a few residents out on the street, and they all seem to be walking in the same direction. Most of them have their heads down, locked in deep conversation, but the few who are looking around and taking in their surroundings seem to be, yes, staring at me. The uneasy feeling in my core deepens the closer to home I get and I find myself subconsciously pressing my foot harder on the accelerator, breaking the sacred 15 mph Kensington Grove speed limit. When I turn the corner into my road, everything seems to freeze.

A crowd of residents are hovering outside my house, and above their heads I can just about see the roof of a police car. I lower my speed to a crawl, approaching the crowd with caution. All heads turn to stare at me. I can't for the life of me think what's happened, but I'm not entirely sure I want to know. In fact, what I want to do is make a U-turn and speed right back out of the Grove, shutting the gates behind me.

Suddenly, the realisation hits me and my stomach leaps into my throat. They're not crowding around my house. They're crowding around next door.

Lacey...

I yank my handbrake on and go to leap out of the car. The seatbelt tightens around my chest, winding me. I scramble with the button. When it releases I practically fall out of the car and, not caring how much of a crazy person it makes me look, force my way through the horde of people. What I see is enough to make me stop dead in my tracks, and for my entire world to spin.

There, on the front of Norah and Lacey's front door in bright red spray paint, are the words 'Shitty Mother'.

PC Harris steps towards me. 'Jodie Anderson?'

Oh no.

Whispers immediately start circulating the group. 'Anderson? Did he say Anderson? I thought her surname was Madison?'

I try not to look at them, just keep my eyes firmly locked on the two police officers in front of me.

'Would you come with us, please?' they say.

'Am I under arrest?'

'Not at the moment. We'd like you to come down to the station for some questioning but you will be free to leave at any time.'

I'm starting to sweat even though it's freezing and my body is shivering. *I haven't done anything wrong,* I tell myself. But the curtains in next door's front window are rippling a little, as if someone has just pulled it open a crack to peek outside and released it again, and all I can think of is Gareth's mum and how he's serving the best part of a quarter of a century behind bars all because of Norah, and now my pulse is quickening and spots are appearing in front of my eyes and it's all I can do not to pass out right on this tarmac.

'Would you like a glass of water?'

I shake my head no. I am thirsty, gasping, my mouth feels as if I've been chewing on sand for the past half hour, but I don't trust myself not to throw up whatever I drink. Instead, I stare down at the table in front of me, trying to stop the room from spinning. Someone has scratched something illegible into the surface. Focusing on trying to figure out what it says is helping.

This isn't like any of the interview rooms I've seen in films. I was expecting dark walls, a huge one-way window, a flickering lightbulb hanging low and casting an ominous glow around the room, a thick metal bar in the centre of the table for attaching handcuffs to. There is none of that here. It's just a plain white room with a table and four plastic chairs. If I didn't know better, I'd say it was one of the mini conference rooms at the office.

DS Wolfe and another officer take a seat opposite me.

'Before we begin, I'd like to remind you that you're here on a voluntary basis and that you can leave whenever you'd like,' DS Wolfe says, the familiarity of her voice sending me straight back to the day she told me Christian killed himself.

I say nothing, just nod. My hands start wringing in my lap of their own accord. I know I need to relax – not to look so bloody guilty – but I can't help it. Them saying my real name has totally thrown me. If it wasn't for my nails digging so deep into my palms it stings, I'd think I was in a dream. No, a nightmare. One where the floor beneath me is going to open up into a huge black hole. I can't talk. I can't think straight. My mind has gone blank.

'I've got a few questions to ask you, if you don't mind, about your relationship with your neighbours . . .' She refers to her notes as if she doesn't know exactly what their names are. 'Norah and Lacey Williams.'

'Wilson,' I blurt out on instinct. If they've found out about my name change, I'm sure as hell going to make sure they know about hers.

'Yes, there's been a lot of name-changing going on, hasn't there? It's made our job rather confusing, to say the least.'

So they already knew. At least that means they're looking into her too. I move my hands up to the scratched word and start tracing it with my nail.

'Where were you today, 13 November, between the hours of 10 a.m. and 2 p.m.?'

Her tone is friendly, encouraging. I presume that's all part of the training. I swallow hard and lick my lips. I can't lie. They'll find out easily enough. They probably already know.

'I was at Ridgemoor prison.' The nerves are evident in my voice.

A wobble I desperately try to stamp out. I swallow. 'I left to go there at about 10.30 this morning and you brought me here as soon as I got back.'

'I see. And what were you doing before you left this morning?'

'Normal morning stuff, I guess. I had a cup of coffee, brushed my teeth, rang to book the visiting slot.'

'Can anyone verify your movements?'

I lower my eyebrows. 'No. I live alone. But feel free to check my car for spray paint.' I don't mean for the words to come out sounding quite so sarcastic, but really, the whole thing is just utterly ridiculous.

DS Wolfe exchanges a glance with the police officer sitting next to her. Not PC Harris. This man is much younger, almost teenage-looking, and has had his head firmly in his notes since we started. He hasn't said a word.

'Look, is all this really necessary?' I say, suddenly feeling as if the room is shrinking around me. 'Seems a bit overkill for a little graffiti.' My eyes flick pleadingly between the two officers. I wonder which of them will play the good cop.

'This isn't just about the graffiti, Miss Anderson,' DS Wolfe says, leaning forward slightly. I frown. It's disconcerting hearing someone use my real name after all this time. DS Wolfe continues, 'There has been an allegation made against you. Apparently, you've been stalking Miss Wilson and her daughter.'

I roll my eyes and let out a half-laugh, then immediately regret it.

'Is something funny?'

'Of course she's going to say that. She knows I'm onto her. She's scared of me.'

DS Wolfe quirks an eyebrow. That was the wrong thing to say.

I sit back in my chair, try to ground myself. The claustrophobic atmosphere of this room is stopping me from thinking clearly, from engaging my brain before I speak.

'What were you doing at the prison, Miss Anderson?'

I take two measured breaths before responding. 'Visiting Norah's husband.'

'I see, and why did you do that?'

'To try and find out more about her. What she was like before she moved to Kensington Grove.' My stomach is constricting and I'm starting to feel lightheaded. 'Actually, could I have some water, please?'

DS Wolfe nods at the young officer and he fetches a bottle of water for me. I fumble with the top and hope they don't notice. The water is ice cool as it touches my lips, a welcome change from the heat spreading through me. DS Wolfe watches me intently while I take a sip.

'Are you aware that Mr Wilson is serving a murder sentence?'

'Yes.'

'So you think a convicted murderer is a good judge of character, do you?'

'I don't believe he's guilty.'

'And what makes you say that? Other than the story given to you by said convicted murderer.'

There is mocking in her tone that makes me want to smack her in the face. Surely that's not professional? Maybe she's just trying to rile me up. I press my lips together and pretend this is just like any other interview that I've done a hundred times before. I'm not nervous, fumbling Jodie but confident journalist Jodie. I know my real answer – I can just tell – isn't going to cut it so I say nothing.

For a few agonising moments we are locked into some kind of bizarre staring competition.

DS Wolfe is the one to break it off. 'Let's explore a different topic. Why have you been using a fake name?'

I blink, slightly taken aback. I don't like where this is going. 'I wanted a new start,' I say. 'As you know my daughter passed away three years ago. I couldn't stand being around the people who knew us, memories of the past. So I came to Kensington Grove to try and move on.'

There is a beat where the air in the room seems to thicken. DS Wolfe is leading up to something that I can already tell I'm not going to like.

'Seems quite a drastic action, changing your surname, don't you think?' she says, and I meet her gaze.

'Have you ever lost a child, DS Wolfe?'

She shakes her head softly. 'No, no, I haven't.'

'Then you have no business telling someone who has how they should or should not act. You can't begin to imagine what goes through a mother's head. Drastic actions are to be expected.'

'It just seems strange that you'd go to such lengths. You moved to a gated community, changed your name . . .' She refers to her notes and starts reeling facts off them as if I don't already know all this. 'Cut off all ties with your friends and family . . . ?'

'You mean, like Norah Wilson did?' I say. And DS Wolfe looks momentarily caught out.

The room falls silent. I take another sip of water, my hand shaking so much the bottle clinks against my teeth. After a long pause I clasp my hands on the table and say, 'My daughter's dad and his family blamed me. I couldn't face them anymore.'

'Blamed you? For what?'

'You know what,' I snap, my voice rising.

'I'd like you to tell me, if you don't mind.'

Oh please, please let me slap her. I focus my glare on my hands, on the chewed-up flaking skin around my thumbnail. I can't look at her anymore. I can't stand the smug expression on her face. She knows exactly what she's doing.

'They blamed me for my daughter's death.' The words come out almost a whisper, and for a moment I'm terrified she's going to ask me to repeat them, but she doesn't.

'Why would they blame you for your daughter's death?'

The room starts to spin again and there's a tightness in my chest as if someone is reaching in between my rib cage and grabbing my lungs and squeezing. There is no control anymore. No trying to be a different person. Everything I've been avoiding since I moved to Kensington Grove rushes back to me like an avalanche, crushing me, suffocating me. Despite every bone in my body screaming at me not to, I break down and sob.

'Because it was my fault.'

Chapter Forty-Seven

Three Years Before the Murder

Jodie

'Where are we going, Mummy?'

The lights of the A-road flash through the car every few seconds, bathing us in an orange glow before plunging us back into pitch darkness. We've been going like this for three hours now. A-roads, motorways, more A-roads. It's surprising you haven't asked me where we're going before now, but that's the wonders of modern technology for you. You've been buried in your tablet, so fixated with bizarre YouTube videos of other people playing computer games that you've barely even noticed we're in the car.

'I told you, we're staying with Aunt Gabbie for a couple of nights.'

I miss the days when Gabbie lived right down the road from me. After I had you she was my saving grace. I don't know what I'd have done without her support in those early days. Those sleepless, exhausting days where my stitches were still healing and my nipples were bleeding and I was never sure if I was doing a good enough job with this tiny human who relied on me for everything.

I'm still exhausted now. For different reasons. I don't have the disturbed nights anymore, I don't feel like a glorified milking cow, but I've got more responsibilities than I did back then. I have a career now, and as great as my boss Dan is about me having a kid and letting me have afternoons off for things like sports days, I'm still expected to bring just as much to the table as everyone else. I have to, if I'm to retain my spot as chief human interest editor.

So this evening I'll be dropping you to Gabbie's and then tomorrow I'll be heading out to interview a couple in Durham, an additional two-and-a-bit-hour journey from Gabbie's house. I haven't told you that your dad might be there. I don't want to get your hopes up. I made that mistake on your eighth birthday. Though I know you're old enough now to understand that your dad only shows up when it suits him, an irrational fear consumes me every time you see him – that you might decide you want to be with him, *live* with him.

This road has looked the same for at least twenty minutes. Just endless tarmac stretching ahead, lined by pine trees, their tips pointing to the stars. We left later than I wanted to, but we haven't got too much further to go. About half an hour if the sat nav is correct. Thank God. I don't think I could do much longer. I've been on the go since six this morning.

I glance over to you. You've abandoned the tablet finally and you're now leaning your head against the window. There are droplets of rain on the glass and every time the streetlights illuminate the car it leaves tiny little shadows on your face. I wish you saw yourself how I see you. You told me a few weeks ago you thought you were 'plain'. Oh, sweet girl, if only you knew. I know I have to say you're beautiful because I'm your mum, but you truly are. Your eyes sparkle with energy, never failing to draw people in. You're going to steal hearts when you're older.

'Look, we're at the ocean,' you say, pointing over at the side of the road. The landscape has changed finally. The trees have thinned and instead we're driving alongside a vast body of water.

'That's not the ocean. It's a river. And that means we're nearly there.'

Returning my eyes to the road I reach over and squeeze your hand. One squeeze asks if you're okay. Two squeezes in return says yes. Three squeezes says no. Our code. I wait to feel your response and smile to myself as I feel two slow compressions. I stifle a yawn.

'Hey, I'm thinking about taking a couple of weeks off in January,' I say. 'I was thinking we could go away somewhere. Maybe get a caravan or something?'

You lift your head. 'What about school?'

I let out a laugh. What other kid would be more concerned about missing school than getting a holiday?

'I'm sure I'll be able to come up with an excuse for your teachers. That is, if you want to go, of course.'

'Will you teach me to swim?'

A pang of guilt hits me. I've been promising you lessons for months but they're all held after school and there's just no way I'll get back from work on time. If it wasn't for the clubs held at school I don't know what I'd do.

'Yes, baby. We'll make sure it's somewhere with a pool. It's a deal.'

My eyelids are heavy. There's a sign up ahead pointing to a service station and I almost put my indicator on so that I can stretch my legs, allow the fresh air to perk me up, maybe even grab a coffee, but we're so close now. I just need to keep going a little longer.

Stifling a yawn, I keep the car straight and we pass the services.

The blaring of the lorry's horn jolts me awake. I don't know where I am or what I'm doing. All there is, is the deafening screech of wheels and crushing of metal and the smell of burned rubber. And then the world is spinning, the stars and the streetlights are whipping around me in a terrifying cyclone. But the stars and the streetlights are not spinning. We are.

A crash like thunder fills my ears as the bonnet hits the lake's surface. My hand instinctively flies to your chest, pressing you back against your seat while I'm thrown forward with such force that my seatbelt slices into my skin. My toes go cold, my fingers damp, as water seeps into the car.

'Baby! Are you okay?' My eyes dart over to the passenger seat, terrified of what I might see. But you're there, alive, staring back at me with wide panicked eyes.

'I . . . I think so.'

'Okay, come on. Let's get out of here.'

I undo my seatbelt and the sight of the water rising above my shins makes me feel sick.

'I'm stuck!'

My body runs cold. Your fingers are grabbing desperately at your seatbelt but it's locked tight around you.

'Sweetheart, you need to calm down. It's designed to lock if it's pulled quickly. Take a deep breath.' I'm saying all this but my body is descending into shakes, my mind wrapped in pure terror. Everything is going too fast for me to think. The water is rising too quickly.

You stop tugging at the belt and I manoeuvre my fingers down to the button. It clicks but doesn't release. Bile collects at the back of my throat. My knees are now completely submerged, and from what I can see of the back window the car is nearly at the bottom of the river. I let out a distraught cry as a torrent gushes from the edges of the doors and roars over us. I tug at your seatbelt, failing to make it budge, and panic floods through me. The water level creeps over our waists, our chests.

You're crying. Your sobs are slicing through me. 'Mummy, I'm scared!'

I plant my feet against the centre console, trying to keep myself weighted, and again I yank at the belt. Nothing. A sound erupts from me that I've never heard before, some kind of animalistic guttural roar.

I start ransacking the car, looking for something, anything that could help us. I take a breath and plunge beneath the surface of the freezing water. In a frenzy I pull open the glove compartment, praying that there would be some scissors or something sharp that I could cut the belt with, but there isn't anything.

I shoot up to the surface, smacking my head against something – the ceiling. My nerves spike as I take in the shrinking distance between the rising water and the top of the car. It will be filled in less than a minute.

'Mum...' You choke and splutter as water laps into your mouth. I grit my teeth and twist my body to face you, my own tears mixing with the river water.

'Listen to me, baby, listen to me. Someone will come. Someone will help us. But until they do I am here with you. I'm not going anywhere.'

You grip onto me and I grip onto you. I hold your face, your beautiful face, in my hands and press my forehead against yours as we cry together.

'I'm here with you. I'm not going anywhere,' I say again.

And then the water rises, sucking up the last pocket of air, and there is silence, the rumble of swirling water barely a whisper. The water around us glows, lit by the car's headlights. The vision is almost tranquil, until I can't see it anymore. I can't see anything anymore.

Please.

I want to see your face one last time.

Just one last time.

Maddie . . .

Chapter Forty-Eight

The Day of the Murder

Jodie

'The name you've been using: Madison,' DS Wolfe says, 'that's your daughter's name, isn't it?'

I nod, my face sticky with partially dried tears. My body is limp, spent. My muscles feel as if I've just ran a marathon. I have nothing left to give.

'They got us both out but it was too late for Maddie.'

DS Wolfe hands me a tissue and for a moment I leave her arm hovering above the table. I don't want anything from her. She has made me relive it after I've spent so long running from it, and I'm overcome with a deep-rooted searing hatred for this woman that I barely know. But then I remember where I am and I take the tissue, wiping at the snot streaming from my nose.

'After your daughter's passing, did you find yourself relying on any coping mechanisms?'

My eyes flick up to the woman in front of me. There's a crack in her tough exterior, a hint at humanity. She fidgets in her chair and exchanges awkward glances with her co-worker.

'I'm not sure what you mean?' I say.

'Well, after a traumatic incident many find themselves using recreational drugs or alcohol to help cope with the pain.'

'I've never taken drugs.'

'What about alcohol?'

I purse my lips, thinking back over the past few months, the times I've drunk and drunk and drunk just in the hopes that I might catch a glimpse of you once more. I think back to curling up on Heidi's sofa with her tangerine-smelling blanket and sipping her tea. Right now I'd give anything to go back there, to have her baby me again.

'No more than anyone else going through a rough time,' I say eventually.

DS Wolfe watches me for a few seconds, her head moving ever so slightly, not quite a nod. She then sits back against her chair and consults her notes, the cracks in her exterior sealing themselves before my eyes.

'We've spoken to a few of your neighbours. There have been reports of you wandering through the estate drunk, making regular trips to the corner shop for alcohol. Apparently, one time you collapsed next to the pond?'

I flush, heat gathering in my cheeks and earlobes. Did Heidi tell them about that, or was someone watching from their window? Not that it really matters. It's not like I've ever felt I could trust any of the other residents.

'I may have drunk a bit too much after Maddie died,' I say, my voice laced with irritation. 'But it's not as if I poured vodka on my cereal. I drink when I need something to take the edge off.'

I don't tell her that I drink when I want to see you. That little detail is just for us.

'Were you drunk on the day you followed Norah and Lacey to the hospital?'

I try to hide my dismay. I'd almost forgotten about that.

'Look,' I say, digging my knuckles into the underside of the table in an effort to stop myself from storming out of this room. 'Norah Williams has made up this stalking story because she's scared of getting found out. You must have the NSPCC report on file.'

'Miss Anderson, it is your behaviour that concerns us, not Norah's.'

'That doesn't mean anything!'

I'm practically jumping out of my chair. DS Wolfe's eyebrows fly up and I know I need to calm down, stop my voice from rising any further. She's baiting me, looking for a reaction, and I'm giving her exactly what she wants.

'Tell me about the hospital,' she says.

'It was nothing. I wanted to see what kind of care Lacey was getting. I'm convinced Norah's making her illness up, forcing the doctors to do procedures she doesn't need. You hear about that, don't you? She never lets her out, never lets her interact with anyone, she's practically keeping her prisoner in that house.'

For an excruciatingly long time DS Wolfe says nothing. The silence hangs between us like a heavy cloud warning of an incoming storm.

'We're going to issue you with a warning,' DS Wolfe says finally, sitting back and closing her notes. 'But if Miss Wilson isn't satisfied with that and chooses to press charges it may end up in the Magistrates' Court, at which point you'll be advised to get a lawyer or we can assign one for you.'

I have to fight the urge to roll my eyes. I may as well not leave. Norah isn't going to be happy with just a warning. I know it, DS Wolfe knows it, even Mr Note-taker beside her knows it.

'In the meantime, Miss Anderson,' DS Wolfe locks her eyes on me, 'you are to stay away from Norah and her daughter. Am I clear?'

I squeeze the bottle of water in my hand. The plastic crinkles under my grip. 'Can I go?'

'You may.'

I want to lurch across the table and shout in her face that she's looking at the wrong person, that she should be at the Williams house protecting that little girl instead of wasting her time with me. But instead I just get up and march, probably too quickly, out of the room.

Toby wraps himself around my ankles the second I enter the house. It's really late. He must have been wondering where I'd got to. I bend down and scratch his chin. He's been left alone so much recently. I'm pretty sure cats are happier being left alone than dogs, but the guilt nags at me all the same.

I scoop him up in my arms and gaze around my house, at the old haggard furniture which doesn't quite look like it belongs in a place like Kensington Grove, at the window I used to chat to Lacey through, at the box of photo frames still hidden in the nook next to the TV. I haven't touched it since that day, that first day that I arrived on the estate. It's sitting there, a visual reminder to unpack it, and I've never been able to. I'm now not sure I ever will.

This house doesn't feel like mine anymore. It feels like I've been living a lie, walking in someone else's shoes. Kidding myself. My attempt at starting again failed. I try to think back, to pinpoint where it all went so disastrously wrong, and no matter how many scenarios I run I'm always brought back to the same moment. The day I let my emotions rule my head. The day I felt sorry for a sick little girl and angled my TV towards her so that she could watch it and unwittingly grew to care for her.

I did this to myself.

Grabbing my laptop I make my way to the bedroom, Toby on my heels, and sit cross-legged with a couple of pillows propped up behind me. The laptop powers up and I log on to Zoopla. I tend to go on this site about once a week, but usually I'm looking at all the million-pound mansions that I'll never be able to afford and picturing what it would be like to live there. Sitting and scrolling through the various houses and flats that are actually within my price range is far less fun.

I add a few bookmarks to pages, then open a new tab and search for local Premier Inns. I need to get out of here. Moving is going to be a process, but a hotel or B&B would do for a couple of nights just to get that much-needed distance and headspace. Toby mews in my lap as if to remind me about him and I sigh and search instead for 'pet-friendly Airbnbs'. There's one not too far from here, about a thirty-minute drive, and it looks nice enough. More importantly, it's fairly remote and off the beaten path.

I book it before I can talk myself out of it, and send a quick email to Andrew at the office explaining I'll need a little more time off. I don't need anyone trying to track me down.

The confirmation email from the Airbnb flashes up on my phone surprisingly quickly and with it comes an almost immediate sense of calm. This is good. This is what I need.

As I sit there, alternating between my phone and my laptop and occasionally getting pawed at by Toby, something nags at me. I attempt to push it away, to focus on the pictures on the screens and begging my brain to switch off, just for an hour or so, but the nagging sensation only intensifies the longer I try to ignore it.

I can't go anywhere without at least checking in with Lacey.

I know I shouldn't. Every cell in my body screams at me not to as I open up Facebook and navigate to my message stream with Jane Smith.

> Hey, you okay?

She's not online. The green dot would be there next to the name if she was.

> I'm going away for a few days but I just wanted to make sure you had my number just in case. If anything happens or you need anything please call me.

I tap out my number and hit 'send', my heart rate racing as I do so. If Norah sees I've messaged Lacey she'll go straight to the police. I should do what DS Wolfe said and steer clear of both of them. Lacey hasn't got anyone else, though.

I reason with myself that Norah doesn't even know about Lacey's secret profile and Lacey's clever. She's not going to be naive enough to read my message while Norah is around. It'll be fine. With that in my mind I haul myself up and start preparing a suitcase. I should really leave it until tomorrow – after my hours of scrolling it's now gone 11 p.m. and I still haven't had dinner – but I want it all ready so that I can head off first thing.

I select the comfiest clothes I own – I don't plan on doing any socialising over the next few days so I don't have to worry about appearances – and drop in any toiletries that I won't need in the morning. Then I grab the essentials for Toby; a few toys, his treats and food pouches, a sealed bag of litter. I balance them all on the counter next to his bed and litter tray so that I don't forget them and he stares at me as if I've lost the plot. I add a few forms of entertainment to my suitcase; I forgo the sewing machine as it's too bulky and instead pack a few books, a puzzle which I've started and abandoned three times before, a couple of DVDs and my notepad. It has the scribbles for a screenplay idea I had once. Maybe that's what I can do. It could end up being my most productive few days yet.

Pleased with my wave of inspiration I return to the bed to grab my laptop and charger ready for packing. Lacey still hasn't seen my message. It's hardly surprising. Last night she didn't start talking to me until gone eleven. She had to wait for Norah to go to sleep before she could log on. Of course she's not going to be checking it yet. I know all this and yet a string of anxiety is coiling itself around my stomach.

I'll just be quick, no one will ever know, I tell myself as I round the corner of my house and approach Lacey's bedroom window. As I move DS Wolfe's words ring in my head, but I just need to check she's okay. As soon as I know that I'll be able to distance myself.

Her window ledge is icy cold as I place the tips of my fingers on it. Frosty. I rub the sleeve of my coat along it to get rid of my fingerprints, just in case. It's a ridiculous measure but Norah has proven herself far more unpredictable than I'd expected. Staying crouched underneath the window, I fumble about in my pockets and find my woollen gloves. Once they're on I try again, using the window ledge to lift myself as slowly as possible so that I can just about peek through the window. I need to be careful in case Norah's in Lacey's bedroom. That would just about seal my fate if she saw me staring in.

She's not in there, though. Lacey is sitting on her bed with her back to me and she's alone. I tap the glass gently and her head whips around. Her face is red and blotchy, her eyes swollen. She's been crying.

I mouth the words 'Are you okay?' to her and she immediately descends into a flood of new tears. My heart aches for her. I want to burst through this window and wrap her in my arms, tell her to come to the Airbnb with me.

'Open the window, Lacey.' I gesture at the handle but she shakes her head, her face pinched. Leaning across to her bedside table, she picks up a notepad and pencil from her side table and begins to write furiously. I can practically see the pencil bursting through the back of the pad. Wiping the tears from her cheeks, she holds the pad up to me.

She's locked me in. Door and window.

Chills slink through my body. My instinct is to look for something I can crack the window with, but I force myself to stop and think. I can't call the police. They won't believe me. They'll think I'm making things up, then probably arrest me for looking through Lacey's window. Heart racing, I creep round to the front of the house and start searching; under the door mat, behind the potted plant, inside the group of ornamental rocks. Nothing. I run my finger along the top of the doorframe, still nothing, then on top of the exterior light. There.

I pull back my hand and stare at the key for a few seconds, a small voice inside telling me to put it back and run. I could go grab my suitcase and Toby and leave tonight. There'll be somewhere with rooms available. But the other voice, the louder voice, is telling me I already know what I need to do. I suck in a breath and slide the key into the lock.

Norah's house looks different in the dark. Now that I'm not being guided by the outside moonlight my eyes are struggling to adjust. I try to remember the last time I was here, to picture where the various bits of furniture are. I shuffle forward at a microscopic pace, pigeon steps. My hand brushes against the breakfast bar and I know I'm not far off the hall. I think of my own floorplan – is Lacey's room on the left or the right of the hallway? Right, definitely right.

As I stand in the hall I pause and listen for any sign, any sign at all, that Norah might still be awake. The house is silent except for a very faint hiccuping sound coming from the other side of the door to my right – Lacey's sobs.

My muscles are quivering, twitching, and it's making me feel dizzy. I take three slow, measured breaths, then with the softest whisper I can muster I say, 'Lacey.'

There's no response. I swallow hard and try again, a fragment louder this time. 'Lacey, it's Jodie.'

The sobs stop. There is the sound of rustling on the other side of the door, then the sound of wheels on floorboards.

'Jodie?'

'I'm here.' I lift my hand and feel around for the door handle. 'Where's the key?'

'I don't know. I think it's with her.'

My blood runs cold and I turn to face Norah's bedroom door. It's ajar. I creep towards it and peer around the corner. It's still hard to see but my eyes have adjusted to the point where I can make out a few shapes. Norah is in bed. I can see the frizzy outline of her hair sticking up.

This is stupid. Crazy. I may as well go back to the police station right now and tell them to lock me up. My heart is beating so hard, thudding in my chest with such ferocity that I'm sure it will wake her. Trembling, I push against the door, widening the gap so that I can squeeze through.

Each featherlight step I take into her room sounds like crashing plates to my ears. I'm aware of every creak of the floorboards, every click of my bones. I pay attention to how my feet are landing on the floor – first the heel, then a slow roll to the ball before carefully transferring the weight. Panic soars through me as I realise how little I've thought this through. What if it's in her drawer? There's no way I'll be able to get it out without waking her. Or what about if it's on a chain around her neck, or in a pyjama pocket? It may not even be in here.

I'm just about to start backing up and retreating from the bedroom when my eyes land on Norah's bedside table. It's hard to make out because it's so dark, but it's definitely what I think it is. A can of spray paint.

Bitch.

But as I move my gaze, I see darkening, a shadow beside the can. It's small, and I'd probably have missed it if I hadn't been actively searching for it, but as I look closer I think it might be a key. My hand reaches out and gently pads along the surface until the cold metal prongs pique my nerves.

The temptation to sprint out of the room is almost too much to bear, but I force myself to take the same slow measured approach as I move further away from Norah. All I need to do is get Lacey out. If I can do that she can come with me to the police and they'll see that I'm not some psychotic drunk stalker. She can tell them everything.

Relief washes over me as I leave the room and turn back to face Lacey's door.

'I've got it,' I whisper.

The key fits perfectly. I chew down on my lip so hard I can taste the metallic tang of blood on my tongue as I pull the handle down.

'Wait!' Lacey hisses.

But it's too late. I pull the door back and the hinges squeak, an earth-shattering groan that fills the entire house.

I freeze.

Seemingly endless seconds tick by, my muscles tensing and burning as if I've just climbed Mount Everest. The urge to check over my shoulder is strong but I remain deathly still, terrified that the slightest movement from me might be my undoing. I'm even scared to breathe. After what feels like hours, my body starts to relax a little. Steeling myself, I reach for the handle once more and edge it open, just wide enough for Lacey to wheel herself through.

No one's coming. Norah is still fast asleep. We have to be quick. I lead Lacey back through the house, out the front door and into the freezing night. Once we're safely down the driveway I stop, squeeze my eyes shut, try to think of the best thing to do. I need to phone DS Wolfe, tell her about Norah locking Lacey in her room. She'll have to start taking me seriously if she hears about things from Lacey's point of view, surely.

'It's so cold...'

I look back at Lacey, whose breath is clouding the air in front of her in misty spurts. Though it's dim in the light of the streetlamps, I can just about see her trembling. She's only wearing a thin set of pyjamas.

'Let's get you into my place,' I start, then immediately change my mind. If Norah wakes up my house is the first place she'll look, and if there's one thing I want to avoid it's a run-in with her, especially now I know what she's capable of. My eyes desperately scan the street and land on the old church spire of the community centre, stretching up above the rooflines of the neighbouring houses like a beacon.

'Actually, come on.'

The smell of chlorine hits me as soon as we enter the foyer. The swimming pool and wellness rooms aren't ready for public use yet. We've been told we are to endure a grand opening ceremony before anyone is allowed to dip their toes, and of course Lacey is to be the first to get to try it out.

'A bit warmer?' I ask her as I press the switch on the wall. We both squint as the overhead lights flicker on. Lacey nods meekly. 'Hang tight while I make a phone call, okay?'

She nods again and I take a few steps away from her, not wanting her to overhear my conversation with DS Wolfe. As much as she clearly trusts me to get her out of this situation with Norah, I don't particularly want her to hear me accusing her mother of child abuse. Bowing my head, I scroll through my previous calls log, trying to remember which string of numbers is DS Wolfe's.

'Mum!'

I hear Lacey's cry at the same time as the sound of the double doors being flung up, crashing against the inside walls. Before I know what's happening hands, sharp nails dig into the tops of my arms and I'm jolted to the side, flung against the nearby wall. Fire explodes in my spine as my neck twists. Pins and needles shoot through every limb, right down to my fingertips and toes.

'Get away from her!' Norah screeches. It's not so much a human sound as some horrid feral shriek.

'I'm not leaving Lacey!'

Norah's face is contorted, veins bulging across her forehead. I press myself against the wall behind me in a feeble attempt to get even a few inches further away from her.

'You have no right! You need to get out of our lives!'

'No!' I'm trying to sound brave to cover how much Norah's expression is making me want to shrink into a ball on the floor. 'I'm not leaving her here with you. I know what you did! You killed your mother-in-law, didn't you? Did Christian know? Is that why you killed him too? And what about Alison?'

I'm treading a dangerously thin wire now, but I need to distract her enough that I can somehow get to Lacey.

'I said, *get away from her*!' Her fist comes flying towards my face. In a heartbeat I dive to the side, scrambling past her, head ducked. Each step is agony but I can't stop. As I clamber towards a terrified Lacey I can hear Norah right behind me, can sense her hands reaching out to grab me.

Before I know what's hit me my foot catches on something – a bulky object of some kind left strewn on the floor – and I'm toppling over, knocked clean off my feet. My hands reach out to protect my face but before my nose can smack against the floor I'm yanked back by my hair. I let out a howl as my scalp burns. My body twists as her weight presses me down. I try to reach behind my head, to prise her grip off my hair.

SMACK!

Her free hand impacts with the side of my face sending my head snapping to the side and my ears ringing.

'You stay away from her! Do you hear me?'

I can't reach her hand so instead I press my palms against the floor and buck as hard and as fast as I can. My entire body lurches backwards in one swift movement. She lets out a grunt as the back of my head bashes her chin and she rolls off me, the pressure on my scalp finally releasing. I scramble up and stagger forwards, the room spinning. I can't get to the main entrance anymore – Norah is blocking the way – but I can get to the emergency exit on the other side of the pool.

I make a beeline for the exit, skidding across the tiled outskirts of the pool, sure that at any second she'll jerk me back. Once I'm nearly within reaching distance of the handles, I open my mouth to scream for help, but the words are ripped from my mouth as I'm shoved from behind. My foot slides from beneath me, twists, and then I'm crashing down onto the tiles.

I'm not sure what hurts more – my back or my ankle. Black spots are dancing in front of my vision, but as I roll onto my back I can just about see Norah looming above me. Her eyes are wild, her chest is heaving. She kneels beside my head and I lift my hands to fight her off, but my arms don't seem to be working right. The pins and needles have turned to total numbness.

'Please . . .' I pant.

Her face is wet with tears, hot angry tears. 'I won't let you take her from me,' she says, though her voice sounds far off in the distance. 'I won't. I wouldn't let Christian ruin this for me and I won't let you.'

Then her hands are on my neck and she's lifting my head, moving it a few inches to the side, and slamming it back down. I brace myself for the pain of my skull impacting with the floor but it doesn't. Instead, water sloshes into my mouth, my nose, my ears. The swimming pool. She's going to drown me in the swimming pool.

Panic takes over. I squeeze my eyes shut which only magnifies the roar of the water around me, that familiar sound, and I'm right back in that car with you. I scratch at Norah's hands, desperately trying to push her off me.

For a blissful second, I break the surface of the water, gulp in air before I'm under again. My head swims. My throat contracts. My lungs are fighting as if concrete has been poured into my airways, screaming out for oxygen, ready to burst right out of my chest while my heart is hammering in my ears. When I can no longer hold my breath I open my mouth, a desperate attempt to suck in air, and cold water rushes in and I know I'm dead. I escaped drowning three years ago, but not this time.

Norah's grip on my throat slackens. The force pressing me down eases. I lurch back up, break the surface and gasp, frantic ragged breaths. I splutter and cough, then retch, a mixture of pool water and vomit splashing out of my mouth.

And now I see her.

Norah is laying on the floor beside me. At first I think she's looking at me but then I realise she's not looking at anything. Her eyes are empty. Lifeless. Blood is dripping from her head, soaking her hair and running in a crimson stream along the pool tiles and into the water where it spreads like a splash of paint, clouding the surface. For a moment I'm transfixed by the sight, partly wondering if I'm imagining things, if my mind has shut down because of the lack of oxygen. I blink and turn my head, the subtle movement sending a jolt of pain through me and making my vision blur. When it clears I see Lacey above me, her hand gripped tightly around something shiny. As my eyes focus I see the glass cabinet housing the asylum memorabilia behind Lacey with its doors flung open, and I realise what it is she's holding. It's one of the metal collars they used on the patients, now dripping with Norah's blood.

And then I realise something else.

Lacey is standing.

Chapter Forty-Nine

The Day of the Murder

Lacey

The collar hangs limp in my hand. It swings gently from side to side, and all I can hear are the chain links grating against each other and a steady drip coming off it. Blood. Mum's blood.

She's lying at a funny angle, the top of her head just touching the surface of the swimming pool. I can't see her face, but I don't want to. Perhaps if I stay very still she'll move, she'll get up and start shouting at me for being so reckless.

The water is turning a deep, deep red. It's the same colour as the new duvet Mum got me.

A tug on the collar makes me jump, and I look down to see Jodie. I'd forgotten she was even here. Meeting her eye forces tears down my cheeks and I start to shake harder than I've ever shaken before. I start letting go of my grip on the collar and Jodie takes it.

'I didn't mean to kill her,' I say, my voice trembling.

She places the collar down on the ground and slowly gets up onto her knees, her hands gripping each of my arms. My eyes drift back to Mum, and I will her to twitch. To do something. Anything. This wasn't supposed to happen.

'Lacey, look at me.'

But I can't tear my eyes away.

'Don't look at her, look at me.' She gives me a little shake and I squeeze my eyes shut, try to block out the images. Maybe I'm having a nightmare. I used to have them all the time. I used to dream about Grandma, the weird look on her face when I found her dead at the bottom of the stairs. Mum would rush in when I woke up screaming and she'd cuddle me and rock me until I stopped.

Grandma... The thought of her turns and twists my guilt into blood-boiling anger. All those years. All those years of Mum telling me it was an accident, that she didn't mean to kill her, that she was only at the top of the stairs that day because she'd tried to grab her and stop her from falling. It was to stay our little secret. All those years of her refusing to let me out of her sight. Never letting me make friends in case I said something I shouldn't. She told me if I ever told anyone they'd take her away, that I'd never see her again. So I never said anything. Although... I almost did. Once. I nearly told Alison, but she died before I got the chance. I never dreamed till today that Mum had something to do with Alison's car accident. I know we fought, but I still trusted Mum was telling the truth, I believed everything she said to me. That she couldn't have killed anyone on purpose. Not my mum. But when I heard Jodie accuse her, it was like all the pieces of the puzzle clicked together in my mind.

I reopen my eyes and my tears splash onto Jodie's face.

'I killed my mum...' I whisper, the reality of my actions sinking over me like a heavy weight.

'Listen to me, Lacey,' she says. 'She was going to kill me. You saved me. Nothing bad is going to happen to you. No one will blame you.'

I can see it now, being dragged into a police car and driven away. I need a way to go back, to undo it. I didn't mean to hit her that hard. I never wanted to kill her. I just wanted to get her away from Jodie. I didn't mean to.

'I just wanted her to stop.' I can't stop sobbing now. It's making it hard to breathe.

'I know you did,' Jodie says, wrapping me in her arms and squeezing me. I want her to take all this away from me, to fix it for me. After a moment she pulls away from me slightly and cups my face in her hands. 'Lacey, how long have you known you can walk?'

I frown. 'I . . . I've always been able to. Mum said . . .' Saying the word 'Mum' makes my face crumple again and I descend into a fresh flood of tears.

'Lacey, I need you to tell me. Please.'

I suck in a shaky breath. 'Mum said the wheelchair was just to stop my muscles getting worse. She said if I didn't use it I could fall.'

Jodie nods, a thoughtful look on her face. 'Okay, listen to me really well,' she says. 'I don't think you're ill.'

My eyes narrow. 'What?'

'I think your mum suffered from something called Munchausen by Proxy. It's where a parent makes up their kid's illness. They make up symptoms and pressure the doctors to perform surgery you don't need.'

My eyes flick from side to side as I replay memories in my mind. All the times I begged Mum to get a second opinion before putting me through any more. All the times doctors told her I seemed to be getting better and she insisted they knew nothing. All the times I told her I could walk and she made me promise to stay in my chair.

'But . . . I have breathing difficulties. I have low blood sugars.'

'You don't know what's in the medication she's been giving you. It could be that that's making you poorly. Maybe even Dr Roth helped her make your illness look worse than it was.'

I shake my head fiercely. 'No. He was always really nice to me. And he wasn't even my doctor for long. Mum broke up with him because . . .'

I trail off, and Jodie leans towards me. 'Because?' she prompts.

'He knew about Grandma. We were the only people who knew: me and Dr Roth. He promised her he'd keep her secret but . . .'

More tears spill from my eyes as I realise just how evil she was. 'Did . . . Did Mum kill him too? To stop him from telling anyone?'

Jodie nods gently. 'I think so.'

This is too much information to process. My head is hurting. First Grandma, then Dr Roth, now this?

I look at Mum's blood-soaked body, then return my gaze to Jodie, my bottom lip quivering.

'So . . . I'm not going to die?'

Jodie's shoulders drop and she pulls me back into her arms. 'I don't think so, no. Not until you're an old woman warm in your bed.'

And as she says that, for one terrifying moment, I'm glad Mum is dead.

We stay hugging for a few minutes, my shoulders bobbing up and down as I cry into Jodie's shoulder. She strokes my hair and shushes me as if I'm a baby, and I never want her to stop. I suddenly feel more attached to Jodie than ever. I want to glue myself to her side and never leave her. She's the only person I've got in the whole world. When we finally pull apart again my tummy aches, a nervy sicky feeling.

'What do we do now?' I ask.

Jodie glances down at Mum. I keep expecting her to get up and start attacking Jodie again, but of course she just lies there.

'We need to call the police,' Jodie says.

I recoil, my face twisting. She's going to turn me in.

'It's okay, it's okay.' She's using her comforting voice again but it's not stopping the panic that's soaring through me. 'I told you, they won't blame you. All you have to do is tell them the truth. Tell them how she's been treating you. Tell them she was going to kill me.'

'And what will happen then?'

She shakes her head. 'I . . . I'm not sure exactly. You'll probably be taken to a foster home while they figure out where you can live.'

'What?' My fingers dig into Jodie's arms, my eyes wide. I'm not stupid. I know what happens to kids who go into foster care, especially teenagers. No one ever wants someone my age. I'll be alone forever. Bounced around the system, from home to home. 'No, I don't want to go to a foster home. I want to stay with you!'

'It's going to be okay. I promise.'

Jodie tries to hug me again but I push her away. I've had enough lies to last me a lifetime.

'How can you promise that? You won't be there! Please, please don't call them. Please don't leave me!'

My voice is getting shrill, echoing through the domed ceiling of the church, and I know I need to be quiet before I attract attention but the panic is taking over. Jodie shushes me, but I can see she's lost for words. She grinds her teeth together and squeezes her eyes shut.

'Please . . .' I beg again. 'There has to be another way.'

Chapter Fifty

Heidi

We're doing tea at my house today at 2 p.m. if anyone wants to join. We'll be holding a two-minute silence for Norah and Lacey.

Marisa

That's lovely, I'll be there.

Sally

I'll be there. I'll try to drag Markus out too. He's been moping around since yesterday. I don't know why this has all affected him so much. It's not like he knew them particularly well.

Emma

It's affected us all, Sally. It doesn't matter if you knew them well or not. It's still right here in our community.

Heidi

It's times like these it's more important than ever we stick together.

Sally
Didn't you have an argument with Norah right before she died @Heidi?

Emma
Time and a place, Sally. Time and a place.

Marisa
Besides, Jodie got arrested not long after they wheeled the body out, didn't she? Pretty sure she's the main suspect?

Heidi
Jodie got released this morning. They had nothing to hold her for.

Sally
Blimey . . . not sure I'm comfortable with her roaming our streets.

Emma
Innocent until proven guilty.

Heidi
Please remember she's in this group, ladies. Let's not point fingers, it won't do anyone any good.

Chapter Fifty-One

The Day After the Murder

Jodie

The woman staring back at me in the mirror looks exactly the same, and I'm not sure how I feel about that. I think I should look different. I didn't kill Norah, but I played a part in her death. A woman is dead because of me. Surely the signs of that should be evidenced on my face somewhere; a few extra lines, deep bags under my eyes, a remorseful expression, perhaps. But no, on the exterior I haven't changed in the slightest.

I finish brushing my teeth and drop my toothbrush and toothpaste into my transparent toiletries bag. I pull my phone out of my back pocket and send a text – On my way – before pulling off the back and sliding out the battery and SD card. I won't get rid of them here. This house will likely be searched top to bottom over the coming days. I'll drop them in a public bin as I drive through town.

Before I leave I take one last look around my home. The house itself I won't miss, with its strange layout and overabundance of windows, but the furniture I will. That old sofa that's come with me to three different homes and whose holes I never did end up patching up. The TV that kept me and Lacey company so many evenings. The cheap table I've sat and drunk my coffee at every single morning for the last four months. Now all I have are the contents of the suitcase in my hand, plus a cat who looks less than impressed to have been locked in a cage.

'You'll be okay,' I say to Toby, slipping him a treat, as we make our way out through the door and load everything into the car.

I keep staring straight ahead as I drive through the Grove, not wanting to catch the eye of anyone lingering about, though I purposefully timed my departure for when the majority will be at Heidi's place. As I pass it, I picture Heidi fussing around with her scones and primping her hair, and silently wish her well before continuing down the road.

It's funny how your actions follow you around. Something you do that seems insignificant at the time comes back to haunt you months later. I wonder – as I pass the eerie Victorian buildings that somehow seem even more ominous than when I first arrived in the community – if I would have done things differently had I known how it would all turn out. Would I have even moved to Kensington Grove at all? Hindsight is a bitch.

When I approach the entrance of Kensington Grove and flash my card to open the gate, I fling it as hard as I can so that it lands in one of the nearby bushes. No turning back now.

The hour-and-a-quarter drive goes surprisingly quickly. I don't listen to music, just enjoy the silence and the occasional annoyed mew from Toby. They're already there when I arrive. I can see Lacey's outline, strange-looking now that she's standing up, as I pull into the car park of the closed-down library we agreed to meet at, roughly halfway between the Grove and Gabbie's house.

'Thank you so much,' I say as I get out of the car, pulling Gabbie into an embrace. It's a wonderful feeling to know that there is someone in the world who, no matter what happens, no matter how many times you lean on them, no matter how many times you try to shut them out, will always come to your aid. No questions asked.

She was the only person I could think of calling last night. I didn't tell her everything. I figured the less she knew the less she'd be implicated if we ever got caught. All I had to say was that I needed her help and she was already putting on her shoes and driving to me. She met us on the east side of the Grove, where the pond runs into the stream and out into the meadow. I'd struggled to think of a way to get Lacey out of the gates without my card registering that I'd left, which would have implicated me in the murder and kidnap, but a flash of inspiration hit me as I remembered that fox on Halloween night. He'd slipped straight under the gate, found the only weakness in Kensington Grove's security. There was just enough room for a petite girl to shimmy under there too.

DS Wolfe nearly had a fit trying to pin both the murder and Lacey's kidnap on me. I could see the frustration bursting out of her as she questioned me. But she didn't have a scrap of evidence to hold me for more than twenty-four hours and she knew it. I'd worn gloves all evening so there were no fingerprints, and any that had managed to creep through or any blood spatters from my fight with Norah were obliterated when Lacey and I scrubbed every inch of Norah's house and the community centre with bleach. We also made sure to check both myself and Norah for DNA links; strands of hair, skin under the nails and such. If they do find anything by then it will be too late.

It's hard letting go of Gabbie. I hadn't realised how empty my life has been at Kensington Grove until I came face to face with her again. I thought she'd hate me for what happened, for giving up on AA, for disappearing like I did, but she was just happy to see me. She never stopped being my best friend.

She gives me a squeeze before pulling away, tears glossing her eyes. 'I'll go grab you the money. It's in the car.'

'I really can't thank you enough. I'll pay you back, I promise.'

She doesn't say anything, just gives me a weak smile and heads to her car. I watch after her, nerves and gratitude and fear and love all swirling, jumbling in my gut. We've agreed to meet back here in exactly one month. I'm not entirely sure what my plan is, how we're going to make this work. We'll stay at a caravan park I've found that accepts passers-by with no credit cards. We'll cut our hair, dye it. I'm going to need to figure out some way to make money, cash-in-hand jobs that won't require using my real name. Or my fake one for that matter. The money I've got in my bag will see us through to begin with, and if we're still struggling next month Gabbie has said she'll lend me some extra cash. We'll be okay. I'll figure something out. I always do.

I glance at Lacey, her bony fingers intertwined with mine, gripping on tight. She looks . . . not happy as such, but at peace. Hopeful. Kind of like she was when I first met her, with only the red rims of her eyes serving as evidence of the trauma she's been through.

'We'll have to make sure wherever we stay has a TV so we can start up our movie nights again,' I say.

'Okay,' she nods, and her voice sounds so small I want to wrap my arms around her and take all the pain away.

'We'll get some popcorn. Make a proper night of it.'

I smile at the thought. Normally during a movie night at home I'd crack open a bottle of wine, but no more. I need to keep my head clear from now on. It's not just me anymore.

Part of me wants to ask Lacey how she feels about Norah, but I don't want to upset her by bringing it up. We'll need to talk about it eventually, of course. What happened is enough to scar anybody, let alone a young girl. But not today. Today can be just about the future.

'Are you okay?' Gabbie's voice snaps me out of my thoughts. I hadn't even noticed she's returned from her car. I look up and force a smile, but it slips off my lips almost instantly. Gabbie's face is different somehow, washed out yet splotched with red. There are beads of sweat breaking out on her forehead and upper lip.

'I'm fine . . .' I say slowly, 'but are you okay? You look like you've seen a ghost.'

'Yeah, yes. I'm just worried about you.'

She's not meeting my eye. Something's wrong. My gaze drops to her hands where there should be the bunch of cash she promised me, but instead all she's holding is her phone.

'Gabbie?'

A sob escapes her throat, coming out as a suppressed, hiccupy gulp. 'I'm so sorry, Jodie.'

The words are almost too quiet for me to hear. I'm hit by a wave of dizziness and my head starts to throb, a dull pulse in the base of my skull.

'Gabbie . . . what did you do?'

'I had to call them, Jode. You're not well.'

It's like the sky above me has turned to a solid mass, lowering itself, crushing me. My body jerks into action. Adrenaline courses through my veins.

'Lacey, get in the car.'

'What's going on?'

'Get in the car now!'

I throw my arm around her and hurry her into the backseat, acid churning in my throat. For a split second I think I'm going to vomit at the sight of a young girl in the backseat for the first time since the accident, but I swallow it down and throw myself into the driver's seat.

'Jodie! Stop! Just talk to the police, please!' Gabbie appears at my window, banging the glass with her fists, tears now streaming down her cheeks. I force my eyes away, start the engine. As I screech off from the car park, ignoring Gabbie's pleading cries, I think I can literally feel my heart shattering into pieces. How could she do this to me? To us?

'Jodie . . .' Lacey sounds like she's crying but I can't look in my rear-view mirror, not while my head is spinning like it is, not while we're powering down a main road. I need to keep my eyes fixed ahead, my hands locked in the ten and two position. *Focus on your breathing, Jodie. In for four, out for seven.*

'Jodie . . . please . . .'

'What?' I snap. I don't want her talking to me right now. I need a moment to think, to figure out what I'm going to do without Gabbie's help.

'I don't feel well.'

My foot eases off the accelerator. A slight tingle brushes through my chest.

'In what way?'

No answer. The tingle evolves, spreading and wrapping itself around my lungs, squeezing. I knock my indicator on, the *tick-tick-ticking* of it pounding through my head. I move over to the slow lane, then to the hard shoulder. The car jolts to a stop as I press too hard on the brake and whip around.

'Lacey! Lacey, what is it?'

The colour has drained from her face. She's not just pale, she's grey, and a glistening film of sweat is coating her forehead. She can't talk, just stares back at me as her chest starts heaving. A horrible wheezing sound escapes her lips, like ill-tuned bagpipes. My brain kicks into gear and I scramble through my pockets for my phone to call an ambulance, and then I realise it's gone, chucked into one of the many public bins we've passed.

She was fine when I looked at her two minutes ago. Two minutes. That's it.

Flashing lights appear in my rear-view mirror. I scramble out of the car. Horns blare as I step too close to the oncoming traffic and I lurch back, body descending into uncontrollable shakes.

'Please!' I scream, frantically waving my arms at the police cars swarming, surrounding us. The officers are out of their vehicles. They're shouting at me, the movement of their lips makes that clear. But I can't hear them properly. Everything is muffled. My mind is a void. It doesn't even feel like I'm the one controlling my movements as I raise my hands above my head. It's like I'm a puppet on string.

'Where are we going, Mummy?'

No. Please, no.

An officer is at the car. 'We need urgent medical care. We've got a young girl in severe respiratory distress.'

Another lunges for me, grabbing at my wrists, yanking them behind my back. At some point the cold metal of handcuffs digs into my skin but I barely notice it. All I can do is stare helplessly at the car, at the officers administering emergency CPR on Lacey.

Norah was right. All this time I wanted nothing more than to save Lacey from her mother, but it was me she needed saving from. In the thick of my grief I've allowed myself to fabricate a reality that I was so, so sure of. I was so convinced Norah had faked her illness, I didn't even consider the possibility that by taking Lacey away I was endangering her life.

Arrest me. Lock me away. Stop me from hurting anyone ever again.

Oh Lacey . . . Forgive me.

Acknowledgements

As I write these words, I remember very clearly starting the first draft of this novel, thinking it would probably never lead to anything. To find myself a year and a half later writing actual acknowledgements to go into my published book is a dream come true. With that said, I first and foremost want to thank you for choosing to read this book.

Of course, none of this would have been possible had I not found my home at Embla Books. Infinite thanks to my agent Emily Glenister, for taking a chance on me and becoming my advocate, my therapist and my friend. I couldn't do this without you in my corner.

A huge thank you to my wonderful editor, Hannah Smith, for loving this story enough to bring it on to Embla's impressive list. And to Emily Thomas, Jon Appleton, Jen Porter, Marina Stavropoulou and the rest of the talented team at Embla for all your hard work on this book.

Thanks also to Lauren North, who chose to devote her precious time to mentoring me and helping me to mould this story into one that (hopefully) people will want to read!

Thank you to Will Dean, Nikki Smith, Jo Jakeman, William Shaw and Alexa Donne for offering me advice and critiques, without which I may not be where I am today, and to Alli Earnest for reading my messy first drafts.

A shout out to my boss Cathy for her endless encouragement, and to Emma for cheering me on.

A very special shout out to my friends and family, who have stuck with me through my many drafting and editing tantrums. In particular my ever-patient husband, my mum (arguably my biggest fan), my super supportive dad and step-mum and my lovely grandad. And finally, to my Nan in the stars, who told me I would one day become a published author. I hope I've made you proud.

Becca Day lives in the middle of the woods in Surrey with her husband, daughters, and cocker spaniel. She studied acting at Guildford College and went on to start her own Murder Mystery theatre troupe. It was this move that inspired her love of crime fiction, and when she sold the company she threw herself head first into crime writing. Her short fiction has won several prizes. Aside from writing, she is also an avid reader and runs Reading Parties with fellow author William Shaw.

About Embla Books

Embla Books is a digital-first publisher of standout commercial adult fiction. Passionate about storytelling, the team at Embla publish books that will make you 'laugh, love, look over your shoulder and lose sleep'. Launched by Bonnier Books UK in 2021, the imprint is named after the first woman from the creation myth in Norse mythology, who was carved by the gods from a tree trunk found on the seashore – an image of the kind of creative work and crafting that writers do, and a symbol of how stories shape our lives.

Find out about some of our other books and stay in touch:

Twitter, Facebook, Instagram: @emblabooks
Newsletter: https://bit.ly/emblanewsletter